Salaam,
with Love

Salaam, with Love

Sara Sharaf Beg

Underlined

Text copyright © 2022 by Sara Sharaf Beg
Cover art copyright © 2022 by Aaliya Jaleel

All rights reserved. Published in the United States by Underlined, an imprint of Random House Children's Books, a division of Penguin Random House LLC, New York.

Underlined is a registered trademark and the colophon is a trademark of Penguin Random House LLC.

Visit us on the web! GetUnderlined.com

Educators and librarians, for a variety of teaching tools, visit us at RHTeachersLibrarians.com

Library of Congress Cataloging-in-Publication Data is available upon request.
ISBN 978-0-593-48262-9 (tr. pbk.) — ISBN 978-0-593-48263-6 (ebook)

The text of this book is set in 11-point Janson MT Pro.
Interior design by Jen Valero

Printed in the United States of America
10 9 8 7 6 5 4 3 2 1
First Edition

For my family, who taught me how to dream.
And for my husband—my partner and best friend
in this life and, insha'Allah, the next.

one

I was rocking out to the radio in my room when my mom walked in. I froze, one foot behind me, and reached up to pull my earbuds out as my mom watched me with a bemused expression.

"Dua, come into the kitchen. Your father and I have something to tell you," she said, the Urdu words flowing like poetry from her lips. "And please stop jumping around like an electrocuted penguin," she added, closing the door behind her.

"Electrocuted penguin," I muttered as I put the earbuds away. Actually, I'd been called worse when it came to my dancing.

"What's . . ." My voice trailed off as I walked into the kitchen and saw the looks on my parents' faces. "What happened?" My heart hammered in my chest. Was this about my music again?

"We'll explain," Mom said gently. "Sit down, please."

I bit my lip. If music hadn't been on their minds, I didn't want to bring it up and cause an argument. Instead, I asked, "Did someone die?"

Dad shook his head. "No, alhamdulillah—all praise is due to God. You remember Uncle Yusuf and his family?"

Dad had seven brothers; keeping all their names and faces straight in my head was almost impossible unless a cup of coffee sat at the bottom of my stomach first. "Yeah, of course. His family visited Dada and Daadi in Pakistan at the same time as us five years ago."

"Dua," Mom said, as if I hadn't even spoken, "as you know, Ramadan starts in a week."

"Yeah," I agreed, my brow furrowed as I leaned forward, waiting for her to finish. I wasn't even sure I *wanted* to hear what else she had to say. "And?"

"Well, Yusuf invited us to come and stay with them for Ramadan," Dad said, a smile breaking out on his face, his teeth startlingly white against his tanned skin. "And we're going to take him up on it."

For a minute, all I could do was blink at him, my mind suddenly blank. Of all the things I expected him to say, this had been nowhere on the list. Once my brain processed his words, I said, "What? Wait . . . *what?*"

"We are going to stay at your uncle Yusuf's for Ramadan," Mom repeated, slowly this time, enunciating each syllable. "Now, please, be happy; we haven't seen them in years."

I would've jumped out of my seat if I hadn't already been in danger of falling off of it. "Exactly! I haven't seen or even talked to Uncle Yusuf or my cousins in five years; that's a long time. How am I supposed to connect with them? What are we going to talk about?"

"There's so much you have in common with your cousins. Your heritage, your faith," Dad reminded me.

I barely held in a snort. Heritage, sure. Faith? Not so much. I knew enough about Islam from what Mom and Dad had taught me growing up, from years of weekends spent at the dining table while they read from the Qur'an or books on prophetic tradition. But Uncle Yusuf and his family were on another level. My cousins grew up going to Sunday school where volunteers would teach them the Qur'an and Islamic history every week. They had Muslim friends from the moment they were born, all the way through university. Compared to them, I wasn't a *bad* Muslim, but the differences in our experiences were huge. Ramadan wouldn't be a quiet, private affair in their household the way it was in my small family.

Like Dad, Uncle Yusuf was a doctor—pediatrics for Dad, cardiology for Uncle Yusuf. Unlike Dad, when Uncle Yusuf wasn't seeing a patient, he was often found attending or listening to Islamic conferences and lectures. A phone call from him meant getting a free lesson on the importance of waking up on time for fajr, the morning prayer. In comparison, I preferred my parents' occasional complaint about my lack of focus during worship.

Sure, my uncle meant well and was kind, generous, and soft-spoken, but I could only take so much preaching before it got on my nerves. I knew enough; I didn't need every moment to become another teaching opportunity. How would I live for a month with him and his family?

"And how do you connect with strangers?" Dad went on, oblivious to the thoughts spinning in my mind. "Just go up and talk to them, but it's even better because they're your family. They'll accept you no matter what.

"You'll be applying for college soon and Mahnoor just finished her bachelor's. I'm sure she'd love to answer any questions you have about college life and the application process."

I didn't respond, recalling the last time I'd attempted to bring up my thoughts about "college life" and the major I wanted. A slight heaviness settled in my stomach, just as it had that evening. As soon as the word *music* left my mouth, Dad had gotten a confused look on his face while Mom chuckled—assuming I was joking. I hadn't had the guts to bring it up again.

"Aren't you Facebook friends with Mahnoor?" Mom asked, reminding me of the dangers of being friends with your parents on social media. Even when you only added them because they wouldn't stop crying that their only child is ashamed of them.

"Yeah, but she's almost never online," I answered. From what I remembered, she'd always been a little on the antisocial side. Plus, I almost never use Facebook anymore. "I think the last time I talked to her was a year ago."

"When she got engaged?" Mom asked, thinking back.

"Right, I reached out to congratulate her, and then we only talked for a few minutes because she was studying for the LSATs." I wasn't exaggerating either. We'd talked for two minutes, and in that time all I'd gotten in was *Hi, I'm so happy for you*, and *bye*. Not that we would have had a lot to say to each other anyway.

"You're cousins, sweetheart. No matter how much time passes, you can always pick up right where you left off. That's what happens when you share blood."

I gnawed on my lower lip as I studied my parents' faces. My mom, with her light brown hair and warm, amber eyes, a smile that could get me to do anything, even the chores I hated the most. My dad, with his thousand-watt grin, merry dark brown eyes, and jet-black hair cropped short and going gray at the temples. I was an even mix of both of them, with my skin tone somewhere between my mom's light complexion and my dad's olive coloring, my eyes an exact match with my mom's, my hair as black and thick as my dad's, and a nose like someone stuck a pear in the middle of my face (I wasn't sure where the nose had come from).

They were being gentle with me, trying to allow me to accept their decision maturely rather than pushing it on me. Not unlike their approach to the options they posited for my future: business, prelaw, or premed. Still, I knew them too well to think that I had any real say in what was going to happen. Family had always been important to Dad, and once Mom made a decision, there was no turning her away from it.

"I can't get out of this, can I?" I asked anyway, slumping in my chair.

"No," my mom said, stopping to kiss me on the head as she got up and left to start packing. "Have your suitcase ready by tomorrow morning, honey. We leave in the evening."

I sat up straight. "You're not even giving me forty-eight hours' notice when you make plans now? I'm your only child—why the lack of communication?"

"We just told you. How much more notice do you need? We're going for a visit. You're not getting married and moving away. You don't have to pack the whole house," Dad said, not getting it, as usual.

I sighed. I just wanted to be consulted for once, to feel like I actually had a voice. "I'm not saying I'm going to New York kicking and screaming, but you could've at least told me earlier. Kat and I had plans for the rest of summer vacation. Now I have to let her down, and we don't have time to hang out before I leave. And what about my birthday? It falls during Ramadan this year, so we're not going to be able to celebrate it together."

"Just celebrate it when we get back," Mom said calmly. "It's only a matter of a few days."

Clenching my jaw, I mulled that over. Kat was more than my best friend; she was my constant companion. We'd played in sandboxes and learned to ride our bikes together. We talked about everything, were always together, always a team. Now our plans were ruined. To my parents, it was only a month, but I felt robbed. Kat knew how to make me forget the stress of trying to deal with everything that came with being different, not just from my non–Pakistani American, non-Muslim classmates and friends, but also from my own family, Uncle Yusuf and my cousins included. Whenever that familiar feeling of not fitting in started to set in, Kat knew how to make me feel better.

"You can invite her for dinner tonight. Your mom's making chicken karahi. Kat loves it, right?" Dad said, like he couldn't get what I was making such a big deal out of. "Try to be happy about this, Dua. I haven't seen my brother in years, and we used to be even closer than you and Kat are now. If you're excited, then Kat will be excited for you too. A month away from your best friend isn't going to kill you." He paused, looking thoughtful, as if he wasn't sure if he should continue or not. "Besides, Kat's a nice girl, but she's not Muslim. There are some things about the way we live that she just can't relate to. You've spent your whole life in this little town, and it's high time you made some Muslim friends."

This wasn't the first time I'd heard this, but it was the first time Dad seemed to be genuinely regretful about it. We'd moved to Burkeville, Virginia, when I was a toddler because of Dad's residency and stayed on because he'd received an offer he couldn't pass up. While Dad had always intended to move closer to his brothers one day, or at least where there were more Muslims or Pakistanis, that day always got put off for one reason or another.

My education. Mom's budding, home-based catering service (any-one craving chicken tikka masala within a fifty-mile radius would be out of luck if we moved). So, Dad put off moving indefinitely. He'd spent almost half his life away from his family. In comparison, one month wasn't much to ask.

"It's not that there's something wrong with your friends now," Dad said softly, almost desperate that I not take his words the wrong way, "but you'll see, it's a little different. You actually belong, unified in a group by our love of God."

I understood what he was saying. It made sense, but I *had* to stop this mini-lecture before it turned into something you might see on Lifetime. "Okay, Dad. I'll call her to come over tonight and start packing right after." I even tried to smile despite the growing knot of dread in my stomach. "I make no promises that I'll enjoy this trip, but I'll keep the complaining to a minimum."

"Good. Ingratitude is displeasing to God," he said, bending to kiss me on the head before going after my mother.

I stared like he'd suddenly turned into a two-headed calf. How were *those* words supposed to encourage me about a trip I didn't want to go on? "God help me," I muttered, plopping my head down on the table.

☾

"New York?" Kat shrieked, almost rupturing my eardrums. "You're going to New York and you're *complaining* about it?" Her eyes were as big as tennis balls, her chicken karahi and roti forgotten.

I stared at her, wondering how her jaw hadn't cracked, she was grinning so hard. "How are you not upset? We were supposed to hang out together this summer. We made plans to go out to the state park, go hiking. My parents didn't care about that."

Her perpetual smile finally slipped. "Yeah, our plans . . . Honestly, I can't remember a time when we've been apart for that long. Don't forget about me while you're exploring New York."

She said it like she was joking, but she looked away, and I could see the tiny bit of skin between her brows wrinkling. She was trying not to cry.

"Oh, Kat." I pulled her close, squeezing her in a hug. "I'm sorry. I'll make it up to you when I get back, I promise. Besides, I don't think there'll be much exploring involved. Everyone's going to be fasting, so we won't have a lot of energy to go out often. Plus, Uncle Yusuf is more conservative than Dad, so I don't really know what day-to-day life is going to look like there." I paused for a moment. "It's going to be so weird for me; I've met Uncle Yusuf and his family five times in my whole life, and now I'm going to live with them for a month. How am I supposed to adjust to that? How am I supposed to relate to *them*?"

She held back a sniffle. "You're overthinking it. It might be weird for you at first because you're not used to having that many people around. Take it one day at a time, and when it gets tough, imagine I'm there with you, like a guardian angel."

"Yeah, I guess you're right," I replied half-heartedly. I wasn't Kat; I wasn't close to my extended family. I was happiest at home where it was just me.

She wiped away a tear. "Of course I'm right." She reached for my hand. "I'm happy for you, though. Really. It sucks about our plans, but honestly, how much are you going to miss? There are only so many things to do in Burkeville, and we'll do them when you get back. Right?"

I squeezed her hand. "Definitely."

She squeezed back. "Come on, I'll help you pack."

Dragging me to my room, she pulled some clothes from my closet and flung them on the bed. Graphic T-shirts with references from my favorite TV shows and movies. Long-sleeved blouses. Jeans.

"Okay, now let's talk about the important thing here." She turned, draping a scarf about my shoulders, checking its hue against my skin. "You have a guy cousin there only a couple of years older than us, right?"

It took a moment to get out of my own thoughts. "Um, yeah. It's not long enough to cover my hair during prayer. I should have some longer ones in the back."

"Yeah, yeah, sure." She whisked it away. "So, your cousin, What's-His-Face, is he hot?"

"Ibrahim, and he's not your type." I glanced down at the long, pale blue scarf in her hands. "That should work."

"Not my type, my butt. If he breathes, he's my type." Kat draped the scarf over my head, checking the length.

"Dua!"

I turned toward my mother's voice, the scarf haphazardly wrapped about my head.

"I brought this in for you," she said, pushing an old suitcase toward me. "Hurry up and get packing." Waves of light brown hair fell from her messy bun, her eyes wide as she perused the mess on my bed. "Where are your shalwar kameez?"

"My closet." Seeing as we never had much occasion to wear

traditional Pakistani outfits, I only had three, all presents from previous Eid holidays.

"Pack them," Mom said, opening the suitcase and folding my jeans into neat stacks. "We might have some dinners to go to. Yusuf and Sadia know quite a few people. If you need them, you can borrow some of mine; I'll pack extra."

"Okay," I agreed, already pulling them from my closet. I folded the matching scarves first, then the trousers, and then, very carefully, the richly colored and embroidered kameez tunics.

Kat grabbed my jewelry box off the dresser and, in a smaller compartment of my suitcase, added a few pieces to pair with the beautiful clothes. "Hey, what about this?" she asked, pulling a gold teeka headpiece from the box, a gift from my grandma on our last trip to Pakistan. "It's so pretty!" She held it up to her own forehead and posed, pouting, the gold beads shimmering against her skin.

Mom smiled brightly. "It looks beautiful on you."

I felt a little twinge, seeing the light in Mom's eyes as she watched Kat twirl before the mirror. Despite admiring the teeka, I'd never been half as excited to try it on. Sure, it was pretty, but I never had much occasion to wear it. If not for myself, I could've worn it for Mom, to make her smile.

We'd always been the only Pakistani family in town, though that never stopped my parents from trying to keep the culture alive at home. I'd worn shalwar kameez every Eid since birth. I'd sit with Mom as she watched Pakistani dramas. Dad was always listening to old Pakistani songs. Yet somehow, Kat seemed more connected to my culture, more willing to embrace my parents' customs and values, than I was.

At home, we only spoke in English on Mondays. The rest of

the weekdays, we spoke in Urdu, and on weekends, Punjabi. Even though we visited Pakistan infrequently, they wanted me to speak and understand both languages easily, so I wouldn't have trouble talking to my grandparents and relatives still living there.

In a way, I understood. If I'd lived half my life elsewhere, I'd want to remember that culture too. Maybe that was part of the reason for this trip: the desire for a stronger connection to our heritage, our family. Dad and Uncle Yusuf weren't far apart in age, so they'd been close as children. Dad must be feeling nostalgic, and I knew Mom, who talked to Aunt Sadia often, longed for friends like the ones she'd had at college in Lahore. She was friendly with all the women in our neighborhood, but they didn't have the comfort of shared experiences and customs.

"So?" Kat said, finally taking the teeka off, her hand hovering over the open suitcase. "Are you taking it?"

I smiled lightly. "Yeah, why not? Maybe I'll wear it on Eid."

"Where's your tasbeeh?" Mom asked. "Don't forget to bring that too."

I glanced around the room. There it was on the windowsill, by my electronic keyboard. I stretched over the length of the keyboard as I reached for the string of black beads, and just as the tassel was within my grasp, my other hand landed firmly on the keys. A single high note rang out, beautiful, but lonely in its solitude. The tasbeeh slipped from my fingers as I caressed the keys. They seemed to hum with anticipation just beneath my fingertips.

"Dua, hurry up!"

"Can I take my keyboard?" The question was out before the thought fully formed, my tongue quicker than my brain.

Mom paused, her forehead wrinkling, eyes slightly narrowing.

"There isn't room in the car, and I don't think there will be in their house either. Besides, are you going to focus on Ramadan or your music?"

Why can't it be both? I wondered.

Mom didn't wait for an answer. As far as she was concerned, the conversation had ended before it began. "Finish your packing; you don't want to forget anything."

I jerked my hands away from the keys, my fingertips tingling. I did as I was told. Although I was careful not to look at the keyboard again, the air hung heavy, thick with the promise of melody.

two

"Dua, I asked you a question."

I turned from the car window, my daydreams dissipating. "Sorry, what was that?"

"Have you given any thought to our suggestion?"

My stomach twisted. I could guess what they wanted to talk about, but I really didn't want to go into that again. Keeping my voice steady, I said, "What suggestion?"

Mom sighed. "The MSA?"

There it was. "Oh. No." I shifted uncomfortably in the back seat, wrapping my blanket tight around myself. Weeks ago, over dinner, Mom and Dad suggested I start a Muslim Student Association at school. I'd laughed it off, assuming they were just giddy from Mom successfully catering a huge house party by herself. I thought it was just a joke.

"Why not? You're going to submit college applications soon, and you need more extracurricular activities. If you start an MSA chapter, it'll look really good to admissions officers."

"I'll be the only Muslim student in attendance."

"True," Dad acknowledged, "but you can spread some positive awareness about Islam, address some common misconceptions."

I thought about it for a moment. I'd pored over all the family photos as a kid, and I clearly remembered the jarring realization that Dad had sported a full beard in all the photos of his arrival to the U.S., with it suddenly missing in all the photos afterward. I'd never seen it in person, and when I asked him about it one day, he simply said it was easier that way. That was a misconception he'd want me to address: just because a brown-skinned man has a beard, doesn't make him a terrorist. With a sigh, I admitted, "Yeah, and I'm sure that's needed, but I don't think I'm the right person to do that."

"Why?"

There were reasons aplenty. As someone who usually missed fajr prayer due to her inability to wake up early, as someone who could barely concentrate during her prayers, why should anyone listen to me about Islam? I wasn't exactly an expert, and it's not like I needed any more attention drawn to the fact that I was the only Muslim kid in town.

"I just don't think it's the right thing for me," I said, hoping to bring an end to the conversation. I just wanted to focus on my music. Why was it *my* responsibility to take a stand, to address misconceptions and prove that being Muslim didn't make me abnormal?

"Okay, but think about it."

"Can we talk about something else?" I just wanted to keep my head down, graduate high school, and be on my way. I didn't want things to be more complicated than they had to be.

"Sure. Do you remember the ages and names of Uncle Yusuf and Aunt Sadia's kids?"

Was it too soon to change topics again? "Yes, I remember. If I forget, I'll ask."

"And you can't sit in a corner and wait for someone to come and talk to you."

"I know, Dad," I replied, fighting the urge to roll my eyes. I'd been getting the same lecture since kindergarten. *Don't be antisocial, Dua. Don't sit by yourself and talk to your imaginary friend, Dua. Do you want to be a loner, Dua? Do you want to live like a hermit?* "I won't do that, I promise."

"We don't want you to be intimidated or retreat into your shell."

"Well, they *are* a little intimidating," I retorted.

"Only because you're not used to it, dear," Mom said, reaching into her purse. "Once you're there, you'll adjust quickly."

"Yeah, Kat said the same thing." I held back a sigh. It was easy for Kat to say; she was the outgoing and adaptable one. In fact, she'd been the one to approach me first, toddling over to me with a big smile on her face and a couple of Barbies in hand, one of which she'd offered to me.

"She's a smart girl." Mom fished out a bag of mini samosas—homemade, of course; you couldn't get samosas anywhere in Burkeville except our kitchen—and offered it to me. "Want some? I have ketchup and chutney too."

I was tempted but could feel my eyelids drooping. "No, thank you. I'm tired; I might take a nap."

"Okay, sleep, then," she ordered. "We should be there a couple of hours after fajr, about seven or so, and you might not get another chance to rest after sunrise. And think about the MSA."

I dozed off the moment she finished that sentence, images of dream-cousins finger-pointing and half-concealed snickers swirling around in my mind.

I awoke as the car screeched to a halt, evil cackles ringing in my ears. Half asleep, I rolled over and fell off the back seat, landing face-first on the gray, fuzzy carpet.

I groaned as I sat up. What a horrible nightmare. I still felt the singe of hot oil on my skin, as Aunt Sadia had been about to fry me up for everyone's iftar.

"Oh, you're up," Mom said brightly, as if she hadn't heard the thump. "Good. We're here."

Rubbing my head, I peered out the window. "This is the city? I thought they didn't have houses here." Floral curtains, big windows, red shingles. Odds were Uncle Yusuf and Aunt Sadia weren't secretly evil cannibals after my blood.

"It's a household of seven people," Dad replied, shaking his head at me. "They couldn't possibly all fit in an apartment. Not comfortably anyway. This is Queens."

Queens? The name sounded a lot fancier than it looked.

Uncle Yusuf, a grayer version of Dad, yanked the door open before Dad could reach for the doorbell, his grin crinkling his eyes at the corners. "Khalid!"

"Yusuf!" Dad exclaimed, his smile quickly catching up with his brother's toothy grin.

I watched my uncle and Dad clap each other's backs and hug, the moment so touching I almost didn't notice how my bags were weighing me down. Almost. I stumbled the moment they parted, my duffel bag slipping off my shoulder and landing on the porch.

At the thud, Uncle Yusuf turned to me. "Dua!" He enveloped me in a bear hug, the smell of cloves and cologne flooding my brain. "Mashallah," he said softly.

"I haven't seen you in years, and now you're all grown up." Uncle Yusuf held me at arm's length and studied my face. "Oh. Are you cold in that?" he said, eyeing my short-sleeved shirt.

"No," I said, immediately wishing I'd brought a cardigan. I'd never even seen Uncle Yusuf in short sleeves before, or anyone from their family, now that I thought about it. They probably always wore long sleeves. "I'm okay."

"Well, good. It's as if I simply turned around for a moment and the years flew by." He sighed, shaking his head. "We must make up for lost time." Seeing my mom, he smiled. "Assalamu alaykum."

"Wa alaykum assalam." Mom returned the greeting.

"Come in, come in." Uncle Yusuf ushered us inside. "Sadia has been waiting for you. Wouldn't let me sleep for her endless questions: What's Dua's favorite food? Does Khalid take cardamom in his chai? Which college is Dua going to? What's Sanam's favorite dessert?"

"Actually, you were the one who wouldn't stop talking." Aunt Sadia appeared with a smile. " 'Everything must be perfect. Khalid is coming; everything must be perfect!' "

Uncle Yusuf laughed heartily. "Of course, anything for my little brother." He clapped Dad on the back again, almost knocking him over.

Aunt Sadia turned to me. "Dua." She hugged me tightly.

"Sanam." She squeezed my mother warmly. "How was your trip?" she asked, pulling back to look at both of us while my dad and Uncle Yusuf retreated to another room to talk.

"Fine." Mom beamed. "Well, maybe not for Khalid. I slept most of the way while he drove."

"Okay," I answered, my mouth stretching in a yawn as soon as the word left my mouth.

"Dua," Mom scolded.

"Sorry, couldn't help it." I covered my mouth.

Aunt Sadia's eyes softened. Unlike my nightmare, she didn't have devil horns sprouting from either side of her hijab. "Come, I'll show you where you'll be staying. The kids put up a fuss if anyone tries to wake them before ten during the summer. You'll fit right in."

"Sadia, she slept for nine hours in the car."

"No matter. Let her sleep a little more if she's tired." She took my hand and led me up a flight of stairs, through the kitchen, and down a hallway lined with photos. She moved too quickly for me to stop and look. "Your parents will be in the guest room, and you'll be staying with Mahnoor." She stopped in front of the door at the end of the hallway. "I hope that's all right."

"Sure." At least with Mahnoor, I was guaranteed some peace and quiet.

Aunt Sadia opened the door and led me inside, hugged me, and then left me to sleep.

I sighed and dropped my bag at the foot of one of the two single beds in the room. A five-foot-something lump rose and fell slightly on the other, a halo of brown hair spread out on the pillow, the only visible part of my cousin.

Changing into pj's, I looked around the room. It wasn't the

largest I'd ever stayed in, but it wasn't small either. Pale blue walls, a desk over by the window, a bulletin board completely covered in sheets of LSAT practice questions, a dresser with photos of my cousins stuck in the corners of the mirror.

Easing my hair out of its ponytail, I walked closer till I could see the photo on the top right corner: a young girl, about twelve years old, smiling as she sat on the hump of a camel. I remembered that photo—it had been hard to smile through the stench of the camel until Dad pulled funny faces and made bunny ears behind Uncle Yusuf's head. That was the last week of our stay in Pakistan. None of us had seen each other since.

I turned back to the window, pulling the curtains aside to peer out. This wasn't the bustling traffic and congested streets I'd been expecting. In fact, the street was so quiet, it reminded me of home. I leaned my head against the glass and closed my eyes, taking a deep breath as I held my frustration in. Except it *wasn't* home. I didn't know my way around here. I didn't have Kat or the coziness of my own room, much less the comfort of familiarity.

Not for the first time, I wished I had Kat's easy adaptability. Instead of longing for the familiar comfort of our tiny town, she'd be making the most of this trip. She'd see all the sights in the city, and drag me along too.

Opening my eyes, I turned away from the window and approached the empty bed, a lump rising in my throat. My fingers hovered over the comforter, moving back and forth in sync with the memory of an old tune. Nothing extraordinary, just a Bollywood song Mom used to play at home when I was little, my eyes unblinking as I watched her hands glide over the keys of the keyboard that now stood in my room. The lyrics had made no sense to me then, but the melody stuck in my brain, soothing me.

Mom hadn't touched the keyboard for years, choosing to fill her time with listening to and reciting Qur'an instead, but I never forgot this song. It had the same calming effect now; my muscles relaxed, my shoulders pulling away from my chin. I sighed as my back melted into the mattress and I pulled the comforter up to my chin. It was practically a reflex, pretending to play piano whenever I felt stressed.

Still, sleep evaded me for what seemed like hours, as a part of my body battled with my mind, trying to make sense of this bed, this room, that was not my own. Finally, after counting at least a thousand sheep, I slipped into oblivion.

three

I slapped myself awake to find a pair of big brown eyes staring at me. I screamed so loudly my ears were ringing by the time I was awake enough to realize it wasn't an alien sent to steal my soul.

"You're ticklish," the little boy announced, a white feather dangling from his fingertips. So that's why I'd slapped myself. I'd felt a little tickle on my nose.

"Where's Mahnoor?" I asked, looking over at the other bed. It was empty, the sheets and comforter neatly tucked.

The boy shrugged. His pale skin stood out thanks to the shock of jet-black hair on his head, his eyes huge and curious. He crept closer and sat in front of me on the bed, staring. "Uncle Khalid and Aunt Sanam got me a present. Are you it?"

I didn't know how to react; I could *feel* how blank my face was as I stared back.

His mouth slipped into a frown and he fiddled with his feather. "Do you have cooties?" He moved closer, till he nearly sat in my lap. "Adam says you do."

"No." I shook my head, laughing. "I definitely don't."

I watched him consider this and lift his chin as he decided I was telling the truth. "You know something? You're pretty."

"Thanks." I could see why my aunt had so many laugh lines. How could you not, when you had this little bundle of adorableness walking around? "You're quite handsome yourself. By the way, I'm Dua."

He nodded, as if he already knew all this. "What *did* you bring for me?"

I thought back to the huge suitcase we'd packed with gifts. "Well—"

"Mahdi!" Mahnoor stepped into the room, dressed in baggy jeans and a sunshine-yellow top. Her eyes, the same shade of brown as her brother's, widened. She rushed to get him off the bed. "Why did you wake her up?"

"It's okay," I said quickly, watching Mahdi clamber off the bed. "He wasn't bothering me."

"See?" He stared up into her eyes, crossing his arms over his chest. "She says it's okay."

"All right." She smiled and touched the top of his head. "Mama's calling you for breakfast. Your favorite."

"Waffles?" His eyes widened. "Bye, Dua." He waved at me and dashed from the room, leaving me alone with Mahnoor.

"Bye." I waved after him.

"Sorry about him. He's easily excited." Mahnoor bit her lower lip. "How was your trip?"

"Not bad," I said slowly. I'd never been the best at small talk. "I slept. A lot. How's your summer been?"

"Good." She tucked a lock of chestnut-brown hair behind her ear. "Hot."

"Hmm." I gnawed on my lower lip as I waited for her to say

something else, urging my brain to come up with something brilliant to add. "So"—she looked up from the floor at the sound of my voice—"where are you going to go to law school?"

She smiled faintly. "Columbia."

"Oh." Ivy League. That'd be something to rub in my face. I could hardly decide on a major my parents would approve of, while my accomplished cousin was becoming a lawyer at Columbia. Music would hardly measure up in comparison. I cleared my throat, hoping it would dislodge some of the resentment. "That's cool. You must have scored really high on the LSATs."

"Yeah, I studied. A lot. And prayed a lot." She swallowed, cleared her throat. "Everyone else is up too. Breakfast is in the kitchen."

"'Kay. Thanks." I didn't know what to say after that. It was the most awkward exchange I'd ever been a part of. If I'd had any doubt before, it was painfully obvious now that we didn't know each other.

"Sure." She closed the door behind her, leaving me alone again.

I took a deep breath and let it out slowly. In less than twenty-four hours, I'd gone from being an only child to sharing a house with seven other people. Even if it was just for a month, it was going to take some getting used to.

I forced myself out of the covers and had just started to make the bed when my phone buzzed. A grin split my face when I saw Kat's latest text.

How's it feel to wake up in the city that never sleeps?!? Remember to get me a keychain before you leave—one that says "I ♥ NY!" Love you!

Typical Kat. *Woke up with the cutest boy ever staring at me,* I texted back.

WHAT?!? Omg what'shisface was staring at you while you were sleeping?!? That's creepy. Unless he's hot. Is he hot?!

I squelched the urge to facepalm. *No, you weirdo! I meant my four-year-old cousin MAHDI.*

Ohhhhhh . . . well, carry on then. Gonna go grab breakfast!

Shaking my head, I left my phone on the bed and headed to the bathroom.

Five minutes later, I entered the kitchen, hair and teeth brushed, wiping my sweaty palms on my favorite blue plaid button-down shirt and jeans. I hadn't been this nervous since the time Jerry Winthrop, the most popular guy at school, had walked up to me in sophomore English to tell me I had a dead bug on my shirt.

"Assalamu alaykum, Dua." Aunt Sadia smiled at me as she flipped an omelet, the edges crisping up, desi-style. "Did you sleep well?"

I forced a smile. "Alhamdulillah. I didn't have to sleep long; I slept so much in the car." Well, at least it wasn't a lie.

I watched her put the omelet on a plate and garnish it with cilantro. As she bent over the plate, I couldn't help but wonder how she seemed to always be smiling.

"Do you want something, Dua?" she asked, looking up at me. "Eggs? Pancakes? Waffles?"

Oops, I thought. *Staring, bad idea.* "I don't want to be too much trouble. Is there any cereal?"

"In that cabinet." She pointed. "Milk's on the table. And it's no trouble. Do you want eggs?"

"No, cereal's fine, thank you." I opened the cabinet, expecting to see Cocoa Pebbles, Rice Krispies, or at least corn flakes. Instead, Raisin Bran, my least favorite, stared back at me, alongside

24

a box of Special K. Even Uncle Yusuf's family's cereal choices were different. I peered at it a little closer. Dark chocolate. Special K it was. I seized the box and was headed for the table when I was assaulted by a raven-haired hurricane.

"Oh my God, you're finally here!" An almost impossibly petite girl crushed me in a hug.

She squeezed me so hard I couldn't feel my hand anymore. A preteen boy watched me struggle for a few moments before he took the box from my hand, placing it on the table.

"Sorry, did I take your cereal?" I wasn't quite as used to sharing as most people since I was the only one who ate cereal with any regularity at home.

"No, you're fine. Let up, Rabs," he said, studying me like I was a blob of goo under a microscope. His hair was gelled up into spikes and, although his face still showed signs of the baby he'd once been, he was almost six feet tall. I barely managed to suppress a gulp. I hadn't expected twelve-year-old Adam to be shorter than me, but this . . . this was overwhelming.

When Rabia kept squeezing me like she wanted to absorb me into her own body, Adam reached out and poked her in the back. "I don't think she can breathe like that. She's actually turning blue."

"Like a blueberry!" Mahdi chimed in, kicking his legs as he shoved another bite of syrupy goodness into his mouth.

I probably *was* turning blue. While Rabia was only sixteen and smaller in build, she seemed to be twice as strong as I was.

She looked up, studying my face intently with hazel eyes as big as Mahdi's. "Oh." She loosened her grip and stepped away, just enough to give me the space I needed to breathe. "Sorry." I watched her try to stay calm, but a grin broke out on her face and her eyes practically radiated sunrays. "I'm so excited you're here!" she squealed. "It's been too long. How are you? How's school? Where are you going to apply for college? I wanted to have you in my room, but apparently I talk in my sleep."

All I could do was blink at her. Wow. I was *not* used to that many words so early in the morning. Was I supposed to have a response ready for each question? When she didn't say anything else, I looked over her shoulder at Adam. "She's done talking," he confirmed. "For now. Rabs, let her eat before you bombard her. Can't interview her on an empty stomach."

"Oh yeah. Sorry. Just let me or Mahnoor know if you need anything. You got some cereal? Good. I'll get you a bowl and spoon." She touched my arm quickly and then went to grab the stuff from a cabinet.

My mouth hung slightly open as I looked at Adam again. I'd forgotten how chatty she was. In Pakistan, our grandmother insisted on always feeding Rabia with her own hands. It was little wonder why; it kept her mouth too full to talk during dinner.

"We tell her to avoid caffeine, but she loves cappuccinos with her bagel," he explained, shaking his head.

"But she and Mahnoor . . ." I wasn't sure what to say. Actually, I had the words; I just couldn't say them out loud. Compared to Mahnoor, Rabia was like a chipmunk on drugs.

"Yeah, it can be hard to believe they're sisters," said another guy, a few inches taller than Adam and clearly older, as he reached for a bagel. "Rabia talks a little too much; Mahnoor doesn't talk enough. They balance each other out." His hand missed the bagel and knocked into the box of cereal instead. Thankfully, it didn't spill. He sighed, straightened the box, and grabbed the bagel. He added, "Don't worry, you'll get used to it. Sit."

I turned to the table. "Where?" There were only a few empty chairs left, and I didn't want to take someone else's spot.

"Here," Rabia said, setting my bowl and spoon across from Ibrahim. "Can I get you anything else? Hey, I was thinking about doing a lot of baking this Ramadan—cookies and cupcakes and stuff. I could use another set of hands."

"Um, can I just eat my breakfast?" I pointed toward the chair.

"Sure." She moved aside, just enough so I could actually sit. "So, what do you say?"

Ibrahim chuckled. From where I sat, I could study him easily. Unbidden, a hundred memories came to mind: Ibrahim hugging me to comfort me when I was five years old and had accidentally run over a lizard with my tricycle. Offering me his lunch when we'd gone on a road trip and I'd forgotten mine in its brown bag at home. Taking Rabia and me to every bakery we could find in Pakistan, gorging on so many treats we had no room left for dinner.

He looked the way I remembered him. His hair, black as night and cropped short, suited him perfectly; his eyes, hazel like Rabia's but lighter; skin naturally tanned, teeth perfect. The neatly trimmed beard was new, though.

He was one of those people who you could just look at and know they were special, his smile gentle. But sometimes, like this morning, he seemed a little out of focus. With a jolt, I remembered how my parents solemnly explained to me, years ago, that Ibrahim was blind and what that meant. Not to be rude or ableist, but always follow his lead. Uncle Yusuf and Aunt Sadia trusted him to take care of Rabia and me when we wanted to visit different shops and bakeries in Pakistan, and that confidence radiated in his every movement. A memory, slightly blurry around the edges, came to mind: a shopkeeper in Pakistan handing him less change, with a smirk. Rabia barely touched the hem of his kurta, and Ibrahim returned the change with a smile and firmly asked for the correct amount.

"Dua!"

"Hmm?" I snapped back into the present and looked at Rabia. Oh, shoot, she'd been talking to me this whole time. "Sorry, what was that?"

"What's your favorite kind of baked good? Cookies? Brownies? Cupcakes?" Her voice was soft, but the question had an edge to it, as if her opinion of me rested on my answer.

"Brownies. Chocolate chip cookies are a close second."

She smiled. "Those are my favorites too. Great, we'll definitely make some."

"Let her eat in peace," Ibrahim said. "You're practically breathing down her neck."

"Right. Sorry." She sat herself next to me.

"I call dibs on the corner brownies," Adam said.

"No way," Rabia replied. "Dua's only here for the month, so she gets the best pieces of everything."

"Oh, come on, that's not fair."

I slumped in my seat, shoving cereal into my mouth as the back-and-forth continued. As if he could feel my discomfort, Ibrahim's mouth lifted in a smile. "Welcome home, Dua," he said softly. "You'll get used to it."

As soon as I finished my cereal, a tug at my sleeve brought my gaze downward. Mahdi looked up at me, a smudge of maple syrup on one cheek. "Present time?" he asked. "Please?"

It might help break the ice with Mahnoor. "Sure."

"Yay!"

"I'll get the presents and meet you in the living room."

"Can you hurry?" He bounced up and down on the balls of his feet, too excited to stay still. "How long is it gonna take?"

"As long as it takes you to get your brothers and sisters in the living room."

He was off like a missile, calling, "Rabiaaa," as he dragged her away from a scintillating debate with Adam on baked goods.

I headed for Mahnoor's room; the gifts had been stashed in a large duffel, now tucked into a corner of her closet. I grabbed it, leaving the room as quickly as I'd entered.

Everyone looked up as I walked into the living room. My steps slowed. I wasn't used to having so many eyes on me at once. My hands were cold as I reached into the bag. I handed Rabia her present first, since she sat closest to me.

"Oh, wow, guitar straps? They're perfect!" she gushed as she picked each one up and studied it. "Thank you so much!" She started to get up, but Ibrahim pulled her back down.

"If you're going to attack her with hugs, only hold on for thirty seconds. Any longer and you'll probably end up rupturing her appendix."

"Hmm." A big smile on her face, she settled for squeezing her new guitar straps.

Pulling the rest of the presents out of the bag, I made myself comfortable on a cushion in the middle of the floor. As soon as I sat down, Mahdi came close, stopping only when he was almost in my lap again.

Without missing a beat, I handed him his gift. He stayed next to me as he tore through the wrapping paper more carefully than I'd ever seen a four-year-old do. "Thank you, Dua!" He grabbed me around the neck in a hug when he saw the Lightning McQueen remote-control car.

"You're welcome, Mahdi," I said, squeezing him back.

"Will you play with me?" he asked, getting off my lap to open the package.

"Sure," I said. "Just not yet, okay?"

He nodded, going over to Rabia so she could open the box.

"Heads-up." I tossed Adam his present.

He caught it deftly, grinning as he looked over the soccer ball. "You play?"

"Sometimes." I didn't add that the last time I'd played, I face-planted in the mud.

"Sweet. Need someone to do drills with that I haven't beaten already." Rabia stuck her tongue out at him. "Real mature, Rabs. You're how much older than me?"

"Ibrahim, this is for you." I didn't let go until I was sure he had a good grip on it.

He ran his hands over it carefully. In his smile, I saw the Ibrahim I remembered: prone to laughter, easygoing, ready to take on the world with nothing more than his smile. I couldn't recall ever feeling that way. "A flash drive?"

"Yes, with music on it. I tried to find songs I thought you'd enjoy learning to play on guitar."

"Awesome." His smile grew. "Thanks."

I smiled half-heartedly. "And this is for you, Mahnoor." I handed her the last present.

"A briefcase?" I couldn't tell if she was happy about it or not. Maybe only old people liked briefcases. I should've gotten her something else, like a gift card to Sephora. Not that she seemed to be wearing any makeup.

"Engraved with your name on it." I pointed out the gold plate with *Mahnoor A. Sheikh* on it in swirling letters.

She ran her fingers over the engraving, the corners of her mouth turning up into a little smile. "My first briefcase. Thank you." Her fingers continuing to trace the letters of her name, she added, "I'm gonna go put this away." She hugged me and left the room before I even had time to respond.

"I'm going to see which one I should put on first." Guitar straps in hand, Rabia left, but not before giving me a hug that nearly pulverized my rib cage.

Adam was already playing with the soccer ball, effortlessly kicking it up and balancing it on his knee. "I need to go out before I break a window. Dua, want to play?"

I bit my lip. "Um, no, not now, okay? Later."

"Promise?"

"Sure, promise."

Then it was just Ibrahim, Mahdi, and me in the living room, nothing but the sounds of Aunt Sadia working in the kitchen and Mahdi playing with his toy filling the air.

I sighed, letting the relative quiet wash over me.

Mahdi's car smacked into my leg, making me yelp. "Oops." Remote control in hand, he came over to me, lower lip sticking out. "Dua, are you okay? I'm sorry." His lower lip trembled.

"It's fine, Mahdi," I said quickly, pulling him into my lap. "Let's work on your driving." He handed me the remote control and snuggled with his head under my chin, his hair tickling me. "I was just distracted."

"You're not comfortable here, are you?" Ibrahim asked matter-of-factly.

I looked up, driving Mahdi's car into a corner.

"I thought you knew how to drive," Mahdi said, tilting his head to look up at me.

"I do. That doesn't happen on the real road," I reassured him, giving him the remote. "Try again." As he fiddled with the controls, I turned to Ibrahim. "Is it that obvious?"

He shrugged. "Maybe just to me. People are often uncomfortable when I'm in the room, so I know what it feels like. It's almost palpable."

My gaze lowered at his frankness. I told Mom and Dad I would try. Was I already failing?

"Is there anything I can do to help?"

I shook my head. "Probably not." I sighed again, a lump forming at the back of my throat, tears pricking at my eyes. I shoved them back. This was difficult to admit out loud; it felt like a betrayal of my parents, of their efforts to bring me up. "I know Ramadan is supposed to be this amazing, special time of year for us. But . . . I don't feel that. And with being here, it's too different. You should hear how Mom and Dad speak of you all—they think you're perfect young Muslims, and that's not me. I don't measure up." My voice cracked. "I don't fit in."

His mouth flattened into a thin line. Mahdi reached up, his hand brushing my cheek to wipe away a stray tear. I smiled down at him, grasping his little fingers in my own.

"Well," Ibrahim said quietly, "I don't quite fit in either, maybe not in the same way as you, but . . . at least you'll have company."

"Hmm." I shrugged, unconvinced.

"Ramadan is about trying, Dua," he said gently. "Trying to be better versions of ourselves, to nurture our faith. It's not impossible, but it is easier if you have others to support you. I'm always here; all you have to do is ask." After a long moment, he added, "Besides, fitting in is overrated. Don't you think so?"

My smile was shaky. It sounded a lot like something Kat would say. "Yeah," I admitted. "I guess it is."

four

On my fourth day in New York, I stood outside the bathroom door. With so many people in the house, bathroom time was tough. Mom and Dad had an attached bathroom in the guest bedroom, which left one for all of us cousins. Ibrahim and Mahnoor never took too long, but Rabia and Adam always seemed to take at least ten minutes. I'd had my own bathroom my whole life; I wasn't used to waiting.

If the door wasn't opened soon, I'd have to start hopping. I crossed my legs and tried to distract myself from my full bladder. So far, my cousins were easier to get along with than expected. Except for Mahnoor. She didn't do anything to purposely make me feel like I was invading her space, but the more time I spent around her, the more distant she seemed. She'd always been on the quiet side, but even five years ago, she hadn't been this reserved.

I didn't want to be rude, but I was tempted to ask if I could move to Rabia's room. Mahnoor nearly ignored my presence, saying quick good mornings and good nights, giving monosyllabic answers to my questions and sometimes acting like she couldn't get away from me fast enough. At first, I found the silence somewhat comforting. But the longer I stayed, the more stifling it became.

Mom's words came to mind: *This trip is about reconnecting, Dua. To your faith, to your family, to your roots.* Mahnoor was part of that. I couldn't force her to like me, but I had to have some sort of a civil relationship.

Rabia opened the bathroom door, and I almost fell in. "I'm sorry. Were you waiting for a while? I was taking a shower and I got some new shower gel—"

"Yeah, it smells nice, gotta go, sorry," I said quickly, pushing past her. If it were a question of what could last longer, my bladder control or Rabia's rambling, then Rabia would definitely win.

A few minutes later, I headed back to Mahnoor's room. I paused for a moment, seeing the closed door. She might as well have put a sign up: No Entry. Sighing, I turned on my heel and headed to the living room.

Mom and Aunt Sadia were watching an old Pakistani movie and analyzing every minute of it. A favorite pastime of Mom's.

Mom glanced up at me. "Come sit with us, dear."

Returning her smile, I made myself comfortable between them, leaning into Mom's side. "So, what's the story here?"

"The main leads are in love, of course, but the heroine's best friend is— Son of a donkey, she is evil!" Mom yelled at the TV, watching as the male lead let go of his love's hand, her "friend" smirking as she looked on.

Aunt Sadia glanced at her, wide-eyed, and then back at the screen. "For a villain, she's being pretty obvious, don't you think?"

"Yes, to everyone but the hero and heroine," she huffed.

"Mom." Mahnoor walked into the room, her face down as she rummaged through her purse. She wore jeans, a fuchsia top, and a navy hijab. Ready to go out. The question was, where? I'd hardly seen her go anywhere except the living room, with an occasional detour via the kitchen. "Do you need me to pick anything up from the grocery store on the way back?"

"No, sweetheart," Aunt Sadia replied. "Why don't you take Dua, though?"

Mahnoor looked up, finally noticing me. "Oh. I didn't know you wanted to go out too," she said, her voice flat.

She was only offering because of Aunt Sadia—if that could even be counted as a real offer—but I couldn't sit in the house all afternoon listening to Mom's commentary. "Actually, I was planning on reorganizing my socks."

All that got was a blank stare. Okay, so humor was *not* the best approach with Mahnoor.

"That was a joke. Sure, I'll come with you," I said. "Let me just grab my wallet."

"Okay. I'll be waiting outside." Slinging the purse over her shoulder, she left the room.

Mom leaned toward Aunt Sadia. "You've done such a wonderful job raising that one," she stage-whispered appreciatively. "She's so sweet, and such a good Muslim."

I could barely resist rolling my eyes as Aunt Sadia beamed. Of course, perfect Mahnoor. She had everything and was the golden child. What was I? I cleared my throat loudly, as if to remind her I was still in the room.

"Do you need any money, dear?" Mom asked. She'd paused the TV, but I knew she was still thinking about it.

I shook my head. "No. Thank you."

She patted my back absentmindedly. "Okay, then. Have a great time."

I sighed. So much for that. I exited the house a minute later, combing through my wristlet, scattering individually wrapped vanilla caramels, my license, and loose change. I offered Mahnoor a caramel, but she shook her head. I paused for a moment, tempted to have one myself. If I were chewing, I couldn't talk to Mahnoor, so it wouldn't be awkward if one of us said something and the other didn't respond.

Mahnoor shifted her weight from one foot to the other. "Ready?" She sounded bored of me already, and I probably wasn't helping by taking forever to decide about my caramel. What was her problem anyway?

I tucked the candy into my pocket, within easy reach if needed. "Yeah, let's go."

She led the way silently.

"Where are we going?" I asked, walking briskly to keep up.

"Pizza place," she replied, both of her hands shoved deep into her pockets.

The only pizza I'd ever had was from Dominos or Pizza Hut, or it was homemade. Nothing close to "New York style." I'd *have* to get my hands on the real thing. "What are we doing there?"

"Lunch and a show." She headed down a flight of stairs underground.

I'd never ridden the subway before, and as we both stood there in the dimly lit, musty tunnel, I realized why. Didn't people tend to get mugged—or worse, killed—in places like this? I moved closer to Mahnoor, leaving her with only the slightest amount of personal space.

"Relax." She took a step away from me, restoring her personal bubble.

"Sorry. I watch a lot of crime dramas. Sometimes I get too paranoid."

She stared at me blankly for a long moment. "We'll be fine."

Once we were sitting down, Mahnoor pulled her hands out of her pockets, and I saw the diamond ring sparkling on her left hand. I knew nothing about diamonds, but even I could tell it was nice. To distract myself from the images of crime scenes floating through my head, I leaned forward to look at it. "Wow, what's his name?"

"Azhar," she answered flatly, glancing at it.

"Azhar." No clue what it meant, but it sounded nice. "How old is he?"

"Twenty-four."

"Hmm. And what does he do?" I was sounding less like myself and more like the older women in Pakistani dramas, always on the lookout for "a good match."

"Electrical engineer."

Typical. There are only two acceptable career options in the desi world—medical doctor or engineer. Sometimes law. A professional degree is always favored, mostly for the money and job security, but also for the respect and social standing. Of course, Mahnoor chose someone who fit the mold, just like she did. I bit my lip. "How'd you meet?"

"Our families have known each other for years."

"What's he look like?" I tried to picture the kind of guy Mahnoor would marry. Tall, probably. Handsome, of course. Extroverted, maybe? Or quiet, like her? Or was she only quiet around me?

"Dua." She looked at me, irritation flashing in her eyes. "You ask a *lot* of questions."

Clearly, my attempts at bonding weren't working. "Sorry." I resolved to stay silent the rest of the way. Getting on her nerves was not going to make the time pass any easier.

The train moved and vibrated constantly, knocking my knees together with every bump. If I hadn't been sitting down already, I wouldn't have been able to hold my balance.

"Here's our stop," Mahnoor announced, readjusting her hijab and standing up.

I got up quickly. Too quickly. The train jerked to a full stop, and I fell back into my seat, flat on my butt. "Oof."

"Dua, come on." She pulled me up, dragging me out. "We'll be late if you don't hurry."

She weaved through the crowd easily; I had to almost run to keep up. Finally, she reached for my hand and pulled me into a pizzeria, letting go as soon as the door closed behind us.

"They're about to start." She turned to face the stage, beckoning for me to do the same. The place was packed, college kids and high schoolers everywhere.

"Hello, Queens!"

I turned my gaze to the stage. A girl not much older than me stepped up to the microphone, wearing combat boots, distressed jeans, and a loose white tunic with half sleeves. Her dark brown hair fell in curls to her waist, black henna tattoos adorned the skin from the backs of her hands to her elbows, and her dark brown eyes sparkled as she held the microphone.

Ibrahim and Rabia stood on opposite sides of her, holding their guitars. Rabia caught my eye and waved frantically, pointing to her new guitar strap. They were in a band? I leaned forward in my seat. This family was full of surprises.

Two other guys were up on the stage, one on drums, the other on keyboard, both as unfamiliar as the girl holding the microphone.

"How's everybody doing today?" the girl asked, smiling as people clapped. Several whistled. "Awesome! We are Sheikh, Rattle, and Roll, and we have an amazing show for you today!"

As they started playing, I found myself studying each of the band members, letting the music wash over me. It was a religious song, but I could hear the pop influences.

The lead singer sang with complete abandon, her voice rich and velvety as she sang of the beauty of the world, and the One who'd created it. She moved freely about the stage, sometimes waving a hand in the air, sometimes whipping her head back and forth. She reminded me a little of Kat: charismatic, energetic, with an I-don't-care-what-you-think-I'm-just-going-to-be-me attitude.

I'd never seen a group like this before. Sure, Mom and Dad played religious music at home, but that was mostly older men with simple instrumentals. This music was different, created with younger audiences in mind. It was refreshing, exciting, and melodious all at once.

Rabia let her guitar do most of the talking. For once. Her fingers moved on the fret board with ease, a grin on her face as she played. Occasionally, she leaned into the microphone in front of her to back up the other girl. Lips moving with the music and lightly jumping in place, her energy perfectly matched the beat.

Ibrahim was amazing. Unlike the rest of the band, he didn't allow anything to distract him from the music, putting all he had into it. Not unlike how I felt when I played, transported. My fingers itched, longing for my keyboard.

The guy on drums was really good, too, clearly the heart of the music. Lightly tanned skin, short dark brown hair, and a slight amount of facial hair. Probably Arab, judging by his facial structure.

The singer skipped over to him, whispering into his ear.

I didn't know what she said, but he looked over at our table and smiled warmly. His eyes, a brilliant green, met mine for just a split second, but . . . Okay, forgive the cliché, but there's no other way to explain it. In that one second, his gaze cut me to the core, seeing into my mind, boring into the essence of my being. It was a strange feeling, yet somehow familiar, like looking into the eyes of an old friend I'd almost forgotten about.

I looked away quickly.

The guy playing the keyboard resembled the singer. Distinctly Arab features, especially the eye shape and high cheekbones. His hair was darker, and he had a light beard, but they had the same nose, the same smile. He was staring at Mahnoor, but not in a creepy way. I leaned closer, watching his hands. There was a ring on his left ring finger.

Mahnoor glanced at me for a second, then looked at the stage before turning back to me again. "What?"

I stared at her, perplexed. "Is your fiancé here?"

"Yeah, why?"

I looked at him and then back at her. "Is that—"

She sighed. "Yes, Dua, that's Azhar, my fiancé."

"He's not Pakistani," I said automatically. Thank you, Captain Obvious.

"I know. He's Lebanese."

Alhamdulillah, God created butts. Without mine, I would have slid out of my chair and landed on the floor.

"Close your mouth."

"It wasn't an arranged marriage?" Every arranged marriage I'd ever seen was between two people of the same culture. A marriage outside one's own culture was usually for love. "I thought it was."

"Why'd you think that?" Mahnoor asked, though she didn't answer my question.

She had a point. *Why* had I assumed? "So how—"

"How was that?" the lead singer asked, finishing the last song. Her huge smile, her eyes crinkling, was infectious. So was her laugh, when everyone else in the pizzeria cheered. "Thank you, you've been a wonderful audience!"

As the crowd began to clap, she held up one hand, quieting everyone. "Just one more thing," she continued, gracefully flicking a lock of hair away from the corner of her mouth. "We won't have another performance for a while. Just a month, guys, that's it," she added, hearing boos. "As usual, we're going to pass around a box for donations. Please be especially generous today; all donations go to help Syrian refugees. Thank you again. We are Sheikh, Rattle, and Roll!"

"Don't forget to grab some pizza," Rabia added, stepping up to the mike. "Ramadan's in a couple of days, so bulk up."

That got a chuckle out of everyone.

Mahnoor dropped a couple of ones into the donation box and passed it over. I put all my spare change in and passed it down, my eyes on the stage the whole time. I couldn't help it; I was staring at the drummer again, but I was trying—and probably failing—to be subtle about it. Seeing as I was the only Muslim teen at home, cute Muslim boys in Burkeville were nonexistent.

"Come on," Mahnoor said, prompting me to finally tear my gaze away from the beautiful back of the drummer's head. "Let's introduce you to everyone." Grabbing my arm, she stood up and led me over to the stage, stopping in front of it.

"Mahnoor!" The lead singer skipped over to us, a huge smile on her face. "You made it!" Sitting on the edge of the stage, she visibly relaxed; shoulders rounding, legs crossed. "Assalamu alaykum," she said, looking at me, extending one hand. "Dua, right? I'm Haya."

"Wa alaykum assalam." I shook her hand. "That was awesome—you're really good."

"Thanks." She seemed more like Aunt Sadia's daughter than Mahnoor did; she couldn't stop smiling. I could've sworn her eyes literally sparkled. "This band is, like, my baby or something. Do you play anything?"

"Piano," I admitted, fondly remembering my keyboard at home. I started when I was six, and I'd kept at it ever since. Whenever I was stressed, every time I touched the keys, my anxieties melted away. I felt content.

"Really?" She leaned in closer to me, so much I worried she'd fall off the stage. "You think you can handle keyboard? Azhar has the oddest notion that he's not going to have time to balance the band, work, and family after the wedding, so we're going to need a replacement."

I opened my mouth to respond, but Mahnoor beat me to it.

"She's just visiting, Haya," Mahnoor reminded her. "After Ramadan, she's going back home."

"Aww." She pouted. "Well, a month is a long time." She winked at me. "We'll see what happens." She jumped off the stage. "By the way, I know Mahnoor doesn't talk much, so let me give you a quick rundown."

"Okay." I stared up at her. She was probably of average height, but compared to me, she was a giant.

"I'm Haya. I'm twenty-one, studying film production at NYU, and Mahnoor and I have been best friends since I was in kindergarten and she was in first grade. We met in Sunday school in Qur'an class." She looked over at Azhar, who was packing up his keyboard. "And soon, she's going to be my sister-in-law."

Mahnoor played with her engagement ring, twisting it around her finger.

Haya didn't notice. "Azhar, this is Dua," she called, putting an arm around my shoulder.

"Salaam," he said, glancing up. "Sorry, I'm a little wrapped up with this." He gestured to the various cables around the stage.

"Of course, you know Rabia and Ibrahim. Over there, looking like he wants to hide behind the drums is Hassan. Hey, Hassan," she yelled. "Say salaam!"

"Assalamu alaykum," he said, looking up momentarily. He and Ibrahim were talking about something.

"Wa alaykum assalam," I replied quietly, forcing my gaze elsewhere. As stupid as it was, I'd never had an actual crush before—one that wasn't on a celebrity, anyway. I didn't want to seem like the weird girl who couldn't stop staring. Haya was a welcome distraction.

"Don't mind him. His heart's in the right place, but he can be a bit shy. Especially when it comes to girls." She folded her arms over her chest. "Trust me, I know. Mom's convinced she's going to have to start looking for a girl for him soon, even though he's only nineteen."

I didn't say anything, not knowing if there was an appropriate response to that. *Pick me!* was off the table, though it was on the tip of my tongue. Fortunately, Haya was still talking.

"Even though he's younger, he treats me like his little sis. You know, going all overprotective-older-brother type. It's annoying sometimes."

"Ready to go?" Mahnoor asked Rabia as she jumped off the stage to land next to me.

"I was planning on meeting up with some friends for lunch." Rabia flashed a smile at me. "I already called Mom, and she said it's okay as long as I get home on time."

"Okay." Mahnoor nodded, still twisting her engagement ring. It was starting to annoy me.

"Ooh, we should go for lunch too. I'm starving," Haya said, slinging a messenger bag across her torso.

"You just ate pizza twenty minutes ago," Hassan said, looking at me for a moment before his eyes found his sister's. She had been pretty loud.

"Yeah, and I'm hungry again. Honestly"—she turned to me— "I don't know how I survive Ramadan every year. At any other time, I need to eat almost constantly. If I go two hours without eating, I'm dead to the world."

"She really is," Mahnoor confirmed as we started walking out, more at ease now that Haya was between us. "It's ridiculous. And she can eat more than Azhar, Ibrahim, and Hassan combined."

"You don't say," I said, only half paying attention, stopping at the door to glance over my shoulder. Hassan looked back down at his drums quickly. Just as fast, I turned back around. I was supposed to be reconnecting with my faith, not my hormones.

"So, where do you want to eat?" Haya asked, turning to me.

I shrugged. Burkeville only had a handful of restaurants. What was I supposed to pick when I had more options than I'd ever known existed? "I'll eat anything spicy."

"Mexican? I know this place, you're going to love it; they make the most fantastic halal tacos." She looked like she was getting puppy-dog-eyed, like how you'd expect someone in a movie to look when they've fallen in love, fantasizing about spicy beef and crunchy taco shells.

"Oh!" Mahnoor bumped into a man, her shoulder smacking into his side. It was no wonder; she was walking in her own little world. "Oh, I'm sorry, I—"

"Watch it, Towelhead!" the man snapped, glaring at her like she was a piece of gum stuck to his shoe.

I stumbled over my own feet in shock. Had I heard him right? *Towelhead?*

Haya, who'd been a couple of steps ahead of us, stopped in her tracks. Turning around slowly, she walked up to the man, face blank, lips pursed. Mahnoor had already stepped away, looking down at her shoes.

Haya folded her arms over her chest, standing with her legs apart, drawing herself up to her full height. Even so, the man was almost a foot taller than her. "You don't need to be a jerk. You wouldn't call a nun 'Towelhead,' would you?" When the man didn't say anything, just glared at her, she continued. "No, you sure as hell wouldn't. You'd be worried about God damning you for insulting a believer."

She leaned in just a little closer. It was barely noticeable, but the man leaned back, away from her. "This girl is Muslim and proud of it, as proud of her faith as any nun. I don't know what you're making such a big deal out of. She bumped into you, and she apologized. You don't have to name-call. You're clearly not in kindergarten anymore." Lowering her arms, she started to turn away, her gaze still boring a hole in his forehead. "Have a nice day."

Mahnoor and I followed her like little ducklings running after their mother. She was still angry, mouth downturned in a scowl. "Haya, that was— Wow. Quite the speech!" I said, speeding up so we could walk side by side. "How did you come up with all that on the spot?" I wished I had the courage to say something, but I'd never expected this. Seriously, who said such ignorant things in the middle of the street? Was this normal now?

Haya scoffed. "It's not really on the spot when it's always on the tip of your tongue, is it? Sheikh, Rattle, and Roll gets a ton of hate messages on our social media, especially our Facebook and Instagram. We delete the comments and block users when we have to, but it's like playing Whac-A-Mole. You eliminate one, three more pop up. You get enough messages, and you start to think about what you'd say if someone had the guts to insult you in public. Every once in a while, you come across someone who is ignorant *and* vocal about it.

"No one deserves to be insulted because of their faith or because of how they choose to dress. It's not right." She took a deep breath. Murmuring a prayer, she turned to look at us. "I lost my appetite."

My stomach growled before I could say anything. Disturbed or not, there was no stopping my stomach when I was hungry.

"We can go home," Mahnoor said. "We have tons of food in the fridge."

"Biryani?" Haya asked.

My ears perked up at the mention of my favorite Pakistani dish—chicken carefully layered with rice and a variety of fragrant, delicious spices.

"Yeah, there's some."

"Sounds good." We changed direction. "Do we have to take the subway again?"

"Yes," Mahnoor replied.

"I'm going to die." How many more times was I going to fall on my butt today?

Haya chuckled. "You'll get used to it."

I couldn't sleep that night. Mom and Dad wanted me to come here so I could see another side of my heritage, faith, and family. Had they known that I'd also inevitably see another side to my fellow Americans? One that I'd known existed, but never actually seen in person.

I put a hand over my chest, feeling my quickened heart, the pit in my stomach. I'd never seen such animosity up close before, not directed at me or someone I knew. In Burkeville, everyone knew my family well. Dad was beloved by all his patients, and Mom's cooking was raved about in every household. Because of these affectionately formed and cultivated relationships, we'd never encountered Islamophobia back home. At least, none that my parents ever let me see.

I shivered despite the warmth of the room. What if I did what

Mom and Dad wanted and started an MSA at school? Would the familiar, friendly faces change? Would they turn on me too?

I turned over. "Mahnoor?" I said quietly, wondering if she was awake.

"What, Dua?" Her reply came seconds later. She couldn't sleep either.

"I'm sorry about what that guy said to you."

A long moment of silence. Then, "It's okay. I'm fine."

"Does this kind of thing happen a lot?" I asked, afraid of the answer. It couldn't, could it? I mean, I'd seen videos of people getting ignorant comments, but it was usually people who put themselves out there—Islamic preachers, scholars, leaders. People who expected it.

She didn't say anything for a long moment. I heard her shifting, turning away from me. "I don't want to talk about it, Dua. Go to sleep, okay?"

The pit in my stomach ached. I couldn't get the idea out of my head—would I be safe if I started the MSA? Had my parents even considered that? I shook my head, as if that would make it all go away. Burkeville was totally different from New York. I'd be fine. And what happened today didn't have to be an indicator for the rest of my time here. We'd all be fine.

My heart still beat too fast, my anxiety high. I sighed, rubbing the back of my neck as I stared at Mahnoor's still form. As a child, Mom taught me all the prayers she knew, the dua for protection among them. I'd spent countless nights reciting the words after her, listening for the whispered sounds, imagining them hovering in a cloud over my little head as I slowly began to dream. Murmuring the prayer now, I closed my eyes and hoped for sleep.

five

Hi, Dua!

I groaned aloud as I read the email from my guidance counselor. It was summer—couldn't she give me a break?

> Your parents reached out to me and said you were interested in starting a Muslim Student Association this year. What a great idea! As you know, we at Nottoway High embrace diversity, and it's important to promote an environment of tolerance and acceptance. Let me know if you need help finding a faculty advisor for the club. I'm sure a few of the teachers will be interested.
>
> Best,
> Ms. Fritz

Great. Mom and Dad weren't going to let up on this MSA business. What was I supposed to do, create a club with only one member? How would that "embrace diversity"?

The fingers of my left hand moved of their own accord, moving to a melody only I could hear. That same song from my childhood.

"Dua." Mahdi stood in the middle of the doorway, watching me solemnly. "Rabia said to tell you to get your butt to the living room. We're all waiting for you there."

I blinked at him, never having heard a four-year-old tell me to "get my butt" anywhere before. He must have repeated exactly what Rabia had said. "Okay, I'm coming." I got up and followed him out.

Uncle Yusuf's face broke into a smile as soon as he saw me. "You're here. Wonderful, we can start now."

Start what? I sat on a cushion on the floor between Mahnoor and Rabia, pulling a passing Mahdi into my lap.

"As all of you know, Ramadan starts tomorrow," Uncle Yusuf began, "and, like every year, it's time to write your Ramadan checklists."

Our *what?* I turned around to look at my mother.

"Just wait a minute," she said quietly, smiling as she touched my shoulder. As her fingers stroked my hair, I turned to face front.

"Who wants to explain the Ramadan checklist to Dua?" Aunt Sadia asked.

Mahdi's hand shot up instantly, waving so close to my face I knew my nose was about to get clocked. Seeing his dad nod, he repositioned himself in my lap, barely missing knocking his head against my chin so he could make eye contact as he explained, "You need to make a list of what you want to do during Ramadan, a list of things you want to accom . . . accom . . . get done."

That helped, a little. "Why?"

"To make sure we have a productive Ramadan instead of just lying around with empty stomachs during the day and full plates at night," Rabia replied.

I could feel the tips of my ears burning. Her description of an unproductive Ramadan sounded a lot like my regular routine.

"Yes, exactly," Uncle Yusuf added. "Ramadan is not just about learning to be grateful for the food and other blessings in our lives, but also about remembering God often and forming good habits, like praying on time and reading Qur'an often." He held his arms out. "Ready?"

"Ready!" Mahdi piped up.

Aunt Sadia passed out lined paper and pencils. I bit back a smile at my dad's face when Uncle Yusuf told him he had to make a checklist too. No one was exempt.

"Are you going to make a list?" I asked Mahdi, who immediately began squirming.

"Lemme go, Dua. Ibrahim bhai is going to help me."

Right. I didn't know what to put on my own list—how would I help him? I let him go, watching as Mahdi sat in Ibrahim's lap.

"Ready?" Ibrahim asked, reaching for his phone.

Mahdi nodded. "Ready."

"This year," Ibrahim spoke clearly, "Mahdi is going to . . ." He passed the phone to Mahdi.

"Memorize the first chapter of the Qur'an," he finished, kicking his little legs.

I looked back at my own sheet.

"Don't worry, the list is just for yourself," Rabia said. "You don't have to show it to anyone."

I picked up the pencil. Mahnoor only had one thing on her

list so far, but Rabia had gone through half a page already. Different goals, different lists. Oh, joy.

Taking a deep breath, I closed my eyes. What did I want to accomplish this Ramadan? Not dying of hunger, same as every year. Next. Hassan's face popped up in my mind's eye. I could find out if Hassan was single, do some sleuthing, maybe get some guy tips from Kat— No, no, no way. Nope. Nuh-uh. I shooed his face into my mental dustbin. Astagfirullah. Holiest month of the year and I'm thinking about a guy. Ugh.

A really cute Muslim guy . . . Nope, not now. I asked myself again, what do I want to accomplish this Ramadan? I needed it to be different this year. Better. Mom's high praise of Mahnoor was at the forefront of my mind, each word a tiny injury against my ego. If Mahnoor was "such a good Muslim," what was I? I already knew the basics of Islam, but I still had a lot to learn. I knew a lot about the stuff I was *supposed* to do—pray, be good to my parents, fast, et cetera—but I didn't know *why* I did those things. In a way, how I'd spent previous Ramadans was superficial because all I'd done differently was avoid eating and drinking for a few hours.

I tapped my pen against my paper in thought. Maybe if I could show my parents I *wasn't* as superficial about Islam as I seemed, I'd have a little more room to challenge their standards for me. Even if they didn't agree with my music, maybe I could persuade them to consider alternatives. Something that didn't bore me out of my mind, at least.

So what could I put on my list that would help me get closer to that? Almost immediately, an image of Mom popped into my head, her own head bent over mine as she recited Qur'an, the flash of disappointment in her eyes barely registering as I scrolled through Instagram. I opened my eyes and started writing. "In the name of Allah, the Beneficent, the Merciful," I whispered to myself.

1. Learn more about Islam and memorize six chapters of the Qur'an.

I paused. What a daunting task. I knew a couple of chapters already, short ones, enough to recite during my prayers. Some chapters were really long, some only as long as three or four verses. Arabic was not the easiest language to memorize something in if you hadn't grown up fluent, which, as a non-Arab whose Islamic education had been through my parents, I was not. While I could read the Qur'an in Arabic, I read painfully slow and my recitation was flawed. I'd have to tackle the shortest chapters first.

I should give myself a deadline. If I leave it as six new chapters for the whole month, I'll put it off, and before I know it, Ramadan will be over, and I'll be lucky if I memorized three.

1. Improve my pronunciation of the Qur'an and memorize six new chapters, at least one a week.

There. Perfect. What else? I thought of Ibrahim, Haya, and Kat. All confident, independent, refusing to let anything except their personal beliefs define them, and always with a smile on their faces. I didn't just want to be like them, I *needed* to be, to show my parents I could do things differently, effectively. There was an expression I'd heard Mom say once, borrowed from a book: "Discover God, and you will discover yourself."

2. Discover myself. What does Islam mean to me, and how can
   I use it to figure out who I am and the future I want for
   myself? Do I want to start the MSA? What kind of career will I
   pursue?

My fingers slowed as I wrote the last bit. I knew what I wanted
to study, but what would I even do with a music degree? Not
knowing wouldn't help me convince my parents. I scrunched my
shoulders in thought for a long moment. When nothing came to
mind, I made myself move on. I'd figure that part out later.

What else? My ears still burned, remembering how Rabia had
described an "unproductive Ramadan." Lying around with an
empty stomach all day and filling it at night was exactly how I
usually spent Ramadan. Occasionally, I'd read a bit of Qur'an, and
I did my best to pray all five prayers, but I rushed through them,
eager to finish and get on to other things. Often, I ended up falling
asleep before isha, the night prayer. That wasn't the point of Ramadan. I'd always known that, but I'd never felt ashamed about it
before, not the way I did now. No wonder I felt less than qualified
to start my own MSA. What kind of example would I be?

3. Learn to focus on the important things. Concentrate on my
   prayer rather than rushing. Pray on time, and don't miss any
   of the five daily prayers.

My biggest struggles were praying on time and lack of concentration. No matter how hard I tried, I couldn't focus on my
prayers for longer than a minute or two. Mom said that would
come once I learned to love God more. I wasn't sure how that was
supposed to happen naturally. What did that feel like? To love

with your whole being, and know without a doubt that the object of your love cared for you more than you cared for Him?

I stopped writing. I didn't know that feeling. I never had. But I wanted it. What else could I do to experience that? I thought carefully before continuing, the deep blue ink smooth on the paper.

4. Don't wait to feel like a better Muslim—actively seek God in both good and bad times, till it becomes a habit.

Dad always said it was easy to seek God in good times, thank Him for that new car or whatever. Thanking Him and making an effort to stay grateful and keep your faith strong even when it feels like your world is about to implode? Not so easy.

5. Get to know my cousins. Be a better relative, friend, and daughter. Learn to be more open, patient, and selfless in my relationships.

How many times had I let Mom fend for herself during Ramadan, letting her prepare every meal on her own, even though her stomach was as empty as mine? And other than talking to Mahnoor last night, what efforts had I made to get to know her? And I thought *she* had a problem because she didn't want to talk? While I wasn't the worst daughter or cousin to have around, I could do better. I could be more helpful, more kind, more patient—and demonstrate that I could care for others as well as myself.

Satisfied, I looked up. Mahnoor was still writing; Rabia set her list aside with a smile. "Look at your list as often as you can," she told me, "preferably every morning when you wake up and every night before you go to bed. Keep your goals fresh in your mind."

"Don't worry if you don't get everything on your list done or if you haven't done it all perfectly," Ibrahim added, ruffling Mahdi's hair. "Allah counts your intentions as well as your deeds. Just make the effort."

"Dua, are you done with your list?" Uncle Yusuf asked. "I can take a look, since it's your first one."

It sounded less like a question than a command. Biting my lip, I passed my list over to him. I watched his face as he read it silently, the paper looking terribly small in his hands.

His brow furrowed—which part made him react that way?— but he didn't say anything. After a moment, he nodded and handed the paper back to me. His own children probably had much more impressive lists. He'd expected more of me. "Set it somewhere you'll be able to see it often, so you always remember it. You can go."

"Not you, Khalid," he said, when my dad tried to get up. "Give your wife company until she's done."

"Thanks, Uncle Yusuf." I rushed past him, list in hand. Despite his less-than-enthusiastic reaction, there was something about having everything down on paper that made me feel better, like I would have a meaningful Ramadan this year. Hopefully, I wouldn't regret any missed chances once it was over.

six

BEEP! BEEP! BEEP! BEEP! BEEEEEEEEEEEEEEEEEEEEEEEP!

"Dua, get up!"

"Allahu Akbar!" I snorted automatically as I jerked awake and sat upright.

Mahnoor stared at me with an *OMG what a freak* look on her face. "Do you always do that?"

"What?" I murmured sleepily, grabbing my phone. It was 3:00 a.m. I'd slept—I did the math quickly—six and a half hours. My eyelids were as heavy as if I'd only slept six minutes.

"Yell 'Allahu Akbar' as soon as you wake up."

"I did what?" I asked, only half listening. Okay, fajr was in forty-five minutes. I had until then to stuff myself. What could I eat in forty-five minutes that would keep me feeling full till sunset? Everything in the pantry, probably.

Except, of course, by stuffing myself I would be completely missing the purpose of Ramadan. Again. *But* if I didn't eat enough, I knew I'd spend the rest of the day either cranky or passed out on the couch, waiting for someone to feed me, and that would also be completely missing the point of Ramadan.

I grumbled as I shuffled into the kitchen, almost walking into Ibrahim as he exited his room. "Hey, 'sup?"

"You sound like you seriously need to get some food in you and go back to sleep," he said, grinning.

"Yup. And you sound way too happy for three a.m.," I replied, stifling a yawn.

He shrugged, smile still in place. "It's not like I can see how dark it is outside. I can't look out the window and decide I should be tired because the rest of the world is still asleep. Either my body's tired or it's not, and right now, I'm not. Ramadan's here. It's exciting, isn't it?"

I paused, mid-yawn, to ponder this. He had a point. Ramadan only comes once a year, and thirty days go by faster than you'd think. It made sense to make every moment count. After all, that was why I'd made my Ramadan checklist.

Number 4: Don't wait to feel like a better Muslim—actively seek God in both good _and_ bad times, till it becomes a habit.

In this case, if I had to get up at 3:00 a.m., I might as well try to find the good in it. I was physically able to fast and reap the rewards of Ramadan, as opposed to those who were too ill to fast and wished they could.

"Dua?" He waved an arm in the air. "Are you still here?"

"Oh, yeah, I'm here," I said quickly. "Thanks, Ibrahim."

"Dua," Aunt Sadia said. "Ramadan mubarak!" Her smile lit up her face as she handed me a plate heavy with turkey bacon, scrambled eggs, and toast.

"Oh, thank you." It looked delicious, but I was used to Mom's freshly made anda paratha—a spicy omelet wrapped in a flaky Pakistani flatbread—for suhoor. Granted, Mom only had to prepare enough for three of us. I couldn't imagine making enough paratha for ten people, especially this early in the morning. I aimed another "thank you" at Aunt Sadia as I sat at the table, tucking into the food.

Allahu Akbar, Allahu Akbar! the adhan rang throughout the house minutes later, courtesy of a special clock.

I looked up from my plate. I could've sworn I'd just sat down to eat. I reached for a date, and Uncle Yusuf cleared his throat. I looked up, noting everyone's empty plates and glasses, their hands in their laps. Oh. They started their fast as soon as the adhan began. At home, Mom and Dad let me sip some water or eat a piece of fruit till it ended. My ears burned. Slowly, I pulled my hand back.

"I intend to keep fast today for the month of Ramadan," I whispered to myself, the Arabic words rolling easily off my tongue after years of practice. This was it. No food, no water for the rest of the day till sunset. I could already feel my stomach twisting painfully in protest.

Allah places no burden on any soul greater than it can bear, the line from the Qur'an popped into my head. I could do this. I'd already done it several times. I could do it again, especially with sincere intentions.

"Get ready for prayer, everyone," Uncle Yusuf said. "We'll meet in the living room in two minutes to pray fajr."

I froze. We'd be praying fajr *together*? Mom and Dad prayed together every morning, but left me to my own devices, which usually meant me praying on my own in my room, half-asleep, or sleeping through it and praying in a rush before I left for school. There were more blessings with praying in congregation, but I found it even more difficult to focus that way.

There's one thing that always gets me every morning at fajr—when I actually manage to wake up on time to pray it. Before we pray, we have to be clean, and that means washing up for prayer. I'm not a morning person, so I'm not happy about splashing myself all over at 3:45 a.m. I get cold, and then I stand there reciting Qur'an through chattering teeth. But unless you've got a good reason for not washing up, like you were in the desert and there was no water available within a five-mile radius, the prayer doesn't count without completing the ablution.

I squeezed my eyes shut. Number 3 on my checklist. Focus on the important things. Concentrate on my prayer rather than rushing. Pray on time, and don't miss any of the five daily prayers. Before I could focus, I'd have to be physically ready for prayer, clean and pure. I took a deep breath and let it out slowly. I'd just make sure the water wasn't cold.

Shaking off the early morning pessimism, I made my trip to the bathroom quick—washing my hands, face, arms up to the elbows, top of my head, behind my ears, back of my neck, feet up to the ankles, rinsing out my nose and mouth—and dried myself well, so I wouldn't start shivering like a bald cat.

I stood between Mahnoor and Rabia, facing toward Mecca. I'd worried for nothing. Uncle Yusuf led the prayer; his voice, strong and melodic, struck me to the core and stirred something in my soul. The verses from the Qur'an sounded better than they ever had before, the way they were meant to sound. Fortifying. Loving.

Oh, Allah, I thought, my head bent to the floor, *please help me make the best of this Ramadan. Help me show Mom and Dad I can make good choices for myself. I don't want to have any regrets when the month is over. And if I cannot have the same kind of love for You that others do, at least help me understand it.*

As soon as the prayer left my mind, my shoulders relaxed, their burden lifted. This Ramadan was going to be *epic*, I could feel it, a promise from God to my heart.

Mahdi kicked up his legs as he watched another episode of *Paw Patrol*, his eyes still on the screen as he leaned forward and opened his mouth. Rabia popped a halved grape into it, watching as he chewed slowly. My stomach growled quietly and saliva began to pool into my mouth as I watched jealously. Maybe I could sneak a grape or two when no one was looking . . . I'd be breaking my fast, and God is always watching, but He's also the All-Forgiving. One or two grapes couldn't hurt.

"What are you reading?"

I peered up at Adam before glancing back down at my book. "Just some summer reading. *The Awakening.*"

"I have to read *A Midsummer Night's Dream.*"

"Trust me, I'd rather read that one," I said, skimming the page. What a much-needed distraction—did I really want to break my fast over a couple of *grapes*? At the very least, I could hold out for some Cheetos. My fingers stilled on the page. Mmm, Cheetos . . .

Allahu Akbar, Allahu Akbar!

Everyone—Mahnoor, Ibrahim, Rabia, Adam, even Mahdi—

sat straighter as Uncle Yusuf reached into his pocket for his phone. "Asr," he noted, turning off his iPad. "Time to pray."

I turned my attention back to my book. I only had a few chapters left, but it was going slowly because I kept getting bored—and thinking of food. It wasn't a book I'd choose to read for myself; I preferred mysteries or a good romance novel.

"Dua."

"Hmm?" I turned the page and looked up to find Uncle Yusuf standing over me with a concerned expression.

"It's time for prayer. Didn't you hear the adhan?"

"No, I did." I glanced around; everyone else had disappeared, presumably to go pray in their rooms.

"I see." Uncle Yusuf's brow furrowed, the concerned look deepening. "Well, go pray. You don't want to be late."

I hadn't been reading *that* long. "The adhan was a minute ago. I still have hours left to pray."

He nodded. "True, but you don't want to put it off; you could forget or get distracted. People accidentally miss asr all the time for that reason."

I blinked at him. I'd never jumped up as soon as the adhan went off. Mom and Dad would remind me to pray, and then leave me alone. Truth be told, sometimes I *did* forget.

I did have it on my Ramadan checklist that I wanted to focus more on my prayer, and praying on time was part of that, right? Plus, based on the look on Uncle Yusuf's face, he wasn't planning on leaving me alone till I agreed. I felt my eye twitch ever so slightly at the scrutiny, my throat somehow drying up even more than it already was. "I'll go. As soon as I finish this chapter," I promised. "I only have a handful of pages left."

He smiled lightly. "Good. Just make sure you don't forget."

"Okay," I replied, readjusting in my seat, trying to get more comfortable.

Long after Uncle Yusuf left the room, I kept checking my phone for the time, all too aware of the minutes ticking away, a headache beginning to pulse at my temples as my stomach continued to growl.

seven

"Got you something!"

I stared at Haya's outstretched hand for a moment before taking the binder, grateful for the distraction from my parched throat. "What's this?" I asked, running a hand over the cover.

"Sheet music, all by different artists: Sami Yusuf, Maher Zain, Native Deen, you know, religious music." She plopped down on the bed beside me.

"Who?" Of those names, I only recognized Sami Yusuf, because my parents always played his music on Eid. I couldn't stop staring at the artwork on the cover. It was so delicate, so beautiful. Dark swirls, reminiscent of Arabic calligraphy, stood out amongst a background with pops of green, red, and white, spelling out *Sheikh, Rattle, and Roll.* A statuesque silhouette—Haya's, probably—melded into the background, one fist punched into the air. "This is great," I said, tracing the figure with a finger. "Did you do this?"

Haya shook her head. "Nah, I wish. I can't do anything like that to save my life. That's Hassan's work; he's a graphic design major at NYU. I like it too. It's simple but makes a statement. Just like the music. Here, go through it a bit." She shuffled through a few pages, her long, dark curls falling to dangle over a few notes. "There's some original stuff too. Think you can play it all?"

I couldn't stop my smile as her lithe fingers skimmed through the pages, caressing each one. I left my keyboard at home, but it looked like I wouldn't have to forget about my music this summer after all. "Yeah, I think so."

She looked up at me, her eyes light with joy. She'd added something to the black henna designs swirling around her forearms. Her name, in curved Arabic script, was now embedded in a rose's petals. A tiny guitar peeked out at me, trying not so hard to hide in a thorn.

"We really are going to need a new keyboardist soon, you know," she reminded me. "You'd be a great addition to Sheikh, Rattle, and Roll."

"Thanks, but I'm going back to Burkeville after Ramadan," I reminded her, flipping appreciatively through the binder. A couple of the songs were familiar, ones that Mom had played around the house before.

"Well, you're going to be applying for college soon, right?"

"Mmm-hmm. George Mason is my first choice," I replied, not looking up. *I can prove to Mom and Dad that I can channel my passion into something they'd consider meaningful.*

"Good school, or so I've heard. If you ever decide to apply to, say, NYU or Fordham, we could work something out. We'd love to have you as part of the band." She tapped the edge of the binder, her chunky bracelets clinking together.

"I'll keep that in mind," I replied, slipping the binder into the duffel bag lying at the foot of my bed. "Thanks."

"Awesome." She clapped her hands together, her whole face lighting up as she smiled. "Okay, I haven't told you why I'm here yet—"

"If it's to talk our brains to mush, we've noticed," Mahnoor piped up without looking away from the magazine she was reading. Some Pakistani bridal thing, I think.

"Nice, Mahnoor, way to be in the spirit of Ramadan," she retorted, rolling her eyes. "Anyway, we're having a little dinner at our house tonight, insha'Allah. Nothing fancy, just our families— to mark Ramadan beginning, and to welcome you. Do you like Lebanese food?"

"Um, I like falafel," I said, almost immediately disappointed in myself. Who *doesn't* like falafel? But it was the only Lebanese food I knew off the top of my head. And hummus. "I'll eat anything that has chickpeas in it," I clarified. "Actually, just give me a bowl of chickpeas with salt and pepper, I'll eat the whole thing."

Haya laughed. "Okay, well dinner's going to be a *little* more elaborate than chickpeas, but I'll keep that in mind. Don't worry, my mom's a great cook. You'll love dinner—I promise. She's making maqluba."

I nodded, finding it easy to believe her, especially considering how hungry I was. You could put a sheep's brain on a platter in front of me in six hours' time, and I'd like it. My parents actually did that to me once. I shuddered. Never again.

"All right, I gotta pee." Haya bounded off my bed.

As soon as the door closed behind her, Mahnoor glanced up at me with a smirk on her face, still perusing her magazine.

"What?" I asked. She was watching me like a black widow about to trap her prey.

"Nothing."

"Okay . . ." I turned toward the bedroom door, hoping Haya wasn't one of those Olympic urinators—the ones who can pee for two minutes straight.

Meanwhile, Mahnoor's magazine rustled as she turned a page. After a long moment, she glanced up at me again. I didn't look at her directly, but I could see her smirk out of the corner of my eye. *First she basically ignores me, and now she's staring at me.* "What?" I demanded finally.

She closed her magazine. "You're making a good impression on Haya, if she wants you to be in their band. And Hassan's going to be there tonight."

I tilted my head to the side. She looked pretty normal. Hair braided, eyes shining. But maybe Haya was right—the hunger had gone to her head. Then again, she barely talked to me and *this* was her topic of choice. Maybe she was already a little strange and fasting made things worse. "Seriously? It's the first day of Ramadan, and you're thinking about boys?" I didn't mention that I was trying not to do the exact same thing. As soon as Haya had said dinner at her house, Hassan's face popped into my head.

"Think you'll freak out if he says *salaam* to you?" she asked.

I didn't bother telling her that I've been known to freak out over less when it came to anyone with a Y chromosome. "Let's hope not." I turned away, signaling the end of the conversation. Then something occurred to me and I turned back to her for a second. Her eyes met mine instantly, as if waiting. "By the way, what's maqluba?"

I'd changed outfits three times before we left, eventually choosing a fuchsia and cream-colored shalwar kameez when I noticed Mahnoor wearing something similar.

"Quit looking so nervous," she said. "It's just dinner. With *my* future-in-laws. I should be the nervous one, not you. Why *are* you nervous anyway? Because of Hassan?"

"Maybe it's the lack of food," I suggested, ignoring that last part, studying my reflection in the mirror. Mascara, check. Lip gloss, check. Face frozen into a mask of terror, check.

"An empty stomach messes with your nerves?" she asked, the doubt evident in her voice. She shook her head at me, all wrapped up in a cream and azure hijab. "Dua, no offense, but you have issues."

"Usually, people try to be nicer when they're fasting, you know," I retorted. Earrings. I needed earrings. My fingers shook a bit, and I stabbed myself with the little hook in one lobe as I slipped on a pair of chandelier earrings.

Still shaking her head at me, she picked up her purse and turned for the door. "Whatever, let's go. Everyone's waiting."

I concentrated on not tripping as I teeter-tottered after her to the car. Uncle Yusuf, bless him, rented a ten-seater for the month. Mom insisted that we could ride the subway, and I had to beg her to take my five-inch heels into consideration. They were the only shoes that matched my outfit, and no way was I going to be able to walk halfway through Queens in them without having to get my feet amputated.

Thanks to Uncle Yusuf, my toes were saved, although I couldn't say the same about my dress. Mahdi wanted to sit buckled into my lap instead of his car seat. Still, thirty-nine pounds of sheer cuteness was worth a few wrinkles.

"How long till we get there?" I asked.

"Fifteen minutes," Rabia answered.

"Is Hassan bhai going to be there?" Mahdi asked, his facial expression matching my own whenever I was waiting for Kat to answer a FaceTime.

Rabia smiled, watching as Mahdi took my phone to play a game. "Yes, he will." She glanced at Mahnoor, who was staring out the window. If a grenade exploded two feet away and her facial expression didn't change, I wouldn't have been surprised. "Azhar bhai too."

Mahdi grinned as he swiped his finger across my phone, slicing through virtual fruit. "Dua, Hassan bhai has this game too. He always lets me play it. He's so fun."

"Oh, yeah?" I squelched the urge to pinch his cheek. It could ruin his perfect fruit-slicing skills. "And what about Azhar bhai? Azhar bhai's not fun?"

"He used to be." Mahdi paused and looked up, pursing his lips. "Well, he still is," he amended, going back to his game. "But now all he wants to do is talk about Mahnoor. Is she happy, what does she like, blah blah blah."

"That's good, right?" I asked him, looking at Mahnoor. She was listening. Her back stiffened ever so slightly. "He's wants to keep Mahnoor happy when they get married."

"Yeah, I guess. Ha!" He waved the phone in my face triumphantly. "Look, Dua, I beat your high score!"

And there went Mahnoor's brain, back to whatever la-la land it'd gotten sucked into in the first place. What was she thinking?

Too bad there wasn't an app for that. A mind-reading app would be *really* useful right now.

I don't know what I'd expected, but it hadn't been Mrs. Mousawi going after me like a lioness tackling an antelope. Except that she hugged me instead of trying to eat me. Not that it made me any less freaked out.

"Haya's told me so much about you," she gushed, squeezing my hands.

I whispered *alhamdulillah* to myself when she let go of me. I had no idea what to say, shell-shocked by her surprise hug attack. People usually didn't hug like that back in Burkeville.

"Hey, assalamu alaykum." Haya seized me in a hug before I'd had time to recover from her mother's. She pulled back quickly, though, to give me a once-over. "Mashallah, you look great," she said approvingly.

"Oh, thanks," I said, adjusting my dupatta over my shoulders. "So do you." Compared to her, Mahnoor and I were overdressed. Haya wore dark-rinse jeans and a plain pink top, her only visible jewelry a pair of tiny faux diamond studs. A simple, no-fuss out-fit, yet she still looked glamorous.

"How much time till we break the fast?" Rabia demanded as soon as Haya was done hugging her. Poor thing looked as hungry as I felt. No matter how many years of fasting during Ramadan you've had behind you, you're always starving the first couple of days till your body gets used to it. Hence the sheep brain debacle last year.

She checked her phone. "Five minutes. Get ready for your stomach to explode," she said, grinning at me.

I smiled back wordlessly. I already knew that would happen if

I didn't get some food in me fast. Five minutes, I just had to wait five more minutes.

"Where's Hassan bhai?" Mahdi asked, staring up at Haya solemnly.

"He'll be out in a minute," she promised, eyes sparkling as she ruffled his hair. "Azhar's here too."

"Hey, Mahdi, what's up?" Azhar appeared behind Haya, all smiles. He tried to hide it, but his dark brown eyes kept roving over to Mahnoor. Not that I could blame him. Something about the colors she wore made her look like she was glowing from the inside out.

Mahdi shook his head. "No, Hassan bhai," he insisted. "You're nice, but you're always getting distracted by Mahnoor now."

Mahnoor instantly went red and blatantly avoided her fiancé's gaze, while Azhar pretended he'd been looking at a floral painting behind her head the whole time. Everyone else, including me, burst out laughing.

"Mahdi," Aunt Sadia scolded, reaching out to her baby. "Shush."

Mr. Mousawi, a grayer, slightly plumper version of Azhar, laughed heartily. "It's all right."

Aunt Sadia ran her fingers through his hair affectionately.

"Let's go. Three minutes left." Haya latched on to my arm, grabbing Mahnoor and Rabia as she led us into the dining room.

I heard Mahdi cry out, "Hassan bhai!" and caught a glimpse of Hassan bending down to his level as Mahdi rushed at him.

"Remember, now's the best time to make dua," Haya said, looking right at me. I snapped back to attention with a quick shake of my head. I was getting too distracted these days. "If there's anything you want," she continued, smiling, "now is the time to ask for it."

Before breaking the fast is allegedly one of the best times to make dua. I'd only have twenty-eight or twenty-nine more chances if I didn't take this one. It sounded like a lot, but I'd realize how little it was when the month was over. My stomach rumbled, and I pressed my hand against it hard, willing it to quiet.

Except I had no idea what to ask for. There wasn't anything material that I wanted. Of course, forgiveness for my sins, mercy, and the chance to enter heaven in the afterlife and all that, but was that all I had to ask for? I wracked my brains, watching the timer on Rabia's phone. A minute left. I *wanted* something. I could feel it deep in the pit of my stomach.

Taking a deep breath, I closed my eyes. "Oh, Allah," I whispered, my voice so low I could barely hear it myself, "please open my heart and mind to You. Help me make the most of this Ramadan, and the rest of my life. I don't know what to do in the future, with *my* future. Please, help me figure out what I should do with school, in life. And don't let me forget You."

Allahu Akbar, Allahu Akbar!

I opened my eyes, the adhan ringing in my ears. Falafel, hummus, pita bread, and tiny samosas were piled high on the table, all steaming and assaulting my nose with their tantalizing aromas. My mouth watered so much I had to reach up and wipe it on my sleeve to make sure I wasn't drooling; I didn't protest when Haya gently pushed me into a chair and proceeded to put a little of everything on my plate.

First, though, she grabbed a couple of dates and shoved one into my hands. A custom from the prophet's time, breaking the fast with a date. I murmured the appropriate prayer as quickly as I could without messing up the words and stuffed the date into my mouth, taking care not to choke on the seed.

I gorged on falafel for the next five minutes, getting in as much as I could before we prayed maghrib, while trying to not look like a pig in front of the Mousawis.

We prayed, and as my head touched the floor, I remembered my supplication. I closed my eyes and thanked God. Despite my headache, I'd made it through the first day of fasting, and now there was plenty of food on the table if we were still hungry.

My eyes fell on the table as we walked back toward it, and they quickly grew to the size of tennis balls when I saw biryani and maqluba. That was a lot of rice and chicken, and it all looked delicious. I happily sat down to eat.

As soon as I'd cleaned my plate, Haya materialized with a tray of ice cream sundaes and nudged my shoulder. "Come on, we'll do dessert in my room."

"Okay." I got up from the table. "But"—I leaned in close to whisper into her ear—"I need to go to the bathroom."

"Down that hall and to your left," she said, smiling as she balanced the tray on one hand and nudged Mahnoor and Rabia with the other. "Then come back here and go through the living room. There's a hall just past, and the first door on the right is my room." Noticing my face, she laughed. "If you get lost, our parents will be hanging out here. Just ask."

I smiled and walked out of the dining room carefully, so I wouldn't trip. The moment everyone else was out of sight, I slipped my heels off and ran till I got to the bathroom. I shouldn't have had so much mango juice.

Two minutes and one empty bladder later, I stepped out of the bathroom gingerly, heels back on my feet. I'd only taken one step when my phone vibrated, sending a tremor down my leg.

Kat.

Guess what?!? she texted.

As usual, she didn't wait long enough for me to guess before she sent another text.

I fasted today too. All day, just like you.

THAT'S GREAT! I yelped with joy as I sent the text, then slapped a hand over my mouth. Too loud. My fingers flew over the keyboard. *How was it?*

I loved *it! Eating and drinking early in the morning was tricky, but not as bad as I thought.*

Then, *I'm almost out of barbecue chips* ☹ *But I felt so good today, I want to try fasting the whole month too. Get some spiritual awareness in me and all that jazz.*

Fasting during Ramadan is an obligation on me, not you, I reminded her.

I'm a believer, too, you know. We're in different states, but we don't have to feel disconnected. I'm here for you, D.

Wow. She was genuinely excited about fasting. More than me. I felt a little twinge of guilt in my belly. Or was that indigestion? *You're awesome. You do realize that?*

Duh. You'd better bring me back something amazing from New York.

Of course. I grinned as I crept through the dining room quietly. The Mousawis sat with their backs to me, so they didn't notice me, but Mom gave me a look like *Really? You're a guest here and you're on your phone?*

Kat, I mouthed. I sighed once the dining room was behind me, not realizing that I'd been holding my breath. I paused halfway down the hall on the way to Haya's room, spotting Azhar's keyboard.

It sat on its stand in a tiny alcove in the middle of the hall. I swear, it was all lit up and glowing when I laid eyes on it, calling to me. My fingertips tingled as I imagined how the keys would feel to the touch, how the music would sound in my ears.

I put my phone away as I approached the alcove, my fingers yearning to get on that keyboard. Yamaha. Not bad. I turned it on, hit the grand piano setting, and stretched my hands toward the keys, elbows and wrists relaxed. My fingertips caressed the keys lovingly like an old friend, whisking me away to my own little world. Not quite home, but without the strange newness of New York.

My fingers went through the movements automatically, flying across the keyboard to match the swift, sweet notes of a Sami Yusuf song floating to my ears. I hummed along quietly, letting myself get lost in it. This particular song, like many of Sami Yusuf's, was all about praising God. One of Mom's favorites, it was the only Islamic song in any of my playlists. My euphoria swelled as the notes did, strong and beautiful. I closed my eyes and listened, my fingers knowing just what to do to keep the music going. My shoulders began to sway slightly, my body shifting in slow, gentle movements. My feet longed to turn round and round like a whirling dervish, in a quickened tempo to match the music. I felt light, untethered. Yet I willed my feet to still, knowing my fingers would have to leave the keys to follow their whimsy. My mind conjured the lyrics to match each note, rising and falling with every description of God and His many names. I picked up speed as I neared the end, my knuckles flexing smoothly to get it just right. With the last note, my hands stilled. The music in my head continued, and I felt the itch to keep going. I lifted a hand slowly, wrist slack, ready to begin again.

Clapping.

I smiled lightly. Is this how it felt for Sami Yusuf, to share every glorious emotion and thought through his music? My heart yearned to capture the feeling, hold on to it like a treasure.

Wait. There was no "applause" button on the keyboard. My eyes shot open and my fingers left the keys, bringing me back to earth, hard. I turned around slowly, my heart pounding so hard, I half expected to see a serial killer standing behind me.

Instead, it was just Mahdi. No, not just Mahdi. My heart rammed hard against my rib cage.

Mahdi and Hassan.

I'd have preferred the serial killer.

"Play it again, play it again!" Mahdi insisted, running up to me to grab me around my knees. "Please?"

"Once was enough," I said gently, focusing on his sweet, innocent face so I wouldn't go all red. Hassan was still there, standing across from me.

"Dua, play something else!" Mahdi tugged on the hem of my pants.

I glanced back at the keyboard wistfully for a moment. Biting my lip, I forced myself to face forward. "I don't think that's a good idea." I moved to touch his head, but he dodged my hand and went to Hassan instead.

"Hassan bhai, tell her to play again!"

He knelt so he was eye level with Mahdi, one arm slung across his knee. "Come on, buddy, I can't make her do something she doesn't want to do."

"But she's so good," Mahdi said, a whine creeping into his voice. "Please?"

Hassan looked at me, just for a second. Still, that was long enough for me to pretend to stare at an empty fish tank. Fascinating. "I don't think now's a good time," he said, turning back to face Mahdi. "Hey, why don't you go find my mom? She made pistachio maamoul last week, and I know she saved some for you."

His eyes lit up, wider than I'd ever seen them. "Maamoul?" he repeated, already headed for the dining room. Hassan kept an eye on him, watching him make his way over to Mrs. Mousawi. Finally, he smiled as he turned his gaze back toward the keyboard. "That one's my favorite. Would've been nice to hear it again."

It would've been nice to play it again too.

He came up beside me, fingers hovering over the keys but never touching them. I took a step back, so his arm wouldn't accidentally brush mine.

"I'm sorry," I said quietly, wringing the edge of my dupatta between my fingers. "I should've asked if it was okay."

He didn't answer right away. His gaze was on the keyboard, but his focus seemed to be directed at me. "How long have you been playing?"

It took me a moment too long to respond. It was, I realized, the first time I was really hearing his voice, aside from that one quick salaam back at the pizzeria. It was gentle yet firm. Pleasant. My heart beat harder. "Since I was six, so eleven years."

He was still studying the keys. "How long did it take you to learn that song?"

"That was my first time," I admitted. "I peeked at the sheet music earlier and—" I broke off when his surprised eyes met mine.

Why? Why did his eyes have to be so *green*? So intense and

deep and— I looked away quickly, focusing on some Islamic art on the opposite side of the room instead.

"It was your first time playing it *ever?*"

I nodded.

"Mashallah. Haya's right. You need to go to college here. Juilliard would love you."

I shrugged noncommittally. "I guess." Now all I had to do was get my parents behind the idea of me applying to Juilliard, or even just studying music as a minor. I'd settle for that.

He cocked his head. "What are you planning on majoring in?"

"Still undecided," I admitted. "I actually do want to pursue music, but you know how parents can be. They think I can't build a career on a music degree. They want me to go into premed, prelaw, or business." I barely stopped my mouth from slipping into a grimace at the thought. "I guess I'll decide once I'm actually at university."

"Well, for what it's worth, I think you're pretty good, and while our parents always want the best for us, they don't always know exactly what that is."

I cocked my head. *Interesting, a different perspective from the "your parents know best" spiel I'd been expecting from Uncle Yusuf's family and anyone who associated with them.* "How did you decide on graphic design? Are your parents supportive?"

"Yes, and"—he looked mildly embarrassed for a fleeting second—"I figured it lets me play to my strengths and passion while paying the bills."

I smiled. "Oh, so you want to be an artist but not the struggling kind?"

He rubbed the back of his neck, mirroring my smile sheepishly. "Basically. My point is, everyone has a certain talent for a reason. Maybe music is worth pursuing after all, even if it's in a different capacity."

"Maybe," I murmured noncommittally. It felt good to be validated for once. I didn't want to get my hopes up yet.

He leaned forward again, and I noticed the ALLAH pendant dangling from his neck on a black cord.

"Where'd you get that?"

He looked down at it, the silver pendant that spelled out God's name in spiraling Arabic letters. "This? Some shop on Fifty-Seventh Street, I think."

"It's beautiful." I started to reach out, then stopped myself, pulling my arm back. I had no business touching a guy I barely knew. Especially an attractive one. Especially an attractive *Muslim* one.

He smiled, still looking at it. Not noticing I'd nearly touched him. "Yeah. I figured since He's closer to me than my jugular vein, I might as well keep His name close to it." He paused, clearing his throat as he ran a hand through his hair. "Sounds kinda weird, saying that out loud."

"No, it makes perfect sense." I allowed myself to study it for one more second before I turned my gaze to the floor. "My mom has one. A pendant, I mean, not a jugular vein. Everyone has those. A gold one on a chain that she got from Pakistan when I was three."

If he thought I was being weird, he didn't show it. "My mom used to bring back stuff like that from Lebanon all the time when we were younger. It's been a while since any of us went back, though. Hasn't been the safest." He was silent as he rubbed the pendant between his fingers. "You don't have one? They're pretty common." He crossed his arms over his chest, his chin lifted as he looked at me expectantly.

"No, I've always wanted one. I'm always forgetting to tell my parents, though. My mom went to Pakistan last year, and it didn't occur to me until she got back." I stopped, the tips of my ears burning as I realized how much I was talking. I wasn't used to talking to guys this much. I backed away quickly. "I gotta go. Haya said we'd do dessert in her room, and my sundae's probably all melted by now."

"Oh." His eyes widened slightly and he dropped his arms to his sides. He opened his mouth for a second, then closed it, as if deciding against saying anything. I couldn't blame him; my awkwardness had that effect on some people. "It's that way." He pointed, then turned his attention back to Mahdi.

"Thanks." I walked away as fast as my heels would carry me, pushing my hair over my ears. It couldn't stop the burning, but at least it would conceal it. Never again. The next time I wanted to play an instrument in someone else's house, I'd stick to non–conversation starters like "Twinkle Twinkle Little Star."

eight

Seriously, what had I been thinking? I stared at my Ramadan checklist, perplexed. *Memorize six new surahs throughout Ramadan.* My memory was *horrible* and my grasp of Arabic even worse. I ran my fingers through my hair, the strands by my crown turning frizzy.

It was already day two, and I hadn't even started yet. I'd have to focus on the shortest chapters first, ones that were only five to seven lines long. I bit my lip, recalling how my usual Ramadan routine was *unproductive* by Uncle Yusuf's standards, like I was a disappointment who missed out on the fundamentals. If I was serious about changing that, I'd have to devote some time to the surahs, not just memorizing them, but studying their meanings as well.

After fifteen minutes, I fell back on my bed, the list on my chest as I stared at the ceiling. Why is Arabic such a difficult language? If you make the slightest, and I do mean the *slightest*, error in pronunciation, you change the entire meaning of what you're trying to say.

I must have sighed, because Mahnoor looked up from her book. "What's wrong with you now?" she asked, as if something happens to me every day.

"I need to memorize six new surahs," I said, still staring up at the ceiling, "and I've checked at least seven different recitations on YouTube for one, and all of them are too fast. I can't understand Arabic even if my life depended on it, and all of these qaris, who've been doing it for years, recite Qur'an like they're in a race." While my parents always stressed to me that the most important thing was to apply principles from the Qur'an to my life rather than just knowing how to recite it without understanding it, having more than a few surahs memorized couldn't hurt. If I could at least remember a few of God's words, hopefully I could remember Him more often too.

Mahnoor closed her book. "If you're having trouble, you can always ask Haya for help." At my confused look, she added, "Haya is a hafizah."

My eyes widened as I stared at Mahnoor. "She has the entire Qur'an memorized?" I'd never met anyone who had earned the title. If you don't think that's impressive, consider my own track record. I've memorized eight surahs. Eight, and the longest of those is seven lines. The Qur'an is divided up into 114 chapters, and the longest one is 286 lines long.

Mahnoor picked up her phone. "Yeah. So does Hassan. The Mousawis have quite a few huffaz in their extended family. Azhar also has about two-thirds memorized."

"Do you think Haya would be willing to help?"

"Maybe. I'll call her, and you can ask if she's free." She tapped the number in, hit call, and passed the phone over to me.

Ring . . . ring . . . ring . . . "Assalamu alaykum?"

That wasn't Haya's voice. I shrieked and automatically flung the phone across the room.

"What the heck, Dua?" Mahnoor went to get it off the floor. "Salaam?" After a moment, she looked at me and rolled her eyes. "Yeah, sorry." She turned so she was facing the wall instead of me. "Where's Haya? Oh. Tell her to call me, okay?" She hung up, turning a disapproving eye on me. "Brilliant, Dua. You couldn't think of a better way to get him to think you're weird?"

"I panicked," I replied defensively, wishing I could put my head between my legs and pretend this whole thing had never happened. My face burned in humiliation. And my neck. And my ears. "Can you blame me? You said you were calling Haya, not her brother."

"Haya went out for groceries with her mom and accidentally took Hassan's phone instead of her own. It happens." I eyed her silently. I wouldn't have put it past Mahnoor to have called Hassan on purpose.

The phone rang in her hand and I tried to make myself as small as possible. Even though it wasn't like whoever was calling would be able to see me.

"Salaam? Hey. Yeah, I tried calling your phone. Uh-huh. Yeah, Hassan told me." Mahnoor looked at me. I scuttled into the headboard. Rolling her eyes again, she looked down at her journal instead. "Dua wants to memorize a few more surahs." Pause. "Yeah, she tried, but she said they all go too fast. Would you mind? Mmm-hmm. Perfect. We'll see you soon, then."

"Well?" I said as she hung up.

"She said yes, so we're going over to their place. Wear green."

My brows furrowed. "Why green?" Was there some religious significance behind it, or would color-coordinating my outfit somehow help me memorize better?

She smirked. "Because Hassan will probably be home; his favorite color is green."

"Is wearing green going to make me seem less weird for screaming on the phone?"

She thought it over for a moment, shifting her eyes. "No."

"Then I'll wear whatever I like."

She snorted. "Sure, Dua. You do know lying breaks your fast, right?"

"Assalamu alaykum!" Haya gave us each a quick hug before ushering us in. "Come in; everything's ready. Except . . ." Her smile twisted for a moment. "I'm sorry, Dua, I don't think I'm the right person to teach you Qur'an."

My heart dropped into my stomach. "What? Why?" My voice came out in a squeak. Why hadn't she told Mahnoor earlier? How was I supposed to get any progress on my Ramadan checklist?

"I thought about it, and I don't think I'm the best teacher. I'm not that patient."

"It's true," Mahnoor agreed, nodding.

I stared at her. *Then* why *are we even here right now?*

"And," Haya added, "you really need someone who'll let you take your time. More importantly, you need to learn how to pronounce the surahs correctly, and while my pronunciation is good, Hassan's is better. He also doesn't go too fast, so you should be able to follow him easily."

I blinked at her. She had to be joking. Concentrating on learning anything in a different language was difficult enough, and now I had to do it *with Hassan*—who was basically one big, life-sized distraction with his green eyes and nice hair? I turned my gaze on Mahnoor.

"What?" She looked at Haya. "We didn't plan this, if that's what you're thinking."

"So, this isn't a setup?" I asked Haya, unconvinced.

Her lips twitched; then she smiled. "Hassan is a better teacher than I am, hands down. His pronunciation is better, too, like I said; we used to do Qur'an recitation competitions when we were younger, and he placed a few times."

She hadn't answered my question, but she did have a point. If I wanted to succeed in my goal, I'd need a really good teacher. I sighed. "Okay, if you're sure this is the best option."

"Definitely," she assured me, her dimple peeking out as she smiled. "Relax; you're in good hands."

Hassan looked up from his laptop expectantly as we entered the Mousawis' living room.

"Dua's ready to start memorizing Qur'an," Haya announced. Glancing at me, she asked, "Do you need to make wudu?"

My heart had jumped into my mouth as soon as Hassan lifted his gaze from the computer. Yeah, this was not going to be easy. "Hmm?" I shook my head quickly. "No, I made my ablutions before leaving."

"Great." Haya beamed. "You can go ahead and get started, and"—she grabbed Mahnoor's hand—"we'll be in the kitchen, preparing for iftar. Mahnoor makes the best mashed potatoes, and I have a craving. It's the next room over if you need us," she said, already dragging Mahnoor away.

That was possibly the most awkward exit I'd ever seen, especially since Mahnoor seemed only partially clued in to whatever was going on in Haya's mind.

"Assalamu alaykum," Hassan greeted me, closing his laptop and setting it aside.

"Wa alaykum assalam," I replied, fidgeting with my dupatta. Again. "I'm sorry, if Haya told me earlier she couldn't teach me, I would've figured something else out. I'm sure you're busy."

He smiled briefly, and my heart practically did a somersault. Maybe I should ask Uncle Yusuf for a consult—if I could without telling him why. I couldn't imagine talking to my own dad about this, let alone Uncle Yusuf. I could imagine the serious, ever-so-slightly disapproving look in his eyes. I saw it so clearly in my head I almost missed what Hassan said next.

"It's fine, I have some free time, and I'd never say no to helping someone memorize Qur'an." Glancing my way, he moved to put the computer away, then stopped. Looking back at me, he slowly took in my appearance. Then, after a moment, as if remembering why I was there, he looked away and cleared his throat. "Are you going somewhere after this?"

"Um, no." I glanced down at my outfit. I was painfully over-dressed. While he was in a simple T-shirt and jeans, I had donned an embroidered powder-blue full-sleeved kameez with a matching dupatta and white straight pants. Clearing my throat, unconsciously mirroring his behavior, I said, "My mother thinks one of the best ways to respect the Qur'an as God's word is by approaching it while wearing nice clothing."

He smiled again, a bigger one this time. A light, genuine, and beautiful expression. He slowly brought his green eyes up from the floor; they practically glimmered, as if they'd stolen all the light from the room for their own depths.

My heart flipped again. Yeah, I definitely needed that consult.

"That's actually a great idea," he said softly. "It sounds similar to the recommendation in the Qur'an for Muslims to stand for prayer in beautiful garments."

I just nodded. Mom insisted I wear this particular shalwar kameez instead of my planned outfit of jeans and an old gray plaid shirt, but if she'd known Hassan was going to be my teacher, she would've put me in whatever outfit most closely resembled a potato sack.

"Are you ready?" he asked, beckoning for me to sit on the sofa next to his armchair. He set a copy of the Qur'an on a stand on the glass coffee table between us.

I stared at it for a moment, tracing the Arabic letters engraved into the cover with my fingers, feeling every curlicue, every dot. This was it, the last guide to humankind, right at my fingertips. So complete, so perfect. I should have done this a long time ago.

Hassan slipped a kufi over his dark brown hair. I followed suit, lifting my dupatta and draping it over my head, in a gesture of respect and reverence for the holy book before us.

"Your goal is to memorize six surahs, right?" he asked.

"Yes." I nodded, nearly blushing as I realized how difficult that would be—and how that must sound like nothing to him, when he had every single one memorized. "I was thinking to start with something short and easy to remember."

He flipped to the back for the index and showed it to me. "You choose."

My fingers trailed down the list as I eyed the titles and the number of lines in each surah. I paused, stopping my finger on the one I wanted. "This one. Surah Al-Qadr, number ninety-seven." I pointed it out to him. It was only five lines long. Manageable.

Hassan smiled. "Excellent choice. Do you know what the surah is about?"

I shook my head.

"It's about Laylat-al-Qadr, the Night of Power, which falls within the last ten nights of Ramadan, on one of the odd nights."

"Oh." I'd definitely heard about that. Mom always told me to spend more time in prayer and supplication during the last ten nights. Sometimes I listened, but usually I'd find an excuse to slack off and binge Netflix.

"No one ever knows which one, exactly, since only God knows that for sure," he continued, "but we know it's the night in history when Prophet Muhammad, peace and blessings be upon him, had his first revelation from God, via the angel Gabriel, of the Qur'an.

"Let's begin. In the name of Allah, Most Gracious, Most Merciful."

Taking a deep breath, I repeated the basmalah after him slowly.

He recited the first line of the surah easily, but not so quickly that I couldn't hear each intonation. His voice rang out through the room, each sound melodious, graceful, every letter precise. It was beautiful, flowing, and pure, exactly how the Qur'an was meant to be read.

He waited for me to repeat after him. I swallowed, staring down at the line in the Qur'an, spelled out in the curving Arabic script I'd been taught to read since I was little, yet still seemed so foreign. Slowly, I repeated the verse. The tips of my ears burned hot in embarrassment, my stomach clenched, every fiber in my being cringing at the clumsy, stumbling recitation.

Undeterred, Hassan recited the same verse again, slower this time.

Again, I repeated after him, the line only slightly smoother on my tongue. My head dipped as a flush rapidly crept up my neck, setting my face on fire. My pronunciation had always been poor, but this was bad even for me. Ashamed, I realized that this was the first time I'd sat down to read Qur'an in a long time. Tears pricked at the corner of my eyes.

In my peripheral vision, I could see Hassan staring at me. Great. My pronunciation was terrible *and* I was about to cry in front of a cute guy. I quickly reached up with a corner of my dupatta to wipe at my eyes.

"Dua," he said softly, "is everything okay?"

I shook my head. "My pronunciation is even worse than I thought. I'm so . . . I'm sorry."

He stared at me wordlessly for a moment. He probably thought I was a freak at best, and a terrible Muslim at worst. I didn't dare lift my gaze from the floor, grateful at least that my dupatta obscured my red ears from view.

Then, sounding perplexed, he said, "Sorry for what?"

I wiped at my eyes again. "That was awful. Your recitation was so beautiful and perfect and mine was . . . not. I'm terrible."

"Stop," he said quietly but firmly.

My stomach twisted and I slowly lifted my head toward him.

His mouth was set in a grim line. "I had to practice for years to get to where I am today. And I still do, just so that I don't forget all that I've memorized. All you need is practice, insha'Allah. Don't give up already."

I shook my head. Verses that should flow like poetry tumbled out in disjointed croaks from my lips. "I shouldn't be this bad at it. I've known how to read Qur'anic Arabic since I was seven."

He was quiet, his gaze focused elsewhere. Slowly, he turned back toward me. "Dua." His voice was soft. "You're struggling with the words and my recitation is, in your own words, beautiful and perfect. But did you know that your attempts to learn and read the Qur'an are more beloved to Allah than my recitation?"

I stared at him. "How?"

He smiled. "Every time you stumble and try again, Allah is rewarding you, and your reward is double that of any reward I get from reciting. You're trying to do better, and no one could possibly love and appreciate that more than the One who created you." He gestured to the Qur'an between us, still lying open. "Think of it like music—if you don't hit the note just so, it won't sound right. If you can play a song you've just heard perfectly on the piano, you can do this. You've got the ear for it."

I mulled it over for a moment. He did have a point. Regardless of how hard it was, I could do this. I wasn't going to quit now that I'd just started. My head dipped in a nod, once. "Okay, let's try again."

"Bismillahi-r Rahmani-r Rahim."

He took me through every single word, not going on to the next line till I had the previous one right. I listened carefully as he recited, listening for each individual sound before I tried it myself. I messed up several more times, but the more I practiced, the more he encouraged me, praising me every time I got it right. Slowly, the words began to flow the way they were meant to. I messed up less and less, and as I did, I felt something in me loosen. Slowly, it became less about proving something to my parents. The words stirred something in me, somehow bringing a sense of peace while making me long for more—lightness, freedom from the burden of others' expectations of who I should be. I kept going. It took an hour, but by the end, the words felt natural, slipping easily off my tongue.

"Great job." Hassan beamed when I'd repeated the whole surah a third time, from memory, without any mistakes. "See? I knew you could do it! Mashallah."

"Thank you." I blushed again, because of the praise and from the excitement of my accomplishment. One surah down, five more to go.

As if on cue, Haya sauntered into the room, Mahnoor in tow. "Mashed potatoes are almost done. They'll be ready for iftar. I didn't realize they'd take so long."

"Generally, the potatoes need more than an inch of water to boil," Mahnoor said dryly.

Haya glanced back at her with a saccharine-sweet smile, then turned to me. "All done?"

"I got one memorized," I replied. "Al-Qadr."

"Yes, and she did a great job!" For a second, Hassan's excitement reminded me of Mahdi. I felt a little flutter in my belly, dipping my head quickly to hide my smile.

Haya quirked an eyebrow, a dimple flashing in her cheek.

His voice lowered. "Do you want to work on the next one now?" Was it just me, or did he sound hopeful?

"Actually, Dua and I should head home," Mahnoor said. "Our moms are preparing for iftar, and Rabia texted me to ask for us to grab some cake mix on our way back."

"Oh, of course." Haya glanced at her brother. "Hassan, be a gentleman and escort Mahnoor and Dua home. I'd do it, but I'm planning on making chicken cutlets to go with the mashed potatoes, and I need to start breading and frying them in a few minutes."

Hassan stared at her for a moment. "Are you sick? Why do you keep smiling like that? And since when do you cook?"

Haya blinked. "I'm fine, and since yesterday. I found a recipe video on YouTube that I'd like to try. Now, go."

Getting to his feet, Hassan looked to Mahnoor. "Cake mix, you said? I'm ready whenever you are."

The subway ride was quick and a little bumpy, but otherwise uneventful. I spent most of it trying not to blatantly gawk at Hassan, who sat directly across from me. Fortunately, he was focused elsewhere, reading something, so I let my gaze linger on the lock of hair that fell over his forehead, soft and dark. What would it feel like to run my fingers through it? His eyes, trained on his phone, really were the most stunning I'd ever seen, their almond shape making the emerald-green irises all the more striking. The left side of his mouth scrunched up in concentration, his brow furrowed. Beautiful.

"Ahem." Mahnoor nudged my shoulder pointedly, bringing me back to Earth.

Right. Staring would definitely not get me any good deeds this Ramadan. Tearing my gaze away from Hassan, I opened up the new Qur'an app I'd just installed on my phone, and began to recite Surah Al-Qadr under my breath, checking the screen at the end of each recitation to make sure I'd gotten it right.

Soon we reached our station, and Mahnoor poked me again. Silently slipping my phone into my wristlet, I followed her off the train. A roar sounded in my ears as we rose from underground. Puzzled, I immediately turned toward the sound, stopping in my tracks as Hassan and Mahnoor slowed ahead of me. My stomach twisted uncomfortably, my shoulders lifted by a wave of anxiety.

A crowd—dozens of people, young and old—stood waving signs and banners, their faces grotesque masks of fury and disgust as they screamed, their voices combining into one incoherent, loud roar. The scrawled messages on their signs stood out, written in bold, thick marker. TERRORISTS GO HOME! SAY NO TO ISLAM! ISLAM = THE DEVIL'S WAY OF LIFE! NO PLACE FOR ISLAM IN AMERICA!

A reporter stood off to the side, calmly facing a camera as she spoke. "The Islamic holiday Eid al-Fitr marks the end of Ramadan. But this year, the three-day festival is reported to begin the day before the anniversary of nine-eleven, and these protestors are *not* happy about it." The words poured from her mouth as easily as if she were describing the bland, overcast sky.

"Dua."

I stood in place, frozen in shock as I singled out faces in the crowd. The tall, bearded man in a plaid shirt and baseball cap could've been one of my neighbors in Burkeville. The screaming blond woman beside him, short and slight, looked like a mother I occasionally babysat for. Worst of all were the elderly couple standing at the front of the crowd, hunched with age, skin wrinkled and withered, their faces red as they shook their fists in anger. Except for the hate in their expressions, they reminded me of Kat's grandparents, a sweet old couple with a fondness for Scrabble and my mother's homemade gulab jamun.

"Hey, Dua!"

A hand seized my arm.

I turned, ready to scream, and my gaze met Hassan's. His beautiful eyes, focused on mine, were determined and strong. His grip tightened on my arm. Somehow that permeated the haze surrounding my brain. Islamically, men and women who weren't immediate blood relatives weren't supposed to touch each other without a valid reason. He wouldn't be touching me *now* if this weren't serious.

"Dua," he said firmly, speaking over the crazed chanting echoing in my ears. "Come on, let's get you home." Gently but urgently, he pulled me forward.

I looked beyond him to Mahnoor, whose face had gone pale, her red hijab stark against her skin. With her in her hijab and me in my traditional shalwar kameez, it wouldn't be long before the crowd spotted us. We were walking targets.

Tears pricking at my eyes and a lump forming in my throat, I forced myself to look away and allowed Hassan to lead me in the right direction. I'd seen protests like this before, but only on the news. Never in person.

A chill ran down my spine as I realized how near they stood to us. Too close to let my guard down, too close to look away. Too close to pretend it wasn't really happening. We were only a few minutes away from Uncle Yusuf and Aunt Sadia's home. All I had to do was swipe my MetroCard, get on the subway, and I would come face to face with these people who were driven so mad by their anger and hatred—and yes, by ignorance—that I wouldn't appear human to them. Instead, I was something to destroy, a pestilence that had to be eradicated, all because I called myself Muslim.

As the tears stung my eyes, I whispered a prayer for protection under my breath, but my heartbeat refused to slow. All these people. Their fury was so real, so tangible. The words on their signs tiny spears thrust at my heart.

Hassan glanced back at me as we left the crowd behind, tugging on my arm until I stepped in front of him, just behind Mahnoor. "So I know you won't get lost," he said softly.

For once, my mood didn't lift at his words. My heart remained heavy long after we crossed the threshold of Uncle Yusuf's house, and we watched Hassan turn back toward his own home, alone this time. I repeated the prayer for protection quietly, reciting it for him. It might take him longer to return home, but I hoped he'd avoid the crowd.

nine

"I hate . . . my stomach," Mahnoor muttered through gritted teeth. She lay in bed, staring up at the ceiling as Haya, clearly disinterested, sat at the foot of the bed.

"I know you do," Haya replied, eyes on her phone. She was browsing through a blog dedicated to Muslim teens and young adults. She'd introduced me to it the other day after iftar; a cousin of hers occasionally posted articles to the site.

"I feel like a gutted fish."

"Stinky?" Haya guessed, focused more on the page than Mahnoor's complaining.

Mahnoor glared daggers at her but stayed as she was. "No, empty. Eight hours left, and my stomach already feels like it hasn't seen food in a week. I don't know how you can just sit there when I think I'm about to die of hunger."

"I told you to stop with the intense workout videos weeks before Ramadan began, but you kept at it. Don't blame me now that your metabolism is almost as fast as Captain America's," Haya retorted, glancing up to smile at me. She mouthed, *Help me.*

I stared at Mahnoor, who was still muttering away. "Why don't you read or something?" I suggested. "You won't feel it as much if you're distracted."

"Five more minutes," she replied, staring at the ceiling as if there was a masterpiece in there somewhere that would appear if she looked long enough.

"Is she"—I leaned in closer to Haya and whispered—"*wallowing* in her own hunger?"

Haya sighed, then cupped her hand over one cheek as she leaned in. "When she gets like this," she whispered conspiratorially into my ear, "she doesn't say what's really on her mind."

I barely stopped myself from doing a facepalm. "So, what's actually going on?"

"The parents want Azhar and Mahnoor to set a wedding date," she whispered, her dark brown eyes sparkling as they widened. "Most girls I know would be excited, but then again, Mahnoor probably has an early case of cold feet."

"It's not weird for you?" I asked. "With Mahnoor being your best friend and Azhar being your brother?"

Wrinkling her nose, she looked down and picked at the unraveling threads in the comforter. "Most of the time, it's awesome. But sometimes it's a little weird. I'm trying not to get involved because, ultimately, it's just about the two of them."

I looked over at Mahnoor. It'd been two minutes since she'd last spoken. But no, she wasn't passed out, just staring at the ceiling, probably quiet so she could hear what we were saying.

I turned away to look at my own lap. "What are you going to do?" I said, not sure whom I was asking. Whoever had the answer, I guess.

"I have no idea," Mahnoor said under her breath, so quiet it was almost inaudible.

I bit my lip, my fingers twitching in my lap. That didn't sound good. As a wave of anxiety washed over me, my fingers mimed playing the Sami Yusuf song—the one I was beginning to think of as *our* song, mine and Hassan's—gliding through each chord. As Hassan's face floated before my eyes, a pit bloomed in my stomach as I puzzled over Mahnoor's lack of excitement. She was getting married to a good guy from a good family, so what was the problem? My fingers moved faster as the tempo in my mind accelerated to match my nerves. I held back a sigh. She didn't even know how easy she had it.

Haya, oblivious to the dark whirlpool of my thoughts, shrugged, then smiled. "I guess we'll see what happens. Even if Mahnoor decides she's not ready at the last minute, we can always get you and Hassan married instead." Her smile grew, eyes sparkling like her irises were full of glitter.

My fingers continued playing to the tune in my head, Haya's words getting lost in the haze. If I were in Mahnoor's place, I'd go about this in a totally different way. But then, I didn't want to be in her place to begin with. "Yeah, su— *What?*" I caught myself just in time, my brain finally processing the joke. "Not funny, Haya."

"I'm just saying." She held one hand up in a half-defensive, half-explanatory gesture, the chunky multicolored bracelets on her arm clunking together. "We wouldn't waste anything or worry about all our relatives coming from abroad for no reason. We'll just get you and Hassan married. Problem solved."

"I like that idea!" a young voice rang out.

Haya and I jumped a foot off the bed. Mahnoor sat up, her

eyes wide. My composure shaken, I leaned down over the side, the ends of my hair touching the floor and the blood rushing to my head, lifted the edge of the dust ruffle, and took a peek under the bed.

"Mahdi, get out from under there."

He crawled out like a cat, his huge eyes blinking at me. After he climbed up onto the bedspread, he paused to ponder whether he should sit in my lap or Haya's. It was adorable, watching the little guy try to figure it out. After a minute, he put his head between us and propped it up on his arms, so one elbow touched each of us.

"What were you doing under there?" I asked, squelching the urge to tickle his tummy.

"I needed someone to help me practice Surah Al-Fatihah," he replied. "Hassan bhai helped me memorize it yesterday, but he said I need to practice so I don't forget." He looked up at me. "When are you and Hassan bhai gonna get married?"

Haya held her hand to her mouth as she stifled a laugh, while Mahnoor was so overcome with a case of the giggles, her bed shook.

I studied him for a minute. His eyes were wide in his eagerness to learn. I could use some of that myself. Number five on my Ramadan checklist: be a better relative, friend, and daughter. Time to put it into practice.

I tucked a lock of hair behind my ear and pulled Mahdi closer to me, gathering him into my lap. "I'll help you."

"But your wedding with Hassan bhai?" he asked again.

I sighed, narrowing my eyes at Haya. "Probably not." I ignored how my stomach plummeted, and the twitch of Mahdi's lower lip. "Go on, get your Qur'an out."

"Mahnoor," Aunt Sadia called. "Come help me in the kitchen, dear."

Suppressing her laughter, Haya followed Mahnoor out of the room, managing to offer her help in between bouts of giggles.

"God, why did You stick me in the middle of those two goofballs?" I muttered to myself, getting out of bed and heading into the bathroom to brush my teeth and make wudu.

When I got back, stray drops of water dripping down my hairline, Mahdi was already huddled in the middle of my bed, a Qur'an propped up in front of him. I sat beside him and opened the Qur'an.

His copy was color-coded, with some parts highlighted in bright blues, pinks, and greens, so the reader would know what kind of sounds to make at certain points. Just like the one Hassan had me practice on at his house.

"Ready?" I asked, looking down at Mahdi.

"First, I have an important question." He eyed me with a serious look on his face. "Can I choose the wedding cake?"

I groaned mentally. *Thank you, Haya, for planting the idea in Mahdi's head. Now I'm going to spend the rest of the day doing damage control.* I sighed, my shoulders slumping in defeat. "Sure, why not?" An image popped into my head, of me in colorful Pakistani bridal finery and Hassan in a perfectly tailored sherwani—the stand-up collar and silhouette of the knee-length coat designed to flatter the wearer. A lovely cream-toned one with pale gold accents was sure to make his green eyes pop. Or black with silver accents! Desi and Middle Eastern men looked *amazing* in black. My mouth curled into a grin automatically, imagining a shy smile playing about his lips as I agreed to the nikkah. *Qubool hai, qubool hai, qubool hai!*

"Dua?"

I jerked upright at Mahdi's concerned poke. He looked down at the Qur'an, then back up at me. Right, Qur'an practice. No time for swooning.

"Okay, repeat that last line," Hassan said.

I did, watching him nod along as every sound dropped smoothly from my lips. It wasn't as melodious as when he recited, but still beautiful.

"Good," he said when I finished. He smiled, his whole face glowing with it. "That makes three surahs memorized, so you're halfway done. Let's go through them again, to make sure you haven't forgotten anything."

I took a deep breath, reorienting myself to the task at hand—ignoring the butterflies in my stomach that fluttered every time he smiled—and uttered the basmalah as I began my recitation. Hassan tapped a finger on the table every time I began a new line, and I kept my gaze on the rhythmic movement as I focused on my pronunciation. Just a few minutes later, I finished the last line of Al-Ma'un, the latest surah I'd memorized.

Suddenly, the room was silent, almost stiflingly so. Hassan stared at the floor, the faraway look in his eyes suggesting that his mind was elsewhere. Mahnoor, who'd been scribbling away in her journal in the corner, was quiet, no more scratch of her pen against paper. Haya, sitting beside her, said nothing.

Had I made a mistake? Had all that time and effort gone to waste? I clasped my hands firmly in my lap, suppressing the urge to wring them.

Finally, Hassan lifted his head and turned to me. "Perfect," he said, so softly I wouldn't have heard him if not for the complete silence. Then he beamed. I felt a flutter in my belly, those butterflies stirring again. "Mashallah. You've come a long way in just a few days."

I let out a small sigh of relief. I'd been practicing every evening before iftar, repeating the lines over and over again till they slipped off my tongue as naturally as a piano melody came to my fingertips.

"Thank you," I said shyly. "You've been a great teacher." Regardless of her motives, Haya made the right choice by having Hassan teach me. It was his calming presence and gentle patience that I'd needed. Well, when I wasn't distracted by the way one corner of his mouth turned up in a half-smile as he listened, or the vivid green of his eyes as he directed me to the color-coded letters to help me adjust my pronunciation.

"Congratulations," Haya echoed, her voice booming in the silence. "So, what are we doing to celebrate?"

"Celebrate?" I repeated blankly, my brows furrowing. The first idea that popped into my head involved a gallon of mint chocolate chip ice cream, but iftar was hours away.

Haya looked at me as if I'd gone daft. "Dua, how many days have you been in the city?"

Oh, how I hate math. I counted quickly in my head. "Eight? Nine?" It'd been a little more than a week.

"And how many days have you spent cooped up either at Mahnoor's house or mine, next to this agoraphobe here, huh?" she asked, pointing at Mahnoor accusingly.

"Do you really have to diagnose me with a new phobia every time you see me?" Mahnoor shoved her arm away. "You called me an arachnophobe yesterday."

"It was a tiny baby spider, and you cried like it was a tarantula."

"Babies grow. Should I have left it in my closet?"

Hassan cleared his throat. "What's your point, Haya?"

"My point, dear brother, is that Dua is only going to be here for a few more weeks." Turning to me, she added, "You can't visit New York and not actually do anything."

She had a point; I hadn't done much sightseeing. I'd meant to, but fasting left me with little energy, so the time I spent between memorizing Qur'an with Hassan and baking with Rabia seemed to pass by in a blur. I hadn't even realized I'd been missing out on anything.

"So where do you want to go? There must be somewhere in the city you've always wanted to visit." Haya leaned back and waited, her gaze glued to my face.

I bit my lower lip as I mulled that over. "I've been wanting to go to the Madame Tussauds wax museum."

Mahnoor stopped writing and looked up at me, staring like I'd announced I wanted to go to outer space and breakdance on Saturn's rings. "You want to go to— But it's so touristy. And the tickets are so expensive."

"We don't have to go, then. I was just—"

"Mahnoor, I would hit you upside the head if it wasn't Ramadan," Haya told her, cutting me off. "It's not like Dua comes to visit every week. If she wants to go, we'll go."

"Great." I glanced down at my shalwar kameez. "I just need to change first."

ten

Remembering Mahnoor's quip about Hassan's favorite color, I'd changed into a forest-green blouse with three-quarter sleeves and jeans. Plain, but I knew the green brought out the golden undertones in my skin.

Even when he wasn't around, I'd sometimes get a whiff of Hassan's scent. It would linger in the air, warm and cinnamony, spicy-sweet, and I'd find myself covering my ears with my hair or a dupatta, knowing that if I thought about it too much, my ears would turn red in a telltale blush.

I shook myself, hoping it would clear my head and bring me back to my senses. I shouldn't be thinking about boys. Especially not during Ramadan.

As we headed toward the subway, we passed the spot where the protestors had been just a few days earlier. My heartbeat quickening and my eyes flicking from one corner to the next, I walked closer to my cousins. Mahnoor glanced at me and then looked away, squaring her shoulders. Rabia reached for my hand, and I squeezed her arm tightly. My free hand tapped a beat against my thigh, a song from my childhood that soothed me, grounded me. Still, I only breathed properly, a nice, deep breath, when we got to the museum.

After the entrance, we split up, each of us meandering through a different section, lingering in the ones we loved the most. Well, except for me. I didn't have any favorites. I was just excited every time I came across someone I recognized and hadn't expected to see, like Lucille Ball or Aishwarya Rai. And, of course, the royal couple.

That was where I found Mahnoor. Everyone else had gone ahead. I'd been looking at wax figures a few feet away, but Mahnoor had been standing in front of Prince William and Kate Middleton for the past ten minutes, playing with her engagement ring as she stared at Kate's sapphire one. When I got closer, I realized that Mahnoor wasn't really staring *at* them so much as *through* them.

She looked distraught, and my Ramadan checklist immediately came to mind. *Be a better relative. Patient and selfless.*

"They look happy, don't they?" I said as I came to stand beside Mahnoor, keeping my gaze on the wax figures.

"Happy?" She stared at me incredulously. "They're *wax*."

I squelched the urge to facepalm. This was going to be harder than I thought. "You know what I mean." I took a deep breath. *Proceed with caution.* "You know, you and Azhar make a cute couple too. He's handsome, tall . . ."

Mahnoor gave me a weird look. Okay, so I was exaggerating a bit. Azhar was about five-seven, which was pretty tall—compared to me. But that wasn't the point.

"Anyway," I continued, pretending I didn't see her staring, "he's handsome, nice, smart, and I've heard he has a killer sense of humor. And you're beautiful, have a good sense of style..." My voice trailed off. Mahnoor continued to stare at me, and I tried not to let my uncertainty show in my face as my brain scrambled to come up with more adjectives. But I didn't have any. At least, none that would be very flattering, so I just finished with, "The perfect couple, Mashallah."

Mahnoor looked away from me and lifted her ring to eye level. After a minute of studying every facet in the diamond, the design painstakingly etched into the white-gold band, she lowered her hand.

"What are you thinking?"

She shook her head, eyes back on the figures in front of her. "Dua, just stop. I know you mean well, but I don't want to talk about this right now."

Abort mission. Abort. Why did I even try? "All right, then." I backed away, putting space between us. But I wasn't ready to be alone yet, so I wandered until I ended up in the music section.

I glanced at Hassan surreptitiously as he walked from one figure to another. As if he could feel my gaze, he slowed and looked toward me. I looked away quickly, pretending to focus on reading the placards by each figure.

Hassan sidled up next to me as I stood by Usher, laughing as Rabia recorded Mahdi doing a little dance. I automatically quieted, hiding my smile and my quickening pulse at his nearness. And then he walked away.

Agog, I watched his retreating back. What was that? I sighed, shaking my head. Never mind waiting for him to approach me. Bolstering my courage, I strode toward him before I could change my mind.

"Who's your favorite?" I asked, stepping in beside him.

He lifted his chin in thought, shaking his head. "Not here."

My eyebrows lifted in curiosity. "Who would that be?"

He shrugged. "Hard to pick just one. I like music that *means* something to me. Sami Yusuf, Maher Zain, Amr Diab, Nusrat Fateh Ali Khan, A. R. Rahman."

"You know Nusrat Fateh Ali Khan?"

He hit me with the full force of his smile, triggering butterfly flutters in my stomach. "Would I be a true Muslim music enthusiast if I didn't? I remember your uncle telling me about his primary tabla player, Dildar Hussain. He was brilliant."

I smiled, crossing my arms over my chest. "So you asked me about my piano before, but you never told me how you got into drums."

"Well, Dad comes from a musical family and we always had instruments when I was growing up. He tried to get each of us into violin and it didn't work. I was his last chance," he laughed, "but I preferred the feel of the drumsticks, the controlled chaos, the varied art of percussion!" He met my eye and smirked. "If you ask Mom, though, she'll just tell you I was hyper and enjoyed being loud."

I giggled. "Yeah, I think mine encouraged me to learn piano so I'd stop fidgeting. She showed me clips of Adnan Sami Khan and I wanted to see if I could be as good as him—he was known as the fastest piano player of his time, at least in Pakistan."

"Hmm. And he's known now for renouncing Pakistani citizenship in favor of Indian citizenship, isn't he?"

I rolled my eyes. "Ugh, yeah. We don't talk about that at home. It's a sore subject."

He chuckled. "Got it. What's the first memory you have of music?"

I smiled, my body pleasantly warm as the remnants of a memory floated to the forefront of my mind—and my ears. "Easy—my mom listening to the soundtrack of *Dilwale Dulhania Le Jayenge* on repeat. Have you ever heard of it?"

His eyes twinkled, a dimple flashing in his cheek. "Yeah, I may have."

I continued. "She was obsessed! I knew all the lyrics by the time I was six, even though I didn't quite get what they meant. The mandolin tune was almost permanently stuck in my head." I chuckled. "Mom basically guilted herself into playing nasheeds, naats, and hamds more often just so I'd have exposure to music that was about spiritual love, too, not just romantic love." I sighed, my chest starting to feel heavy as images of the protest flashed through my mind. "People don't always see that side of Muslims, do they? The lightheartedness, the passion."

"The sincerity," he added, a somber expression snatching his smile. "People believe what they want to believe. But we can be better than what they think we are. We have to remember that we're representing Islam to others, whether we like it or not."

I looked down, the wheels in my head turning. "My parents want me to start an MSA at school. It's not a bad idea, but what if someone takes it the wrong way? I've never been a target before, but I've never drawn attention to myself or my religion before either."

He didn't say anything for a beat. Then, his voice soft, he said, "Maybe take a break, then revisit the idea. Sometimes it's better to distract yourself, think about something else for a change. Then you'll be able to make the decision with a clear head."

I blinked up at him. "Great, how do I do that?"

He opened his mouth, furrowed his brows as he realized

something, then closed it. "Actually, I was hoping you could tell me. I'm better with vague witticisms than concrete advice."

I couldn't help but laugh at the bewilderment on his face and his straightforwardness. The tightness in my chest loosened, my heart lifting.

His eyes softened, a smile spreading across his face. "You have a nice laugh."

I bent my head, allowing my hair to fall forward, covering my blush. "Thanks."

"Hassan bhai!" In a blur, Mahdi attacked his legs. "Come look at this with me!"

"Do you mind?" Rabia asked, looking harried. "He's been asking for you for ten minutes."

"Sure, no problem." Flashing his smile at me, he said, "Maybe we'll talk later?"

There went the butterflies again. Did I detect a hint of hope in his voice? "Later," I agreed. "Insha'Allah."

"Insha'Allah." He allowed Mahdi to lead him away. As he left, he whistled a tune that felt all too familiar. It took me a few moments, then I had it. My favorite from *Dilwale Dulhania Le Jayenge*, the one where the leads realize they've fallen for each other. He whistled the chorus perfectly. *You've fallen in love, sweetheart. You may deny it a hundred thousand times, but, darling, this is love, sweetheart.*

My heart seemed too big for my chest, swollen with joy and hope. Did this mean what I thought it did? Did he have feelings for me too?

As if she could read my mind, Mahnoor materialized before me, mouth downturned in disapproval. I automatically stepped back. "What?"

"Be careful, Dua." She'd heard.

I stared at her. "Is that a threat?"

She shook her head. "Of course not. The Mousawis are wonderful people, incredibly loving. But unless you're willing to reciprocate, don't let yourself get too close to them."

My voice sharpened, defensive. "What makes you think I won't reciprocate?"

"You're going back to Burkeville," she reminded me, "and you have no idea when you'll be back, if ever. I'm just saying, is it worth taking up space in their lives if you're just going to leave a void?" Her voice cracked.

I cocked my head as I studied her. Somehow, I had the feeling this wasn't really about me at all.

"Just . . . try not to hurt anyone. And don't put yourself in a position to be hurt either." With a final shake of her head, she turned on her heel and walked away, leaving me to stew in my feelings: confusion, indignance, disbelief. And, as my mind replayed Hassan's whistled tune over and over, hope.

eleven

"One more time," Hassan said.

My head bowed, I repeated Al-Humazah, the fourth surah I'd memorized. This one was a little longer than the rest and had taken me twice as long to learn. Finally, after two grueling hours of practice, the Arabic verses flowed from my lips, lilting and smooth.

"Good," Hassan said, satisfied. "Now recite all the surahs you've learned, from the beginning."

I obliged, reciting slowly but letting the words flow naturally, as he'd taught me. All the hours of practice paid off; my recitation wasn't at his level, but it was significantly improved from when I'd first started. And I was actually enjoying it more than I thought I would.

"Excellent, Dua." Hassan smiled, his eyes sparkling like an anime character's. I could get lost in them easily if I didn't stop myself. So much so, I almost missed what he said next. "It's the tenth day of Ramadan. You're more than halfway done, and you've got plenty of time left to memorize the other two surahs. You can do more if you want."

I blinked, momentarily overwhelmed by his catching enthusiasm. "Maybe just six for now. I don't want to get overconfident and forget to practice them all."

He nodded, still smiling. "Fair enough."

I sighed in relief, the upturn of my mouth mirroring his. "Thank you, again, for teaching me. I wouldn't have been able to do it without your help."

His smile widened as he lifted a hand and placed it over his heart. My stomach twisted, recognizing the genuine kindness in the gesture; it was how Mr. Mousawi had greeted us the first time we entered their home. Yet somehow, it felt different coming from Hassan—more intimate. "No problem," he said. He lowered his hand to the table, and I couldn't help but notice how near his outstretched fingers were to mine—not touching, but so near I could feel their warmth. Yet, his eyes were on me, and I wondered if he'd noticed the proximity of our hands. His eyes unwavering as they met mine, his eyebrows rounded as he opened his mouth. I could practically see the words ready to tumble off the tip of his tongue.

The front door swung open, and Mahnoor, sitting a few feet away from us, automatically turned toward the sound, her journal forgotten. I self-consciously pulled my hands into my lap, lowering my gaze, but not before I saw Hassan clamp his mouth shut.

A moment later, Azhar walked in, his shoulders slumped. He must have had a long day at work. Then he spotted Mahnoor, and a warm smile split his face, his eyes crinkling at the corners. He stood taller, reenergized.

"Assalamu alaykum," he greeted Mahnoor first, who responded quietly and with a small dip of her head.

Turning to Hassan and me, he greeted us, nodding at me. "How are you doing, Dua?"

I couldn't help but return his smile. "Good, thank you."

"At the rate Dua is going, she'll accomplish her goal of memorizing six surahs in no time," Hassan informed him, an unmistakable tinge of pride in his voice.

"Mashallah, that's great." As if magnetically drawn toward Mahnoor, his gaze landed on her again. His eyes softened. If he didn't truly love her, he certainly cared for her, at the very least. "How is your fast going?" he asked her. "You look a little tired."

"I'm a little low on energy today, but otherwise fine. Thank you."

"I'm glad I made it home while you're still here. Are you staying for iftar?"

If my ears were any longer, they'd be standing up. I held my breath, listening for Mahnoor's response.

"No." She shook her head firmly, and my hope deflated almost as quickly as the excitement on Azhar's face. "I promised Mom I'd help prepare iftar tonight. We've been here a couple of hours already, and we were about to leave, now that Dua's done with her lesson."

Azhar's shoulders slumped. I didn't blame him a bit; my own shoulders had begun to droop under my dupatta. "Oh. Well, I'll drive you home."

"There's no need, thank you," she said, still not looking at him. "I'm sure you're tired."

Come on, Mahnoor. I winced internally. At least give the guy *something* to hope for. I didn't want to be in his shoes right now, especially since there were witnesses to Mahnoor not so subtly shutting him down.

Still, I had to give him props for being tirelessly chivalrous. "No, I'm fine. Are you ready to go? I'll get the car started while you put your things away."

My gaze nearly bore a hole into Mahnoor's back. *Say yes,* I willed, not least of all because it would mean avoiding the subway tonight. I wasn't ready for another bumpy ride.

Mahnoor nodded. Slipping her journal into her bag, she stood up. "Sounds good. Come on, Dua. Thank you for everything, Hassan."

I exhaled, louder than I'd intended. "I'll be there in a sec," I called after her, watching her walk out the door just behind Azhar. I bit my lip, glancing back at Hassan. "Was that as awkward as I thought it was?" I asked quietly.

His shoulders stiffened, pulling up by his ears for a moment in a tight shrug. "I'd rather not comment on their relationship, but . . . yeah. Azhar's just excited. He takes after our dad with the romantic side of things."

And you? I bit my lip, hard, before the question popped out. Instead, I said, "Relationships are hard. Harder still if you're Muslim, it seems."

I saw a flash of something in his eyes, just for a moment. "I guess it depends on the relationship," he replied, his voice soft.

"Maybe." Before I could stop it, my tongue betrayed me. "What do you see yourself doing?"

The skin between his brows wrinkled in confusion. "With what?"

Stupid, stupid, stupid tongue. "Like, do you see yourself with someone you've known all your life or meeting someone new?" Then, trying to make the question seem less random, I quickly added, "My parents had an arranged marriage. Sometimes it's difficult to wrap my mind around the idea."

His forehead smoothed. "Did it work out as well as it seems? They look quite happy together."

I grinned, seeing them in my mind's eye—the way they balanced each other out, and never failed to tag-team on me when needed. "Oh, definitely."

He smiled. "That's great. I'm open to whatever is meant for me, I guess. Sometimes you meet someone and . . . you just know." He paused for a long moment. "Of course, they'd have to feel the same way."

"Right," I admitted, my voice barely above a whisper as I recalled his whistled tune yesterday. Of course, there was a chance he was just being friendly and showing me he knew the same music I did. But, my heart hoped, there was also the chance he meant something by it. With Mahnoor's warning echoing in my head, I was questioning everything.

He cleared his throat. "Azhar and Mahnoor must be ready to leave now; we're probably holding them up. You've improved a lot in a short time." He moved to place the Qur'an back on the bookshelf behind him. "Mashallah. Don't forget to keep practicing."

"I have you to thank for it." While his back was turned, I slipped a package, wrapped in brown paper and tied with a simple white ribbon, out of my purse.

"I'll walk you to the door." He turned toward the door, not seeing the package.

I followed him, clutching it tightly.

He opened the door for me, but I didn't move. "Hassan," I addressed him softly.

He turned toward me then, his eyes falling on the package.

"This is a small token of my appreciation," I said, my arms steady as I held it out to him. "As thanks for all the time and effort you're putting in with me." Dad always said, never let a kindness go unpaid, and I'd known exactly what I wanted to get for Hassan.

"Dua, no. I can't."

"Please," I said, offering it again. I stared at the floor, not quite able to meet his gaze. "It's just a small gift, nothing at all compared to what you've given me. Please, take it."

He didn't move, just for a moment. Then, slowly, he reached out and wrapped his hands around it. "Thank you."

I lifted my gaze from the floor. "I hope you like it."

He bent his head over the package, a lock of shiny brown hair falling over his forehead as he gently pulled at the ribbon and slipped off the paper. His mouth curved into a smile, and when he lifted his head, his eyes were shining. "Sami Yusuf," he noted.

"I know it's not much, but . . ." My voice trailed off, the thought not fully formed.

"It's perfect," he said, his voice thick as he pressed the CD against his chest. "Thank you."

I returned his smile. I'd chosen the Sami Yusuf album that featured our mutual favorite song. Briefly, I'd wondered if I should have gotten him something else, worried that he already had that album, or that he didn't have a CD player, but nothing could have been better than this. "You're welcome."

"Dua!" Mahnoor called, leaning out of the car, her eyes searching for me. "Come on!"

"Coming!" I slipped past Hassan and onto the front porch, turning toward him as I did. "Assalamu alaykum."

"Wa alaykum assalam," he replied, leaning against the doorjamb, his eyes locked on mine till I finally turned away.

twelve

Hi, Dua!

Hope you're enjoying your summer. I've got great news for you! I contacted some of the faculty and Mr. Smith, your history teacher, volunteered to be the faculty advisor for your Muslim Student Association. I'll have the paperwork ready the first week of school, so you can get started right away. Please come see me so we can go over all the details.

Regards,
Ms. Fritz

My eyebrows seemed to have settled into a permanent frown. No, no, no! I hadn't decided if I wanted to go through with it yet, and Ms. Fritz was running ahead at full speed. I pressed my phone against my forehead, eyes shut, holding in a frustrated grunt.

"Hey, Dua, are you okay?"

I barely registered Adam's voice. I shook my head firmly. "No, and I don't have the mental bandwidth to talk about it."

A pause. "Ooookay. I hope it works out."

I grunted in frustration again, the fading sound of his footsteps barely registering. The moment passed, and my hunched shoulders relaxed. I'd deal with this MSA business later, once I was back in Burkeville. I had until then to decide, anyway. No matter how prepared she was, Ms. Fritz couldn't force me to start a club.

I stood in the hallway outside Mahnoor's room. The door was closed. Again. But I was too tired, too frustrated to figure out somewhere else to go. With a quick knock, I let myself in.

Mahnoor sat on her bed, eyes closed as her hands tapped out a beat on the legs of her jeans. Her lips moved in a soft song, notes of praise and love resounding in the Urdu lyrics. No music accompanied her, but she didn't need any.

I stood, transfixed, till she finished her song.

"Wow."

She opened her eyes slowly. The coldness from the museum had vanished from her face, a gentle peace softening her features. The unsettled sensation in my body lightened. I stepped toward her.

"That was amazing," I said, my voice barely above a whisper, so in awe of what I'd just heard. "Musical talent runs in the family, I guess."

A blush colored her cheeks. She lowered her head, letting her hair fall forward to hide her smile. "Thanks, but Ibrahim and Rabia are the real talented ones. I just like to sing sometimes. It makes me happy and calms me down when I'm upset. Like I'm at peace."

"That's *exactly* how playing piano makes me feel!" I climbed up beside her on the bed, without waiting for an invitation. "And your voice, it's just beautiful! I wish I could sing like that. What song was that, anyway?"

She eyed me for a moment, as if momentarily unnerved by my closeness. Then she flashed an uncertain smile at me. "Oh, just the title song from a Pakistani drama. You've never heard it before?"

"No, I haven't. Definitely not the way you sang it."

Her smile widened, her eyes sparkling. For a moment, I could see what Azhar saw in her. Yes, Mahnoor had always been quiet, but she had also always been pretty, especially when she smiled. A smile that reached her eyes would make it seem like her whole face was glowing with happiness. It was a smile worth almost anything.

"The lyrics are lovely," I added, "but I'm not sure I fully understood. What's it about?"

"It describes God as the painter of life. You know, filling our lives with color and purpose." She chuckled. "That's one thing I love about Urdu—there are so many deep, powerful things you can say that you never could in English."

"Will you teach me? The song, I mean?"

She studied me for a moment. "Okay, I guess. Sure."

Just like that, she began to sing again. Her voice was soft and sweet, rising and falling with the ebb and flow of the distinctive Urdu lyrics. But this time, she paused between the lines, waiting for me to repeat after her.

I was fine with the first line but stumbled over the next. This was poetical stuff, not the typical Urdu I was used to.

"Try again," she said, repeating the line in her lilting voice.

I tried again, and while I got the lyrics right, it just didn't sound the same.

"Listen for the rhythm. You're good at that." She sang the first two lines again, tapping out the beat on her leg.

Following her lead, I let my hands take over. Even though my tongue had stumbled over the song, my fingers recognized the rhythm, playing it out on an imaginary piano. This time, my voice fell in sync with my fingers. I wasn't as good as Mahnoor, but there was no denying the beauty of the song as she joined in with me.

"I don't know why Haya's trying to recruit *me* for the band," I told her when we'd finished. "You could join yourself, or you and Azhar can make your own little duo."

The sparkle in her eyes dimmed, her smile fading. She wrapped her arms around her knees, tucking into herself, like a cocoon. "Haya's right," she whispered. "I'm afraid that Azhar may not be the right guy for me. It all happened so quickly, and now I'm terrified of spending the rest of my life with the wrong person."

Mahnoor looked at me, and for the first time, I saw my cousin, really saw *her*—not the flawless, unattainable image I'd had of her—when I looked into her big brown eyes. My heart went out to her. I reached for her hand to give it a squeeze.

Words gushed out of her at my touch, a dam breaking. "Azhar isn't what I'd imagined my husband would be like. You know how every girl talks about wanting to meet someone tall, dark, and handsome? That's what I wanted. I had it all planned out. If not at university, then I'd meet a great guy at law school, a handsome desi guy who had the same goals and dreams I did, who could relate to my family and me. Someone I could fall in love with, and who would fall in love with me."

I felt a hot, sharp pang of tension between my shoulder blades.

Azhar did love her—I was sure of that—but it wasn't enough. He didn't fit the description Mahnoor had in her head for her future husband, and never could. "But, Mahnoor, if that's the kind of guy you wanted, why did you agree to marry Azhar in the first place?"

She stared at me for a long moment, like I'd asked her why the sky was blue. "You really haven't grown up around other Muslims, have you? We're primed to start thinking about marriage since preschool, practically. It's the way things are supposed to be. Grow up, finish college, get married—that's the timeline. I already did the first two."

I bit my lip. I may have gotten the diluted version compared to Mahnoor, but I knew what she meant. Still, I could never imagine myself saying yes to someone unless I was really sure. But maybe that's why my parents admired Mahnoor so much—in their eyes, she was the ideal daughter—balancing professional goals with parental expectations. They just didn't know how much that cost her.

She sighed. "I thought it would make everyone happy," she admitted, crestfallen. "I had no idea Azhar liked me that way, and when he and his parents first came over to ask about me, I was in shock. Aside from saying hello and a smile, he hadn't noticed me much. At least, I never thought he did. Sometimes when I was at their house, Mrs. Mousawi would get Azhar to go on a grocery run, and every single time, he made sure to bring back some dark chocolate gelato, my favorite. I always thought he was being nice to me because I was his sister's best friend. I never thought there was anything more to it.

"I had this epic boy-meets-girl love story in my head; I'd never even considered marrying someone I've practically grown up with. And my parents, they were so thrilled. They love the Mousawis. I didn't want to disappoint them. I thought maybe I was wrong, that I was dreaming about someone who doesn't even exist, so why should I say no to a perfectly nice guy? I thought I could get used to the idea of marrying Azhar. But I haven't."

Her voice breaking, she tried to hide her face with her hair, but she didn't move quickly enough. I could see the tears pooling in the corners of her eyes, ready to fall any second. "Now, with the Mousawis waiting for me to pick a wedding date, I don't know what to do. How am I supposed to have my dream wedding without my dream guy?"

I didn't know what to say. I could tell her to break it off with Azhar or stick it out, see if her feelings changed. I could tell her that no matter what, everything would turn out okay. But why should she listen to me? I wouldn't take my own advice on relationships; I didn't know how to make eye contact without getting butterflies in my stomach, let alone how to settle an unhappy engagement.

As I stared into her eyes, I realized I didn't want to play the comparison game anymore. I didn't want to live my life by someone else's standards, and I didn't want her to hurt because of them, either. That left me to do the one thing I could think of: offer comfort. As my cousin broke down in front of me, I wrapped an arm awkwardly about her shoulders. She moved in closer, sobbing. *Ya Allah, please help her through this.*

thirteen

"D! Pick up, pick up!"

Mahnoor flashed a puzzled look my way.

"Kat set my ringtone, so I always know when she's calling," I explained, getting into a wrestling match with my earbuds, the wires wrapped around my phone.

"Kat, what's up?" I said, excited despite the dull pain threatening to erupt at the back of my head. The hunger was really getting to me today, but half the day was already gone. Thank God. I would finish my fast or lose my head trying. No pun intended.

"D! Ohmygosh, ohmygosh, ohmygosh, I'm gonna explode with excitement!" she squealed, talking so fast her words blurred together and it took my brain a minute to process it all.

"Kat, slow down!" I put a hand to my temple and took a deep breath, allowing the pain to ebb as I exhaled slowly. To her credit, she did stop talking, but the silence buzzed. "Okay. What were you saying?"

"Word is going around that you're starting an MSA at school," she said, barely pausing between words. "D, why didn't you tell me? Can I be VP?"

I groaned. That's the problem with small towns—news travels fast. "How many people have heard?"

"Enough to have a good presence for meetings, I think. You know Mia?"

"Of course; she's our class president." And it was a pretty small class too.

"Yeah! Well, she texted me to ask if it was for real, but I didn't know enough to tell her the whole story."

I gritted my teeth. Wonderful. "I would've told you, but honestly, I haven't decided for sure. My parents want me to do it and Ms. Fritz is all gung ho, but I don't think it's the best idea. It'll single me out more than I already am."

"Oh. I mean, I can't tell you what to do, but I do love the idea, and there's a lot of interest. I can help with whatever's needed to get started."

"Thanks. I'll keep that in mind."

"Keep me updated, okay?"

"Okay. I'm going to go, Kat. I have a headache."

"I'm sorry, D. Take it easy. Enjoy your fast."

"You too. Bye."

"What was that about?" Mahnoor asked, looking up from her Qur'an.

"Kat found out about the MSA thing." I stretched across my bed, facing her.

"You still haven't made a decision about that?"

"No. On the one hand, it'll be a little weird being the only Muslim in a *Muslim* Student Association. On the other hand, it gives me a reason to learn more about Islam and stick with the things I've learned from my checklist after Ramadan ends."

"That's true. But?"

I sighed. "But people are already talking about it. Soon they'll be talking about me, if they aren't already, and I don't know if I can handle that."

"Hmm." She furrowed her brows.

"Topic change, please," I groaned.

Like she'd been summoned, Rabia poked her head into the room. "Get ready! The Mousawis are coming over for dinner."

Mahnoor ducked her head, but I could clearly see the glow fading from her eyes as her smile dimmed. "When will they be here?" she asked, forcing her voice to sound light.

"Just in time for iftar."

Mahnoor nodded. "I'll be ready."

"Good. Dua and I are in charge of dessert." She looked pointedly at me. "I've got all the ingredients for fruit trifle. Meet me in the kitchen in ten minutes."

I smiled, eager for a distraction. "Yes, ma'am. Dessert duty it is."

As soon as Rabia left, I looked at Mahnoor. There were traces of her happy glow still left, but they were so faint, they looked like they would completely fade out soon. I climbed over onto her bed and wrapped an arm around her. Her shoulders stiffened, making the hug even more awkward than it already was. Still, I kept my arm where it was. "Are you going to be okay?"

Her shoulders lowered and she squeezed me back with surprising warmth and force. "I don't know," she admitted. "We'll see. I'm just glad knowing that you and Allah are with me."

Once again, I was left with nothing reassuring to say as I squeezed her tightly.

All evening, the house was filled with the aroma of Pakistani spices as Mom and Aunt Sadia prepared dinner. Thanks to Rabia's expert dessert skills, the fruit trifle was done and in the fridge in twenty minutes, freeing us from the kitchen before the smell of the food got too tantalizing to resist.

Which meant I had enough time to get ready, according to my mother. While she'd told me I didn't need to get too fancy with my outfit, the faded blue jeans and dark blue-and-pink-plaid button-down shirt I wore didn't make the cut either. With some help from Mahnoor, I came up with an outfit that wouldn't make my mom put a hand to her chest, look to the heavens, and cry dramatically, "Allah gives me one child, one daughter, and she can't even dress for company without looking like she's ready to go outside and play kabaddi."

I'd chosen from the few traditional Pakistani clothes I had, settling on an emerald-green shalwar kameez with gold trim and embroidery, with a matching gold dupatta with green trim. My jewelry was simple: thin gold hoops in my ears and a delicate heart pendant on a gold chain—borrowed from Rabia—around my neck. I smiled at my reflection, turning to check different angles. I looked pretty good, if I said so myself.

Mahnoor raised an eyebrow. "Green again. Are you hoping someone will notice? Someone whose name starts with *H?*"

"Maybe, but if you tell anyone, I'll deny it." For once, the throb of my head was a welcome distraction from the blush creeping up my neck. It sharpened every now and then, lying in wait for the right time to strike. I ignored it, focusing instead on making sure I remained presentable—that is, not tripping over my own feet and ripping something.

Mahnoor was breathtaking, though. She'd taken extra care with her appearance tonight, lining the corners of her upper and lower lids to make her eyes look bigger, applying lip gloss with a light hand, and arranging her sky-blue hijab in a new style that flattered her face. I couldn't help but wonder what she was getting so dressed up for, if she was still torn about the engagement.

A sick feeling settled in the pit of my stomach. Of course, everything would be okay. The only reason I had a bad feeling about the whole thing was because I was clueless about relationships. Especially ones as complex as Muslim marriages, where relationships weren't just about the two people getting married, but also the two families coming together.

Deep breaths, I reminded myself. Mahnoor wasn't freaking out, so why should I? *It's the calm before the storm,* my brain offered. I shoved the thought into my mental dustbin, shaking my head to clear it. No, everything was fine. Tonight was going to be about food, friends, and fun, not freaking out.

Iftar was at 8:37, and the Mousawis arrived right on time, just a few minutes before.

"Assalamu alaykum, how are you?" Mrs. Mousawi grabbed me on sight and squeezed me so hard I could feel my brain being deprived of the oxygen it so desperately needed, especially with my headache.

"Good, alhamdulillah," I replied when her grip loosened enough, my voice slightly muffled since my face was pressed up against her shoulder. "What about you?"

"Alhamdulillah, thanks for asking," she replied, releasing my torso from her hug trap to grab my head and kiss me on each cheek before passing me on to Haya.

"Salaam." Haya squeezed me tightly, though not as tight as her mother, and smiled as she pulled back. "You look beautiful. How was your fast?" she added, squeezing my hand. There was a new addition to her black henna tattoos tonight, a flower with six intricately drawn petals and a pink rhinestone set in the center. Note to self: Find out who does Haya's henna.

"Pretty decent. I can't wait to eat. Now I feel bad. Should I not have said that? I mean, there's people in the city who are starving, and who knows when they'll get food and—"

I stopped talking as my brain zeroed in on something beyond Haya's shoulder. Hassan was greeting my dad. Oh, lovely. He was wearing a polo shirt, just the right shade of gray to bring out his eyes and make them stand out even more in a roomful of brown-eyed people.

Haya squeezed my hand again, bringing my brain back to reality. I hoped she didn't notice me practically ogling her brother, though I doubted she'd mind even if she had.

"Slow down, Dua," she said, and before I could rush to explain myself, she continued. "You must be hungry. You're barely pausing between sentences."

"Right," I said slowly. She hadn't noticed. Phew. The last thing I needed right now was for her to crack a joke about Hassan and me, right in front of my parents. "Sorry, sometimes I talk too much when I'm hungry. Hey, show me your henna. Do you do it yourself?" I pulled her arm toward me and bent over it, forcing myself to focus on the beautiful designs against her skin instead of Hassan. No distractions tonight.

Allahu Akbar, Allahu Akbar!

"Oh, Allah, I fasted for You and I believe in You and I break my fast with Your sustenance," I murmured, the Arabic words barely spoken when I stuffed a samosa into my mouth. It was still hot, and that first moment when my mouth held that delicious combination of crisp pastry and spiced potatoes, if anyone had asked me how I was feeling, I would've said something about falling in love with a samosa.

"I think Dua was hungry today," Aunt Sadia observed with a laugh.

I smiled sheepishly and took a sip of water. "These are my favorite samosas."

Ibrahim pushed the platter closer to me. "Don't forget to save room for dinner." He smiled as he reached for another samosa from his own plate.

After eating, we prayed maghrib together in the living room. I intended to pay attention through the whole thing, and I really tried, but as my head dipped in sujud, it filled with visions of the delicious meal we were about to have. As Uncle Yusuf led the end of the prayer, turning his head to the right and then the left, I couldn't tell you which surahs had been recited, but I knew exactly what was on the dinner table.

"Astagfirullah, Allah forgive me," I whispered to myself. I'd have to try harder. Slipping the dupatta off my head as I approached the dining table, I eyed the food. I tried not to put a mountain of biryani and a mound of chicken saalan on my plate, but I still ended up with two decent-sized piles when I dug in.

I hadn't been paying attention to the conversation at the table, but when Aunt Sadia said the words *wedding dress,* I immediately stopped stuffing myself and looked up from my plate.

"Insha'Allah, we'll go dress shopping as soon as Ramadan is over," she said, replying to something Mrs. Mousawi had said. "We were thinking of a traditional Pakistani dress for the wedding and a white dress for the reception, if that's all right."

"Of course, whatever Mahnoor wants," Mrs. Mousawi beamed.

"Sweet! You know I have to come, as your best friend." Haya grinned, nudging Mahnoor's elbow.

Mahnoor smiled faintly but kept her gaze down on her plate. She'd barely eaten anything this whole time, moving the small amount of food that *was* on her plate around so it looked like she was eating, as if she were making sure there weren't any cardamom pods in her biryani. You don't want to bite into one of those, trust me. One second, you're eating a delicious spoonful of biryani, the next you have cardamom seeds all over your mouth, ruining the deliciousness.

"Don't worry," Haya added, sneaking a sly glance at her brother and leaning into Mahnoor to whisper not-so-quietly, "I know what Azhar likes."

Mahnoor dropped her fork. *Oh, jinn poo.*

"I think we should hold off on the wedding dress shopping for a bit," she said, still staring down at her plate. *Major jinn poo.*

"Why, beta? Are you waiting for the latest fashions to come out?" Aunt Sadia said, going back to her biryani like nothing had happened.

Wait, I don't think jinns even go to the bathroom.

Mahnoor waved Rabia's hand away when she offered her a clean fork. "No, Mom, I don't care about that."

Everyone's eyes were on her now, but only Azhar appeared

132

more concerned than confused. He'd forgotten his dinner alto-gether, a mix of fear and anxiety in his eyes. "What do you mean, Mahnoor?" he asked quietly.

"We can check out some options online to get an idea of what you like, and if you don't like anything in stores, I'm sure we can figure out something," Haya said.

"Doesn't your cousin Hiba design wedding dresses in Paki-stan?" Mom leaned over to ask Aunt Sadia.

"Oh, yes, we can ask her for help. She makes—"

"Mom!" Mahnoor's voice boomed. "Stop. I don't want any help from Hiba Auntie. I don't want any help, period." She glanced at Azhar. "I'm sorry."

Mrs. Mousawi's lips twitched in a smile. "Sorry for what? Habibti, what's going on?"

"I can't do this," she said, slipping her engagement ring off her finger and placing it on the table. "I can't handle talk about wedding dresses and invitations and things like that anymore. Not now."

She turned to Mrs. Mousawi regretfully. "I'm sorry. But I can't go through with this wedding." She pushed her chair away from the table and stood up. "Please excuse me. I'm very sorry," she offered again, walking away. She didn't look at Azhar.

Azhar looked stricken. He ran his hands through his hair, making it stand up. His eyes roved about the room, unseeing as he muttered to himself, "No, no, no."

Everyone just sat there for a few seconds, too shell-shocked to move. You could've heard someone bite a cardamom pod open, it was so quiet. But then my headache came back with a ven-geance, slamming into the back of my head like a sledgehammer. I couldn't hold back my grimace in time.

Aunt Sadia got up from the table with a determined expression. "Please excuse us. Yusuf"—she tugged on my uncle's sleeve to get him up—"come."

"Perhaps we should discuss this," Mr. Mousawi said as he stood, nudging Azhar to his feet.

"Yes, of course," Aunt Sadia said. "The rest of you, please eat, enjoy your dinner. Someone get Dua an Advil. We'll be back soon."

I downed the Advil Adam gave me like my life depended on it. The only sound was the occasional louder-than-expected exhale as we all stared at our own plates, aside from Mahdi, who still joyfully dug into his biryani, totally oblivious to the seriousness of what had just happened. Although, I guess in his four-year-old mind, it wasn't a big deal.

Eventually, Dad, at the end of the table farthest from me, picked up his fork and started to eat again, and soon the rest of us were doing the same, though it did little to alleviate the awkward silence that had spread through the room like a plague.

"At least she said it before we ended up spending serious money on a wedding dress," Adam muttered under his breath.

Everyone heard it despite how quiet he'd tried to be, but when Mahdi spoke next, he made no attempt to be quiet or subtle.

"It's okay if Mahnoor and Azhar bhai don't get married. We'll just get Dua and Hassan bhai married instead!"

Right at that moment, I bit into a cardamom pod. Hassan, who'd been taking a sip of water, coughed as it went down the wrong way, and we both ended up doubled over in front of our plates, choking on opposite ends of the table while everyone stared at us.

Mom stopped mid-chew to look at me with concern, but my dad? Oh, boy.

He paused, his fork halfway to his mouth. "Who is thinking of marrying my only child?" he demanded, his accent going full-on desi. Oh no. Normally my dad speaks flawless English; when he suddenly gets an accent, prepare for trouble.

Hassan stopped choking, but his face had gone a little red. I didn't even want to think about what shade my face must be.

The chicken fell off my dad's fork, and he put it down to aim a stern glare at me. "Dua, what is the meaning of this?"

I spit the cardamom into my napkin and looked at him, forcing my voice to be calm. "Nothing, Baba. I bit into an elaichi." I hadn't called him *baba* since I was five.

"Then why are the two of you blushing like you've been caught red-handed?"

"Khalid, stop it. Her head's been bothering her the whole day," my mom said, trying to pacify him by putting more biryani on his plate.

It didn't work. "Sanam, she is turning eighteen at the end of the month. If there is any hanky-panky going on, I need to know about it."

Oh, God, he broke out the *hanky-panky*. My eyes met Hassan's, as wide with surprise as my own, and I couldn't stop the giggle that escaped my mouth. It only took one to lose my composure, and soon my laughter was joined by Hassan's. Of course, like everything else about him, his laugh was as sweet as a note of music. My heart lifted like I'd just listened to a hundred Bollywood love ballads.

Dad, ready to fulfill his role as Overprotective Brown Father, cleared his throat loudly. My romantic daydreams dissipated instantly, leaving a void in their wake. Catching my eye, Hassan lifted a hand and fake coughed into it, hiding his smile. There was no hiding the way his eyes sparkled, though. Lowering my head, I nudged Ibrahim with my foot, willing him to say something, anything, to reassure Dad. He had a gift for communicating to our elders, old soul that he was.

He caught on quickly. "Uncle, Mahdi loves Hassan like an older brother," Ibrahim explained. "And he loves Dua too. It's nothing more than a case of a child wanting to see two of his favorite people together. Children do it all the time."

"You see, Khalid?" Mom gave him a disapproving look. "There's a perfectly reasonable explanation."

"Hmm." Dad went back to his biryani, appeased. "But if anything is going on," he said, pointing his fork at me, "I want to know about it."

Sure . . . once I figured out what *was* going on. There was no sense in getting him involved prematurely and scaring Hassan off. "Of course, Baba." I released a breath I hadn't realized I'd been holding, whispering a quiet *thank you* to Ibrahim.

Rabia clapped her hands together and stood up from the table, a big grin pasted on her face. "Who wants dessert?"

fourteen

The engagement was officially over. No more ring, no more dress shopping, nada. Everyone walked on eggshells around the house. Rabia whipped through her summer reading like there was nothing better than having your nose stuck in a book all day, and Adam spent most of his time outdoors with a soccer ball or inside playing video games. He'd asked me once if I wanted to play Mario Kart, but I hadn't been feeling up to it.

On the plus side, Mahnoor wasn't staying up all night crying into her ice cream. On the negative side, it'd been three days since that catastrophic dinner, and no one had heard from the Mousawis. It was weird, expecting Haya to drop by any second, only to realize that that wasn't going to happen. Even weirder was the realization that I'd gotten used to having her around.

Mahdi missed his Hassan bhai and kept asking Ibrahim to call him, but Ibrahim just ruffled his hair and gently explained that everyone was a little confused right now, and it was best to give them some time and personal space. Mahdi's lower lip trembled every time he heard this, but he bravely held in his tears. I couldn't blame him. I didn't dare admit it to anyone, but I missed Hassan too. Butterflies fluttered in my stomach whenever I thought of his eyes meeting mine, the gentility of his voice. If he felt just a little bit of what I did, how could he possibly be comfortable with this silence and distance?

No one else may have noticed my aimless shuffling at home, but my parents certainly did. They were doing all they could to avoid the subject of the engagement altogether—at least in front of Uncle Yusuf and Aunt Sadia. In front of me, not so much.

"Dua!" Mom called me from her room.

"Coming!" I called. I was in the kitchen with Rabia, frosting cupcakes. Even though it made me super hungry, it was better than sitting around thinking about how hungry I was, and there was only so much of that I could do before my legs got restless and I had to move. If I didn't, I'd go berserk.

"Dua!"

"I don't think she heard you," Rabia pointed out. "It's hard to hear from the kitchen all the way at the end of the hall unless you're using a bullhorn."

I stopped frosting the cupcakes on my side of the counter—chocolate, it's always chocolate with me—and went to my mom's room as fast as I could, calling, "Yes, Moooooom?" the entire way.

"Come in, beta."

Before I could answer, Mom grabbed me by the arm and pulled me inside, closing the door behind me.

"Mom, are you okay?" I asked, noting the somber expression on her face. It wasn't often that I saw her looking so serious, without a hint of a smile.

"Of course, sweetie," she said, cupping my cheek in her palm. "But my hair's gotten so dry, and so has yours. Let's fix that."

She sat on the bed and pulled me down beside her, gently tugging my hair free of its ponytail and running the ends through her fingers. Excuse or not, she was right. My hair had seen better days.

She plucked a bowl of oil from the table beside her. I breathed in the strong coconut scent. She must have just heated it up. "You've been spending so much time with your cousins lately, not that I'm complaining, and I realized we haven't really sat together this Ramadan," she said, dipping her fingertips in the warm oil and massaging it into my scalp. "I missed you."

I leaned my head back into her hands, the movements relaxing me.

She sighed. "Remember when I used to do this for you when you were younger?"

"Mmm-hmm," I replied, closing my eyes. Regular hot oil treatments ensured that my hair was always healthy and shiny, and Mom's massages were the best.

"I miss those times. You're grown now, Mashallah. Pretty soon, it'll be time to look for a good match for you."

My heartbeat quickened, but I didn't say anything. I'd hear her out.

"You know, that's one of the reasons I wanted to come here in the first place. It's hard to find a good match these days, and for you, especially, it'll be difficult since your father and I don't know many Pakistanis. I'd hoped that through Sadia and Yusuf, we could get to know a few families, and maybe in a few years' time, we could find a good boy for you."

I didn't say anything for a moment. I'd always known that my parents' marriage, like many other Muslims, was arranged. But from how often I'd heard Mom tell the story, I also knew that they'd been attracted to each other since they first met, and the mutual attraction quickly blossomed into love. Kat would sometimes remark that seeing my parents together was like seeing a Nicholas Sparks novel come to life. Even when they argued, they couldn't hold a grudge against each other for longer than an hour. Arranged marriage had been the right option for them, but that didn't mean it was for me.

"Mom," I said quietly, "do I *have* to have an arranged marriage?"

She shook her head. "No, sweetie, of course not. We're just looking so that the route will be available to you in the future, if you choose."

I heaved a little sigh of relief, but then I thought of Mahnoor and Azhar's relationship. Arranged from Mahnoor's perspective, for love from Azhar's. Some marriages could be both, arranged and for love, but not like this.

As if she was thinking the same thing, Mom said quietly, "Poor Sadia. She's trying so hard with Mahnoor, but the whole situation is complicated. Marriage is not easy these days."

Mahnoor had been confused, in pain, and now everyone around her felt the same way. Unbidden, Hassan's face came to mind, his soft, patient voice and his warm, kind eyes. I couldn't even imagine what he must be thinking.

"Mom?"

"Hmm?" Her fingers moved from my scalp to the ends of my hair.

I paused, making sure I used the right words. I'd been reading some blogs and sites geared toward young Muslim women, and from many of those posts, I'd gleaned that Islam approved of interracial marriages and Prophet Muhammad (peace be upon him) actively encouraged them. However, contemporary Muslims, fearful of losing their individual culture, often disapproved of and even forbade such marriages within their own families. Not always, but often. Obviously that wasn't an issue in Mahnoor and Azhar's case, but I couldn't assume that Mom and Dad would be as enthusiastic as Uncle Yusuf and Aunt Sadia, who'd known the Mousawis for well over a decade.

"What is it, darling?" Mom prompted when I didn't say anything.

"If I wanted to marry a non-Pakistani, what would you do?" I said quietly. "He'd be Muslim, but what if he wasn't Pakistani?"

Her hands, running a comb through my well-oiled hair to coat every strand, stilled at my back. The silence, however brief, was deafening. "Well," she said finally, getting back to work, "that would be *different*, but as long as he has good character, I don't see why not."

"What if I really like him, and you don't approve?" I said, a lump rising in my throat, so many other girls' stories coming to mind.

After a beat, she replied, "Your father and I raised you right. I have full faith that you will never bring someone to us that we couldn't respect. Insha'Allah, whoever Allah wills for you is whom you will end up marrying. All we can ask is that He wills the best person for you."

Neither of us said anything for a few moments.

"Dua. That boy, do you like him?"

I felt a blush creeping up my neck. "Who?" I said, fighting to keep my voice neutral.

"That boy." She gestured with her comb, as if he were sitting in the room. "The short one with the green eyes."

"Mom, he's not short," I retorted automatically. "I know he's not six-two or whatever Ibrahim is, but Hassan's not short just because he's . . ." My voice trailed off as I realized I'd given my mother exactly what she wanted to hear. Oops.

Her hands gently pulled my hair into a braid. "I knew it," she replied, her voice low.

"Mom." I made a face and tried to shrug it off, but my blush betrayed me. "Okay. Yes, Mom, you're right. I like him."

She didn't say anything for a moment. Then, her voice low, she asked, "Does he like you?"

"I'm not sure," I replied honestly. The only way for my over-thinking mind to be *sure* would be if Hassan stood in front of me with a sign spelling out his feelings. Besides, the song he'd whistled hinted at me falling in love, but it said nothing about how *he* felt. Still, I'd seen something in his eyes, I think. I added softly, "But I think he does."

"You'll tell me if anything happens?"

"Okay."

"Promise?"

"Promise," I assured her. Although, if Hassan was seriously interested in me, that disaster at dinner probably scared him off. He'd seen how the idea of me getting married sent my dad into overprotective Papa Bear mode. And, after Mahnoor's decision, would the Mousawis consider creating another tie to our family?

Mom swiftly secured the end of my braid with a ribbon hair tie, letting it fall against my back. "Well, he seems like a nice boy." As if she knew what I was thinking, she added, "I don't know what will happen now after Mahnoor, but we'll see. I am always pray-ing for you."

"Thank you for being so understanding."

"Oh, Dua." She turned me around and pressed her lips to my forehead, the kiss gentle but firm. "You are my only child, the coolness of my eyes. You arrived into my life as the answer to my prayers, the physical manifestation of my duas. Your dad and I will always want only what is best for you." She cupped my cheek in her palm. "May Allah bless you with the best of this world and the next, with love, health, wealth, and the utmost happiness."

I sniffled, tears pricking at my eyes. "I love you, Mom."

"I love you too, sweetie." She kissed me again, then gently nudged me toward the door. "Now, go and finish helping Rabia. Don't forget to wash the oil out in an hour."

"I won't," I said, dropping a quick kiss on her cheek as I left. My lips lifted into a smile, but my shoulders still sagged. My parents were reasonable about this, but what if they couldn't be as understanding about the MSA? Or studying music? It was just one hurdle down with more still in the way. I had no choice but to take them one at a time.

"What did Aunt Sanam want?" Rabia asked. She'd already frosted my half of the cupcakes as well as hers, leaving me with nothing to do but roll up my sleeves and wash the dishes.

"Nothing, she just wanted to talk. Have a little mother-daughter heart-to-heart."

Rabia was up to her elbows in suds as she rinsed out the cupcake trays. "My mom's probably going to want to do that with me next."

"Probably," I agreed. There was no use sugarcoating it. Mahnoor's decision was going to affect everyone, whether she liked it or not. She had to be patient with everyone else, and everyone else would have to be patient with her, or we'd never get through this in one piece.

Rabia reached up to brush her hair out of her eyes, leaving a tiny trail of soap on her forehead. "I just hope it all works out, insha'Allah."

"Insha'Allah," I repeated, reaching over to brush the soap away. "It will," I added, not entirely convinced myself. How, exactly, was this going to work out? With Mahnoor and Azhar back together? With the Sheikhs and Mousawis torn apart forever? Whatever Allah willed was what was going to happen. But what if patching up a rift between the families wasn't His will?

"Sorry," Rabia sighed. "This was supposed to be an enjoyable trip for you. We've managed to turn it into a Pakistani soap opera."

"It's fine," I reassured her. "A little drama never hurt anyone, and this has been a good visit so far."

Rabia smiled. "Then we'll make it better. We'll go to Central Park tomorrow."

"Really?" I grinned.

"Great idea," a voice said from out of nowhere.

I jumped, spraying stray droplets from my dishrag.

Mahnoor smiled. "Sorry. But like I said, that's a great idea. You've been cooped up inside too long."

She wasn't totally off about that. The house hadn't been the most comfortable place lately; we all needed a little break, a distraction. "Will we go to the zoo?" I asked hopefully.

She laughed, and I could see why. I sounded as excited at the prospect of going to the zoo as Mahdi. On him, it was cute. On me, not as much. "If you want. So insha'Allah, God willing, we'll

144

go tomorrow, and maybe stop by a gift shop on the way back. You wanted to get something for your friend, right?"

"Right." Kat had been super-specific about what she'd wanted me to get her, and if I forgot it, she wasn't going to be happy. "So, we're going?"

Mahnoor's smile grew. "Sure. Rabia, you coming?"

"Obviously. It was my idea," she replied flippantly, though she smiled. "But," she added, turning to me, "if you start acting like a four-year-old, I'm going to pretend I don't know you."

"Deal. But you buy me ice cream tomorrow, after iftar."

Rabia rolled her eyes. "God really broke the mold when He made you, Dua."

"Don't worry, Dua," Mahnoor reassured me, "if she doesn't buy you ice cream, I will."

I smiled. Only God could fix this mess that we were in, but ice cream wouldn't hurt. "What about Ibrahim, Adam, and Mahdi?"

"Ibrahim will be busy; he's taking some Arabic classes so he can understand the Qur'an better, so he'll be online all day tomorrow," Mahnoor explained. "And Mahdi has a playdate. I guess Adam's free, though."

"I can ask him," Rabia said.

"Let me." I'd been wondering how Adam was doing; he hadn't said much since dinner the other day.

Adam was lounging in the living room, slumped in a beanbag chair. The TV was on, but he was on his phone. Mom and Aunt Sadia must have watched it last; a Pakistani drama was playing. The camera zoomed in on the lead actress's face, the huge tears falling from her kohl-rimmed eyes.

I sank into the beanbag chair beside his. He didn't look up from his game.

"We're planning on going to Central Park tomorrow. Are you coming?"

He shook his head, his fingers flurrying across the screen. "No, thanks."

I watched him quietly, the furrowed brow, his messy hair, the way he bit his lip as he concentrated on the screen. In that moment, he seemed much older than twelve. "Adam, are you okay?"

He didn't say anything for a few moments, and as I began to wonder if he'd even heard me, he sighed. Tossing the phone into his lap, he looked up at me. His eyes were red, as if he hadn't slept properly. "You're actually asking?"

"Yeah, I am."

He ran a hand through his hair, making it stick up more. He needed a comb, badly. "This whole thing with Mahnoor and Azhar, everyone's upset, and I don't know what to feel; I don't know where I fit in with all this. I can't even keep my own brother entertained without him asking for someone else."

Wow. It had never occurred to me that Adam felt this way, or that we were all too busy with our own problems to stop and ask how he was doing. "I'm sorry, Adam," I said sincerely. "But everyone cares about you. They're just hurting right now. But know that I'm here, and I care. You're just as much my family as any of them are, and I'm sorry if I didn't give you that impression before."

The tiniest smile appeared on his face. "Thanks, Dua. I appreciate that, honestly."

I smiled back. "So, are you coming to Central Park with us tomorrow?"

He shook his head. "No, thanks. Ibrahim mentioned his Qur'an classes the other day and asked if I wanted to sit in with him for a couple. I think I'm going to take him up on that tomorrow. Get some quality time in with my brother."

I smiled. "That sounds good. Do you want us to bring anything back for you tomorrow?"

"Um, ice cream, if you don't mind."

I laughed.

fifteen

I get it now. I studied the Alice in Wonderland statue quietly. For the first time, I truly understood the story. I hadn't fallen down a rabbit hole, but I *was* visiting a new, strange world.

"Dua," Mahnoor addressed me.

"Hmm?" Somehow, I hadn't expected the Mad Hatter to be so short.

"You're happy, right?"

I smiled at her. "Yeah. You know, I used to wonder what it would be like to have siblings, have a huge family together for dinner, getting ready for iftar, fighting over who got the last samosa."

Mahnoor smiled. "Mahdi. Mahdi always gets the last samosa. It's the puppy-dog eyes."

I turned back to look out at the grass. It was just so beautiful. So calm, even with tons of people around. I blinked. Speaking of people. "Is that Haya? And Hassan?" My heart leaped into my throat as his name fell from my lips.

Mahnoor followed my gaze. The two figures I'd spotted were

a bit far off, but still close enough to be recognizable. And they were walking right toward us. "Yeah." She nodded, her voice lowering.

"Should we say hi?" I said, my hand already up in the air, ready to wave.

Rabia shook her head. "Dua, there's a *reason* we haven't been talking. We should probably go. Come on, Mahnoor."

I hesitated, still eyeing Haya and Hassan from a short distance. It didn't feel right, being so close for so long and then suddenly not talking. But this was about Mahnoor's feelings, not mine.

I turned to go.

"Watch out!" Hassan's warning rang in my ears, a few seconds too late, as I hit the ground.

"Dua!" Hands lifted me up into a sitting position. I blinked as I touched my head, felt the bump. Haya had called out my name, alarm in her voice.

A circle of people surrounded me: Mahnoor, Rabia, a guy I had never seen before in my life, and Haya and Hassan.

"Ow," I muttered over a stream of muttered apologies. "What happened?"

The strange guy looked sheepish. "My friend and I were fooling around with a Frisbee. I'm really, really sorry. Are you okay? How's your head?"

"I think I'll be okay," I said. "I just want to stand up now."

They gave me a little space, Haya and Mahnoor holding on to my arms as I stood up.

"Thanks," I murmured as Hassan handed the guy his Frisbee, his mouth a thin, firm line.

I looked at Haya. Something was missing. The sparkle was

gone from her eyes. Surely, she must be yearning for Mahnoor and the rest of us as much as we were for her.

Time for a little help from my Ramadan checklist. I had to be a good cousin, but also a good friend. If I couldn't handle not talking to the Mousawis, I could only imagine what Mahnoor and Rabia were going through.

Still staring into Haya's eyes, I smiled. Beamed the biggest, most good-willed grin I could muster in her direction. It took a moment, but she smiled back faintly.

"Assalamu alaykum," I greeted them.

"Wa alaykum assalam," Haya and Hassan replied at the same time, voices low. I let my gaze linger a moment too long, catching Hassan's eye. He clenched his jaw, eyes brimming with concern. And maybe something else too—I wasn't the only one having trouble looking away. Slowly, he gestured to his own head and mouthed, *Are you really okay?*

I nodded. My heart was beating a little too fast, but my head was just fine, if a little tender.

His mouth quirked in a small, sad smile. He lowered his gaze, finally breaking eye contact. I sighed in a moment worthy of a Bollywood Filmfare Award, and if anyone else noticed, they didn't say anything.

Mahnoor finally looked at her best friend. "How are you?"

Haya held her gaze for a moment. "Okay. Thanks for asking."

"Of course," Mahnoor said. "How's everyone else at home?"

Haya's lips twitched. "They're okay." She exchanged a look with Hassan. "We were on our way out of here. It's nearly time for iftar."

"See you later," Mahnoor said quietly.

"Yeah, sure," Haya said noncommittally, reaching for her

brother's arm. "Assalamu alaykum." They trudged past us, eyes straight ahead.

Rabia sighed. "That could have been worse."

"You think so?" I murmured, touching the tender spot on my forehead.

"Now what?" Mahnoor asked quietly, looking defeated.

"Now we go home. And make sure Dua doesn't have a concussion."

As we walked away, me lagging behind Mahnoor and Rabia, something willed me to turn around. I glanced back, my eyes meeting Hassan's. He looked at me over his shoulder, Haya's arm still on his. Our gazes remained on each other until the distance between us was too great, our forms mere specks across the park.

☾

"Ow!" I bumped into Ibrahim on my way in as he exited.

"Are you okay?"

"Fine," I muttered, rubbing my forehead for the second time today. A new record, even for me. "Where are you going?"

"Presentation on the life of the Prophet Muhammad, peace be upon him, at the mosque," Adam replied, appearing behind him.

"Oh. Nice." I stepped aside, giving them enough room to pass through.

"We'll see you there later, insha'Allah," Adam said as they stepped out.

"At the mosque?" No one had told me anything.

Ibrahim smiled. "Ask your mom. Assalamu alaykum."

"Wa alaykum assalam," I replied, watching their backs as

they moved away. I stared at their kufis, blindingly white against their jet-black hair, seeing tiny smiley faces in the lacy pattern.

"Mom?" I stepped into the open doorway of my parents' room. No sign of her.

My dad was sitting on the bed, though. He looked up from his Qur'an and smiled, and I realized that his hair wasn't as dark as it used to be. When had all of this gray come in?

"Baba," I said, walking toward him. Ever since dinner, I'd reverted to calling him Baba to his face. He liked it, I could tell. Every time I said it, his gaze would soften, and he would smile brighter. "Ibrahim and Adam mentioned the mosque?"

"Right. We're going there for iftar tonight, insha'Allah, and to pray maghrib after."

"Oh." Iftar at the mosque would mean good food—my mouth was already watering as visions of fresh samosas, falafel, and naan swam before my eyes—but I'd already gathered that it also meant huge lines as everyone waited to fill their plates.

"Dua." Mom emerged from the bathroom, towel-drying her long, thick hair. "You're still sitting here?"

"I just got—"

"Don't make us late. Go get ready."

"But iftar's two hours away." I don't know why I was arguing. You'd think I'd have learned by now.

"Exactly, now go, get ready. You smell like dirt. What did you do, lie down in the grass and roll around in it?"

Not quite what had happened, but she wasn't that far off. I sighed, getting up to drag myself to Mahnoor's room. "Okay, Mom."

After a quick video chat with Kat for advice, I chose a shalwar kameez I'd previously worn last Eid, a deep purple with tiny flowers embroidered all over in pale pink and gold thread. I'd barely finished putting it on when the bedroom door opened with a bang.

"Dua!"

"Yes, Mom?" I turned around, and my smile faded at the look on her face. Fear. Worry. Pain. "Mom?" I didn't recognize my own voice; it sounded so small.

"Adam's in the hospital."

sixteen

We must have looked a strange sight, seven of us trying to cram ourselves through the hospital entrance at once, me getting my dupatta caught in the sliding doors.

"Stay there," Dad commanded, pointing us to the waiting room. "All of you kids."

We tried to argue, but our parents were gone before we could get a syllable out.

As we sank into our chairs, oblivious to everything except each other, I snuck a glance at each of my cousins. Mahnoor. Rabia. Mahdi. All of them wide-eyed, the same haunted look on each of their faces. Did I have that same dread in my eyes, the same hopelessness?

Adam had been *fine* when he left. Better than fine. His face popped into my head, the way he'd shoved the kufi haphazardly over his gelled hair. My brain couldn't make sense of the situation, like it was suddenly broken. How was I supposed to accept that one second Adam was safe and sound, and the next he wasn't?

"They need to tell us what's going on," Mahnoor said, voice

raspy, blinking back tears as she gripped her seat so tightly her knuckles turned white.

"They will," Rabia replied quietly. "I just hope Adam . . ." Her face crumpled as she sobbed. "God, I wish I didn't annoy him so much this summer."

Regret stung in my stomach. I'd barely spent any time with him this summer. I'd worked at getting to know Mahnoor, Rabia, Ibrahim, and of course, Mahdi. Yet, Adam was always there, hanging around in the background. I'd told him I cared about him, but I hadn't shown him.

"You're here."

I looked up, the pain etched on Ibrahim's face, the redness of his eyes hitting me full-force. He knew. He knew what happened to Adam. I swallowed against the lump in my throat, taking in the tearstains that marked his face from his eyes to the very edge of his chin. It was bad.

Really bad.

"Ibrahim"—Mahnoor's voice cracked—"what happened?"

"Adam . . . Adam was . . ." Ibrahim reached up and wiped his eyes on his sleeve.

"Was *what?*" Mahnoor demanded, crossing the room. "What?"

Her tone unnerved him; he flinched, taking a step back. "Don't yell at me. Please." He shook slightly, a tremor traveling from his shoulders to his knees.

"Mahnoor!"

Haya's voice.

I turned around. And there she was, along with Azhar, Hassan, and their parents. All with the same exact look of terror that was in our eyes.

For once, Mrs. Mousawi didn't crush me. Instead, she and her husband said their salaams and hurried off to find Uncle Yusuf and Aunt Sadia.

"Ibrahim bhai, what happened?" Rabia demanded, her voice softer than her sister's had been. Mahnoor hadn't spoken a word since the Mousawis had walked in.

"Adam was shot," Ibrahim said finally, his voice so quiet I almost didn't hear him. But I did.

Shot?

My chest hurt, a sharp, burning sensation by my heart. It hurt so much, I wanted to cry.

I wasn't the only one barely holding myself together. Mahdi, who'd stretched out on a chair, started bawling, looking more confused and afraid of our own pain than anything else. Mahnoor rushed over to him, but Hassan got to him first. Carefully, he cradled my baby cousin in his arms, nodding at Mahnoor, allowing her the space she needed to process her own anxiety and grief.

Rabia couldn't hold in her tears anymore, filling the room with the gut-wrenching sound of her sobs. Mahnoor put her head in her hands, her body shaking as she cried noiselessly. Haya had gone so white, the black henna tattoos on her arms looked like a schoolkid's doodles on paper. Azhar clenched his jaw as he stared down at the floor. We stayed that way as Ibrahim began his story, his voice cracking.

"We never made it to the mosque. Not even close. We were in the subway tunnel, waiting for the train. I felt Adam get closer to me, and he whispered that this guy was staring at us. We tried to keep a distance, but he came after us. He had a gun, I think— I felt the barrel. He pushed it right here." He lightly touched the center of his belly. "He demanded our phones, our wallets. Adam was frantic; I could hear it in his voice. I thought when we gave the guy everything, if we stayed as calm as we could, he'd leave. But he didn't. He just kept standing there in front of us, staring at us, and then he said, 'You're Muzlims, aren't you?'"

I closed my eyes and toyed with my dupatta, concentrating on the feel of the fabric instead of the horrible picture in my head.

"We didn't say anything," Ibrahim continued. "We were too scared. Adam put his hand in mine, like he used to when he was five and needed me to help him cross the street. He was shaking. I begged him to leave us alone, but it wasn't enough. He started yelling at us, calling us terrorists, saying we're the reason nine-eleven happened.

"I couldn't say a word. I was too scared, so I just started praying to myself, quietly. Praying for the guy to get out of our faces, for him to leave us alone. Then . . ." He paused, swallowing loudly. "There was a loud bang. My ears were ringing, he was gone, and Adam . . . He was on the ground. He didn't answer me, and when I touched him, my fingers were wet. I could smell his blood." He started to sob. "There was so much blood."

The pain in *my* chest intensified, like a thousand blades in my heart, and I bit my lip to keep from crying out. I'd never been so scared before, so much I thought I might die from fear alone. Out of all of us, Adam deserved this the least.

☾

Allahu Akbar, Allahu Akbar!

Azhar pulled his phone out of his pocket, the adhan stopping automatically after the first thirty seconds. "Time for maghrib," he said quietly.

Time to break our fasts. My stomach had stopped trying to

catch my attention ever since we left the house, so instead of having a stomach that was trying to eat itself, I had an ache in my chest that refused to go away.

All desire to eat gone, I pulled my knees to my chest and, closing my eyes, rested my head on them. I didn't want to sleep, and I didn't think I could anyway, but I had to block myself off. I longed to hear nothing, see nothing, feel nothing, *think* nothing. I sought peace in emptiness, and my brain wouldn't let me have it.

How was Adam doing? Why wouldn't someone tell us? He couldn't be feeling anything. He was unconscious, wasn't he? Could he hear anything, like the voices of the surgeons around him, the beeping of the machinery? Was he dreaming about something, or was it just a black hole enveloping his consciousness as he slept? If he was dreaming, was it pleasant, or a nightmare, a reliving of getting shot? My heart seized at this thought. *Please don't be that.* "Dua."

I kept my head down, tightening my arms around my knees. My brain wasn't the only thing that wasn't letting me have peace.

"Dua. I know you're awake."

Hassan. Unwilled, his name popped into my head as my brain finally recognized his voice. Opening my eyes slowly, I lifted my head from my knees.

He stood over me, his eyes overflowing with pain and worry as they met mine. Wordlessly, he extended his hands out toward me. I stared at the offering without moving to take it, the small, flimsy paper plate with three dates on it and a cup of coffee. The coffee's scent wafted to my nose, sweet yet bitter.

I shook my head and turned away. Adam was fighting for his life; how could I concern myself with filling my own stomach?

But Hassan didn't walk away. He knelt before me, so our eyes were level. "Dua, please. You need to break your fast." As always, his voice was so gentle, but today, it was also weighed down with sadness. I couldn't meet his gaze. "Here." He proffered the dates and coffee again.

I couldn't refuse him again even if I wanted to. "Thanks," I said, so quietly it was almost a whisper. Hassan returned to his seat as I lifted one of the dates to my mouth. "Oh, Allah, I fasted for You and I believe in You and I break my fast with Your sustenance," I whispered, the Arabic words heavy on my tongue today. I took a bite, knowing the fruit was sweet, yet not tasting it.

"I spoke to a receptionist," Haya said, walking into the room. I hadn't even noticed she'd left. "There's an empty room we can pray in."

Mahnoor stared at her for a moment before standing. "Come on," she said quietly, glancing first at Rabia, then at me. "Let's make wudu."

Rabia sniffled, wiped under her eyes with the back of her hand, and stood without a word, looking like she would burst into tears again as she followed Mahnoor and Haya out of the room. Swallowing my last sip of coffee and with date in hand, I slipped out behind them.

I didn't dare glance at my reflection in the mirror when we walked into the bathroom, immediately turning on the faucet and sticking my hands under the stream. I didn't need confirmation I was a mess.

When I began, the water was lukewarm; by the time I wiped water over the top of my head, it was so hot my hands turned red, but I didn't try to cool it. I cherished the heat, how it made my whole body feel warm by its touch. Like a heat pack, it warmed my chest and eased the pain, finally letting me breathe without feeling as if I were suffocating.

"Ready?" Mahnoor asked, watching me.

Slowly, I pulled my hands out from under the faucet and shut off the water. "Ready," I replied quietly. I recalled my Ramadan checklist—pray on time, and don't miss any of the five daily prayers. *Focus.* No matter how terrible I felt, I couldn't let go of my prayer. I'd never needed to seek God's mercy as badly as I did now.

We walked into the room and took off our shoes, setting them in the corner. The adults were already there, my parents and the Mousawis laying out prayer rugs for everyone.

I joined Rabia, Mahnoor, and Haya in a line behind my mom, Aunt Sadia, and Mrs. Mousawi. Mr. Mousawi led the prayer. I closed my eyes and concentrated on my own breathing, the rise and fall of my chest, and imagined I was the only one in the room, with nothing at all between me and God.

"Allahu Akbar." Placing my hands on my chest, I recited Surah Al-Fatihah quietly. My fingers trembled. "You alone do we worship. You alone do we ask for help."

Allah doesn't burden any soul with more than it can bear, Mom's voice, a memory, reminded me, recalling the verse from the Qur'an she'd reference whenever times got tough. *I know You won't try us with more than we can take, oh Allah,* I thought as we knelt with our foreheads pressed to our prayer rugs, *but, please, give us the patience to get through this.*

After the prayer ended, I lifted my hands to supplicate. *Ya Allah, please take care of Adam. Heal him. Please, help us through this. Ameen.* I swept my hands over my face and opened my eyes to see Dad walking toward me.

"Baba." I stood slowly, then bent to fold the prayer rug I'd been using, finding it easier than making eye contact with anyone. "How's Adam now?"

He sighed. "Still in surgery. Insha'Allah, he'll be out soon."

Feeling more tears on the way, I turned my head away, using the other prayer rugs as an excuse as I folded them. "Insha'Allah," I echoed quietly.

"Dua, go home."

"But, Baba—" I turned toward him, tears forgotten.

"It's late, sweetheart," he said, cutting me off. "Sitting and worrying in the waiting room all night isn't going to help anyone. It's not just you, Dua. All of you need to go home and get some rest."

"What about you and Mom?" I asked as Mrs. Mousawi took the stack of folded prayer rugs from me.

"We're going to stay with Sadia and Yusuf tonight. The Mousawis too."

"But—"

"Dua, please. No arguments. Not here, not now."

Looking down, I found myself nodding. "Okay."

"Good." Looking away from me, Dad called out, "Azhar!"

Breaking away from Haya and Hassan, Azhar came to stand beside me, though there were several feet between us. Not knowing what else to do with myself, I looked down at the floor and stayed where I was, like a statue.

"Azhar, you all need to go home. Here." The change in his pocket jangled as he reached in and pulled out a set of car keys. "Take the van."

Of course. They wouldn't possibly let us ride the subway this late, especially not after what had just happened.

"Okay, sir," Azhar said, pocketing the keys. "Haya, Hassan. Come on, we're going." He looked at Mahnoor—okay, not *at* her, just in her general direction—and Rabia, Ibrahim, and Mahdi. "You too," he said, quieter than before.

We piled into the van somberly; the vehicle seemed to echo our despair, the engine sighing after Azhar turned the key in the ignition. Mahdi laid his head in my lap and stretched out on the seat, falling asleep in seconds. For five minutes, the inside of the van was silent as a coffin. My chest tightened again at this thought, and this time it felt like someone squeezed my heart.

"Mahnoor," I heard Haya whisper from behind me. "I'm sorry. We all are. We should never have cut ourselves off from you like that. I feel so bad. I mean, of course Azhar's my brother, anything that hurts him is going to hurt me, but you're my best friend. You've always been there for me, and I should've been there for you—"

"Haya," Mahnoor said softly but firmly, interrupting her. "It's okay. Sometimes a little space is necessary. But you're here for us now, when it matters most. Thank you. If you weren't here, I don't know what I'd do."

Letting out a breath I hadn't realized I'd been holding, I closed my eyes and stroked Mahdi's hair as my thoughts turned into a stream of automatic prayers. *Please, Allah. Thank you, Allah. Please, Allah. Thank you, Allah. Please* . . .

I stirred at the sound of Mahnoor's voice, opening my eyes as we pulled into the driveway. "We should get some rest," she said, looking unconvinced. If any of us—other than Mahdi, who dozed soundly—managed to fall asleep, it'd be nothing short of a miracle.

"Can I sleep over tonight?" Haya asked as she jumped out of the van.

Mahnoor smiled faintly. "Of course. Have I ever said no to you before?"

Mahdi and I were the only ones left in the van now. Slowly, I gathered him into my arms and stood, shoulders hunched and head ducked so I wouldn't hit the ceiling.

But this *is* me we're talking about. I can't call it a day till I've tripped or gotten in a sticky situation. Before I could step out of the van, my dupatta got caught, leaving me halfway out of the van with a child in my arms and a dupatta that was about to choke me.

"Here, let me take him." Hassan stepped forward, arms open wide.

Cradling Mahdi's head, I passed him into Hassan's waiting arms carefully and turned to see what I could do about my dupatta. The edge of its purple-and-gold border had snagged on a lever underneath one of the seats. I tugged at it, but somehow that only made it worse, the edge tangling and threatening to rip.

"Oh, Dua. Never a dull moment with you, is there?" Haya clambered back into the van, reaching for the fabric.

"You know," she whispered as her fingers wrapped around it, her head bent toward mine, "if life were a Bollywood movie, your dupatta would fly off and land in Hassan's face."

I would've laughed if I'd been in a better mood. The dupatta came free in her hands, and I smiled a little at her as I turned and stepped down from the van.

"I'll take him now," I said to Hassan.

He lowered Mahdi into my arms. "Looks like it's been too

much excitement for him today." He started to pull back, then stopped.

I stared at his puzzled face for a moment, then looked down. Mahdi had grabbed hold of the front of Hassan's shirt in his fist, and it didn't look like he was going to let go any time soon.

"You'd better take him." I took a step toward him, my heart quickening as I realized how close we stood.

Slowly, Hassan took Mahdi into his arms again and put space between us.

Mahnoor smiled. "I guess"—she cleared her throat and looked at Azhar—"you two can stay the night too."

"I'd get the pillows and blankets so we can camp out in the basement but . . . uh"—Hassan looked down at Mahdi, who'd clutched his shirt even tighter.

"I'll get 'em," Azhar said, pointedly not looking at Mahnoor as he walked into the house.

"Great," Hassan said quietly, muttering something in Arabic under his breath as he followed.

Lifting the heavily embroidered kameez above my knees, I walked up the steps to the door as quickly as I could without falling over. Heels and me, never a good idea.

Except, I realized as I stepped inside and bent to remove my shoes, I hadn't been wearing heels. This entire time, I'd paired my semi-formal shalwar kameez with a pair of old, dirt-crusted sneakers. I half laughed, half cried as I thought, *I wish Adam could see this.* Something in me felt empty, longing to see his smile and hear him laugh beside me.

seventeen

I sat on my bed with my knees to my chest, my chin on my knees as I stared at the comforter, looking but not seeing. My dupatta slipped from one shoulder and was just barely hanging on to the other, trailing on the floor beside the bed. These clothes would wrinkle if I didn't take them off and hang them up, but I had no desire to get up. My whole body was beginning to fall asleep, the numbness starting from my feet and slowly creeping upward. Pretty soon, I wouldn't feel the difference between these and my softest pajamas.

A sob threatened to rip out of me, my throat heavy with my grief, but I forced it back down. It wasn't fair. Adam never bothered anyone, never hurt anyone. He didn't deserve this.

Neither did the Prophet Muhammad, peace be upon him, the little voice in my head reminded me. It was starting to sound like Hassan, but it was right. Before his prophethood, Muhammad, peace be upon him, was known as Al-Amin, the Trustworthy, but after his first divine revelation, the same people who had once praised his trustworthiness called him a liar. People who didn't know him personally but hated what he stood for threw trash and stones at him. Those who had once respected him turned against him and drove him out of his beloved hometown. Yet still he didn't complain, never let his faith in Allah waver.

No one ever said life was easy. No one ever said *being Muslim* was easy, or that seeking the truth and sticking to it was easy. Being hard doesn't make it wrong. No matter how you look at it, it's still the right thing to do. But it is so, so difficult. Painful, even, at times. My chest felt heavy as I sighed, invoking a strength I didn't feel.

Bzzz. Bzzz. Bzzz.

Taking a deep breath, I let it out slowly and reached for my phone. It vibrated on the bed where I'd forgotten it, the same way I forgot my clothes and my heels and everything else.

A close-up of Kat's grinning face flashed at me. I let my phone continue to vibrate in my hand as I stared at the screen. As soon as I answered, she'd know something was wrong. She would start worrying. I couldn't handle my own grief and hers too.

"Are you going to answer that?" Haya asked, moving to sit at the foot of Mahnoor's bed.

Shaking my head, I dropped my phone into my lap and watched as Mahnoor plopped down on her bed. "No," I replied softly, shifting my gaze back to my phone. It vibrated again, and then Kat's flashing grin was gone. I looked at Mahnoor. "Can you turn the lights off? I wanna lie down."

"Yeah, of course. All of us need to." She turned away from me, casting us all into pitch-black darkness. "Good night."

"Good night." Letting my dupatta finally fall to the floor, I stretched out on my side, hand under my cheek. But I didn't dare close my eyes. In the dark, listening to the soft sounds of our breathing, there was nothing to distract me from the grief that sat curled up at the bottom of my stomach. Tears fell from my eyes and I sobbed as quietly as I could. Allah would never burden me with something I couldn't handle. But this?

I turned my face into my pillow, pouring all my sobs into it. How could I possibly be strong enough to handle this when I'd never had to handle anything worse than the occasional bad grade on a test? And even then, a bad grade was enough to make me cry my eyes out for hours.

But all too soon, my tears dried, my sobs dying in my throat as anger welled up in me, bright and hot. I gritted my teeth and clenched my hands into fists as my body shook. How dare that man, that coward, shoot Adam? What kind of person shot a twelve-year-old? It had to take a special kind of hate, a truly heartless person, to attack a *kid*.

I clenched my fists so tightly my nails cut into the skin of my palms. What does it matter to anyone if we're Muslim? It's a free country; we have every right to practice our beliefs peacefully, just like anyone else. But no, as long as we exist, people have a problem with it. Without knowing what Islam *really* is, without knowing what being Muslim *really* means, people pass judgments and think they're qualified to do so. How had I never seen that before?

True, people in Burkeville weren't that bad. But that didn't indicate a lack of judgment—just that the judgment was covert, below the surface. Or maybe it wasn't judgment, but ignorance.

No wonder my parents were so in love with the idea of the MSA. Maybe it would be the only voice of knowledge, the only accurate source of information on Islam in our tiny town.

Ya Allah. I clenched my fists even tighter. *Is there no limit to the cruelty of this world?* A lump rose in my throat, and I slowly pulled my face away from my pillow. The darkness, trying to hold in my anger, it was all suffocating me. I had to get out of it.

Ignoring the fast rise and fall of my chest, I sat up and swung my legs over the side of the bed, my heart fluttering as I lifted my dupatta from the floor and lazily draped it about my shoulders. The blood rushed in my ears as I walked to the door, each step more painful than the last, but I had to get out. I needed some air, some space, *something*.

Mahnoor was awake. I could feel her gaze burning into my back, but I knew she wasn't going to say anything. Swallowing against the lump in my throat, I stepped outside and closed the door behind me without looking back.

The floor creaked under my feet despite the care I took to step softly, the sound making me wince as I walked down the hallway.

The lights blinded me when I entered the kitchen. Automatically, I put a hand in front of my eyes to shade them, squinting as my eyes were forced to get used to the light after being in darkness for so long.

Hassan. I smelled him before I saw him, his warm, cinnamony cologne. My heart beat faster, and I turned back around. Between the tears and my anger, I was already confused enough emotionally. I didn't need a fresh stream of hormones right now.

"Couldn't sleep?" His voice was soft, as warm and gentle as a hug.

I stopped myself from running back down the hallway, back into the safety of Mahnoor's room. I shook my head, my heart still beating hard.

"I'm making hot chocolate. Want some?"

My stomach growled, reminding me that I hadn't eaten any-thing since fajr except three dates and some coffee. Slowly, I turned around.

He stood by the stove, shoulders squared as he waited for my answer, the jug of milk in his hand tilted toward the saucepan in front of him. I couldn't see his face, thank God. That would've made everything so much harder to handle.

I took a step farther into the kitchen. "Sure." The moment the word came out, I wished I hadn't spoken. My voice was so pitiful. I sounded broken.

"Would you mind grabbing a couple of mugs?" he asked, swirling the milk around the saucepan.

Keeping my mouth clamped shut, I pulled two mugs down from the middle shelf of the cabinet and put them on the counter next to him.

"Thanks." He glanced at me, and I noticed how stark the em-erald of his irises were—and the red veins surrounding them. Clearly, Mahnoor and I weren't the only ones losing sleep.

"Mmm-hmm." I lowered my gaze, watched as he poured the hot chocolate into the mugs. One, I noticed, he'd filled higher than the other. What was I supposed to do now? I stood where I was for a minute, but it felt too weird. I leaned against the counter instead, my fingers toying with the edge of my kameez.

"Whipped cream?"

I shook my head, but his back was to me. Sighing, I opened my mouth. "No. Thanks, though."

"You don't have a peanut allergy, do you?" he asked, moving over to the toaster just as four slices of toast popped up.

"No." My fingers moved nimbly across the table in an imaginary rendition of our Sami Yusuf song. I glanced at the toaster. *Four* slices? "Were you really hungry?"

He paused. Slowly, he turned around, crossing his arms over his chest. "No, not really," he said quietly. "But I had to eat, and I had a feeling someone else would need to eat too."

"Oh. Mahnoor and Rabia are trying to sleep, but I can ask them if they want anything."

He blinked, then leaned back, the rounding of his shoulders mirroring mine. His mouth quirked at the corner, so slight I would've missed it if I hadn't been looking right at it. Well, not that I had any business looking at his mouth . . . "Actually, I was talking about you," he said, his voice low but clear. "You barely ate anything earlier."

He'd noticed. I didn't realize I was speaking my thoughts aloud until the words rang in my ears. "Why do you care?" I lifted my hand to my mouth. I hadn't meant to be so blunt.

He opened his mouth, but nothing came out. He closed it, his jaw working as he lowered his arms, his expression unreadable. After a long moment, he said, "Is there a reason I shouldn't?"

I felt my lips curl into a half-smile. "That is such a therapist answer. Are you sure your major is graphic design, not psychology?"

He rubbed the back of his neck, sheepishly returning my half-smile as his eyes met mine. "I care because I do."

"Thank you," I said simply, not knowing what else to say.

"You're welcome," he replied.

The room was silent for a long moment, both of us staring at our feet.

"Just give me a minute," he said finally, turning around to

spread some peanut butter on the toast. I should have helped him, since he was doing so much already, but I didn't have the heart for it.

"No problem," I replied, my voice unsteady, even as I sat and tapped my fingers on the table.

"Mom used to make me hot chocolate and peanut butter toast whenever I had nightmares and couldn't get back to sleep." He turned around and set a mug and a plate down in front of me. "Obviously, this is worse than any childhood nightmare I've ever had, but I didn't know what else to do." He seated himself across from me with his own toast.

"Thanks." My stomach growled, but I didn't move. My mug was fuller than his, the hot chocolate forming a ring of foam around the top. I looked down at my hands; they'd slowed, nearing the end of their "song."

"Are you practicing the surahs you've memorized?"

"Yes." I nodded. I hadn't gotten any practice in today; I'd been too overwhelmed. But I was trying.

"Good." He looked up at me, his eyes deep and dark with regret. "I'm sorry this whole thing with Azhar and Mahnoor interrupted our lessons; it shouldn't have. Just let me know whenever you need to work on a new surah, and I'll make sure it gets done."

"I'll take you up on that. I've had my eye on a couple of sections. How is Azhar, by the way?"

A muscle twitched in his jaw. "Hurt, I guess," he replied, taking a sip from his mug. "He's barely said anything, but I doubt he's jumping for joy on the inside."

"Of course. I'm sorry," I murmured. My stomach growled again, but my hands stayed in my lap.

"Don't be." He reached for his toast. "He'll be upset for a few days, but if it's not meant to happen, it's not meant to happen. How much can we fight for something we're not meant to have?"

He looked up at me then and swallowed his bite of toast. "Why aren't you eating?"

"Oh." I reached for my mug and took a sip. The hot chocolate, sweet and milky, dissolved the lump in my throat and warmed my insides as it descended into my stomach. "It's good."

His gaze didn't move from me. "You know, if Adam knew you weren't eating because of him, he'd be upset." Looking back down at his plate, he took another bite of toast.

I took a long, slow sip of my hot chocolate before I answered. "I can't shake the idea that I took him for granted. I didn't really take the time to get to know him." I had gone five years without seeing him, and then when I finally did see him, I didn't do anything about it.

Hassan paused, his voice going soft. "We all take each other for granted at some point. I'm sure he knows you care."

"I wish I could be half as sure." I reached for my toast and took a bite half-heartedly, the peanut butter sticking to the roof of my mouth.

"You will be. You'll see when he wakes up, insha'Allah. He doesn't get mad easily." Hassan chuckled, setting his mug down. "Although, trust me, you don't want to see it when it happens. He gets this unreadable look on his face and goes all quiet; he doesn't even acknowledge that you exist till he's forgiven you. He's like a little Hulk, but less smashing, more brooding."

I ran my finger along the rim of my mug. "Speaking of anger..."

"What?" He lifted the mug to his lips, eyes focused on his drink.

I opened my mouth but paused, then slowly closed my mouth.

How should I phrase this? Taking my finger off the rim of my mug, I looked up at him. "Do you ever get so angry at the world that you just want to grab the Earth and shake it like a snow globe, hoping that your shaking will erase all the hatred, all the violence and prejudice from the minds of everyone in the world?" I didn't even know if I was making any sense, but I had to ask. If there was anyone who could give me a proper, sincere answer, it was Hassan.

He stopped, still holding the mug to his mouth, and looked at me again. Slowly, he set the mug on the table and rested his hand beside it as he glared at the floor, his hand clenching into a fist.

"Almost every day," he replied, his voice gruff as he looked up at me again.

I stared at him. I couldn't picture him angry any more than I could Adam—or anyone in Uncle Yusuf's family, for that matter. Even now, as Hassan looked at me, there was no trace of anger in his eyes, just pain and sadness. "How do you cope without it, you know, taking over you?" *God, I sound like I turn into She-Hulk when I get angry.*

He glanced at the table, a muscle twitching in his cheek, but then his eyes were back on my face and he replied, "Unfortunately, anger, hatred, and prejudice are part of this world, and you have to do all you can to make it better, instead of adding to it. Countering all that anger you see outside of you with more anger isn't going to do any good, and for something good to happen, you have to put good into the world. And you have to remember that you're never alone. Allah's with us no matter what. All you have to do is talk to Him." He reached for his mug. "I don't know, does that even make sense?"

"Yeah," I replied quietly. "You sound like Ibrahim."

He smiled faintly, looking down into the mug as if there were tea leaves at the bottom instead of chocolate milk. "Yeah, well, we've been best friends for years. It was bound to rub off sometime." He looked up, and the smile faded. "Something else bothering you?"

I watched the steam rising from my mug. "I'm still conflicted about the MSA thing. What is one person's voice, *my* voice, going to do to dispel misconceptions about Islam?" I paused, swallowing. "Won't that just make me a target for more hate?"

"I doubt your parents would suggest it if they thought it would put you in any danger," he said softly. "And sometimes, one person's voice is enough. But after all this, I don't think anyone will object if you want to lie low. You have to decide for yourself."

I closed my eyes for a moment, remembering the second item on my Ramadan checklist. *Discover myself.* What does Islam mean to me, and how can I use it to figure out who I am and the future I want for myself? The MSA was part of that now. Would it help prevent situations like what happened tonight with Adam, or make things worse? Could I actually educate others, or would I just shine a bigger spotlight on myself?

I lifted the mug to take another sip, pausing only when I noticed Hassan staring at me with an alarmed look on his face. "What?"

"What did you do to your hands?" he demanded, pushing his chair back.

"What?" I took my hands off the mug and looked at them. Oh. I'd had my hands clenched so hard, my nails must have cut in deep; there was blood all over my palms, and I'd gotten it all over my mug without even realizing it.

Before I could say anything, he was standing over me, looking down at my hands. "Dua, how . . ." Shaking his head, he went and got something from a cabinet.

"No, really, I'm—"

He ignored me, placing the first-aid kit in front of me and taking out a couple of alcohol swabs. He stared at my hands for a moment, then his own. "I'll be right back."

"But—"

"Don't touch anything," he called back, already walking down the hallway, his back to me.

Moments later, a tired-looking Haya walked into the kitchen, Hassan just behind her. "Oh my God, Dua!" Pulling a chair next to mine, she sat down and reached for the alcohol swabs. "Rabia can't talk, Mahnoor can't stop crying, Ibrahim's wandering around like he's never going to sleep again, Mahdi looks disturbed even when *he's* asleep, and now you're dabbling in self-mutilation. Adam's going to kill us all when he gets better, insha'Allah. I mean, insha'Allah to the when-he-gets-better part, not the killing us part." She gently touched an alcohol swab to my palm, but it stung so fiercely I couldn't stop myself from wincing.

"*Okay*, Haya, just clean her up and get some Band-Aids on her fast." Hassan picked up our mugs and plates and put them in the sink.

"I'm doing it, Mr. Bossy. She'll be fine."

Turning away from the sink, he looked at me for a moment, then looked away. He shuffled on his feet uncertainly. "Are you sure?"

"Well, I'm not a surgeon"—Haya rolled her eyes—"but yes, pretty sure I know how to put a Band-Aid on. Get some sleep; I have it covered from here."

He looked like he wanted to argue, but he set his jaw and sighed. "All right, I guess." He lifted his gaze, meeting my eyes. "Good night."

"Good night," I replied quietly, watching him leave.

Haya looked up at me, smirking.

"What?"

"Nothing. So, should I keep calling you Dua or start calling you Dua bhabhi?"

Bhabhi. Sister-in-law. I would've done a facepalm if I had a free hand to do it with. Haya was totally going to get me in trouble one day with her big mouth. "Haya?"

She smoothed the last Band-Aid on my palm and looked up at me, grinning. "Yes, bhabhi?"

"Shut up!"

"Whatever you say, bhabhi."

eighteen

When I dragged myself into the kitchen hours later for suhoor, it was obvious none of us had gotten any sleep. We were all still in our clothes from the night before, our eyes swollen and bloodshot, everyone's hair sticking up all over the place.

I stifled a yawn as I zombie-walked to the table and sat beside Mahnoor, who stared at her cereal like she was waiting for something to jump out at her.

"Any updates?" I asked. She'd called her parents while I was in the bathroom.

She shook her head. "They got the bullet out, alhamdulillah. Doctors think he'll be okay, but he lost a lot of blood, so they're not sure yet." Her voice cracked. "He hasn't woken up yet, and my mom's starting to panic."

If Aunt Sadia was *just* starting to panic, she was a lot stronger than the rest of us. *Insha'Allah may her strength be rewarded,* I thought, grabbing a date.

"Oh my Allah, Dua, what did you do?" Mahnoor cried, grabbing my hand.

Now everyone was looking at me. Except for Haya, who was clearly still half asleep. *Thanks, Mahnoor.*

"I waited too long to cut my nails," I said by way of explanation, popping the date into my mouth and shoving my hands under the table. "Now, can we stop focusing on me and get back to eating? Thanks."

"We're going to have to prepare iftar ourselves tonight," Mahnoor said, dragging her gaze away from my hands and shoving a spoonful of soggy cereal into her mouth.

"I know how to make pakoray," I said, reaching for another date. Pakoray were basically the only Pakistani thing I really knew how to make, thanks to multiple exam seasons spent frying up the gram-flour fritters with whatever was on hand. "What?"

Rabia blinked, breaking her stare, and looked at her plate. "Nothing. Just pakoray are Adam's favorite. Sorry."

I swallowed my half-chewed date and pushed the plate away, even less hungry than before. I studied her quietly, noting her bloodshot eyes as she stared down at her breakfast. I'd never seen her so miserable as she pushed her food around the plate with a fork.

A muscle twitched in Ibrahim's cheek as his frown deepened, a grim transformation of his features. "It's not fair," he said quietly, though his voice rang out in the quiet room. "Adam is just a kid. I mean, who shoots a kid? If it'd been me, it—"

"Ibrahim," Mahnoor admonished quickly, "don't talk like that. You're fine, thank God." Her voice broke. "You're safe. Adam will be, too, insha'Allah. He has to be. He's strong."

"No, you don't get it," Ibrahim said quietly. "I can hear the sound of the gun going off all the time, like a ringing in my ears. I can smell the blood. I can *feel* him no longer standing next to me."

Rabia touched his arm gently. "I can't imagine how horrible that must be. I wish I could take that feeling away from you, but I can't. None of us can. We can only pray that Adam gets better soon. We'll get you what you need to heal, I promise. But Adam needs to get better. Be strong."

No one said anything after that, and I thought Haya had actually managed to fall asleep, when she said, "It's the twentieth day of Ramadan. Mashallah."

The room went quiet again and you could almost hear what everyone was thinking: *Ramadan is going by so fast. Only ten days left.*

I finished my glass of water in silence. It was amazing, how quickly the time had gone by this month. I'd thought it would drag on, especially because of the summer, but the opposite had been true.

Hassan's words on the last ten days of Ramadan came to mind. Specifically, Laylat-al-Qadr, the Night of Power. The most powerful night in the whole year, better than a thousand nights. The night Prophet Muhammad, peace be upon him, first received revelation, the very first portion of the Qur'an. There was no better time for prayers to be answered.

Mom always encouraged me to pray and read Qur'an more, especially during the odd nights within the last ten days—any of which could be Laylat-al-Qadr. Sometimes I'd read a surah or two, or make a short dua, but most times, I'd just go to sleep, wasting the opportunity.

But not this year. This year, I'd do better. For Adam. For Ibrahim. For myself. For the first time in what felt like days instead of hours, my heart lifted. Yes. Everything would work out, insha'Allah.

Quickly, I finished my suhoor and headed straight to the bathroom to wash for prayer.

Mahnoor and Haya walked into the room just in time to see me trip over my dupatta from last night as I unfolded my prayer rug.

"What's got into you?" Mahnoor asked, following my every movement with wide eyes.

"Last ten days of Ramadan," I replied breathlessly. Of course, all the dates I'd had probably didn't help—too much sugar.

Haya smiled. "Aww, how cute. Bhabhi's excited."

Mahnoor looked at Haya before glancing back at me. "Dua, did you and Hassan have some secret marriage ceremony I don't know about?"

Haya mock-gasped. "I thought that was suspicious at dinner when they both started choking at the same time. They must have been remembering their nikkah."

"Astagfirullah." I shook my head at them as I put my hair up. "*Please* never say anything like that in front of my dad. Or Mahdi. Or Hassan. And you"—I turned to look Haya in the eye—"don't call me bhabhi. You're making me feel old."

"Oh, so that's why you don't like it?" Haya lifted her eyebrows at me and grinned.

"Astagfirullah." I turned back to my prayer rug just in time to hide the smirk that I'd barely managed to hold in. *Focus, Dua. Ramadan. Prayer. Worship.* Clearing my throat, I lifted my hands to ear level. "Allahu Akbar." Placing my hands on my chest, I began my prayer.

When I put my knees and forehead to the floor, there were only two words on my mind: *Thank you.*

Thank You, Allah, for making sure Adam got to the hospital. Thank You for keeping him alive. And thank You in advance for his healing. Please, help Ibrahim too. Help him feel better, help him move on. Please.

Thank You for Ramadan, for giving me the chance to get closer to You. Thank You for this trip. I didn't want to come, but I needed to. Please make my last days in New York blessed.

Thank You, Allah. Thank You.

With my forehead pressed to the floor, I felt a hand stroke the top of my head.

"It's all right, Dua," a deep voice not unlike Uncle Yusuf's said. *"You're safe. Everything will be all right. Hold on to your faith—everything will be all right."*

"Dua."

I blinked until Mahnoor's face came into focus. The sisterly touch of her hand on my head was unexpected, unfamiliar. "You fell asleep on your prayer rug. Are you all right? You were talking in your sleep."

I sighed, sitting up. "I don't know who I should worry about most; we're all so messed up. But I'm hopeful that—" I stopped myself, my fingers clutching the fabric over my heart. *Hopeful* wasn't the right word. "I *know*. I just have this feeling that Adam's going to be all right. I just know Allah's going to heal him. So, I shouldn't worry because I know he's going to be okay.

"But at the same time, I can't stop myself from worrying. There's a part of me that's so scared that I'm going to be wrong. That Allah might choose not to save Adam just because I don't totally believe it." Again, I stopped myself and squeezed my eyes shut.

Mahnoor shook her head. "Allah isn't petty, and it's not your job to will Adam into healing."

My eyes burned with tears. "It feels like it, though," I murmured. "Thank you, Allah," I whispered, my voice dropping as I rocked myself, counting the number of times I said my thanks on my fingers. "Thank you for his healing. Thank you for his healing. Thank you for his healing." I couldn't let myself just give up. I had to believe that he was going to be okay; I had to believe that Allah would choose to shower His mercy down on us and save Adam, the way I'd been so eager to believe it this morning.

For a long moment, Mahnoor didn't say anything. Her fingers shook a little bit as she rested her hand on my knee. "May Allah grant everything you ask for."

"Ameen."

Like she knew we needed the comic relief, Haya's giggle floated to my ears as she walked into the room. "Wallahi, I just took one look at my reflection and screamed so loud Azhar almost had a heart attack. You should've seen him; every hair was standing up!"

Mahnoor chuckled half-heartedly. "Yeah, and he sees you every morning before you've brushed your hair and put on makeup. Imagine what would've happened if he saw me. He might have fainted."

I had to admit, they both looked ten times better. The dark circles were still there, but less obvious, and they were in clean clothes that weren't wrinkled. I should freshen up too.

"Well, at least we're all cleaned up now," Haya said. "We won't scare our parents when we head over to the hospital before maghrib."

I glanced at the clock. How was it noon already? "That reminds me, I should start preparing the batter for the pakoray. It always tastes best if it sits for a few hours before frying."

"Yum." Haya had a mischievous twinkle in her eyes. "Hope you're going to add lots of onions; onion pakoras are Hassan's favorite. I'm sure he'll like the ones you make, bhabhi."

I rolled my eyes. "Don't call me bhabhi."

Haya blew an air-kiss my way. "Think about it, you won't find a better sister-in-law than me. Isn't that right, Mahnoor?"

"Uh . . . right." Mahnoor shifted, looking uncomfortable. "Oh, by the way, we're going to need more food over the next few days. The uncles are coming tomorrow."

My forehead creased in alarm. "What, *all* of them?"

She nodded. "And the aunts and their kids, of course. Every single one."

"Great, more Sheikhs!" Haya said, grinning.

Mahnoor eyed her warily. For once, I knew exactly what was on her mind. Altogether, at least twenty individuals were about to descend on their home. While our family was incredibly loving, we were a handful on our best days, and this was *definitely* not one of our best days. "Tonight might be Laylat-al-Qadr. I'm going to pray we get through this in one piece."

"Ameen to that."

☾

I was about to fry the last batch of pakoray when Rabia shoved a change of clothes at me and pushed me away from the stove. "I'll finish. Go, freshen up."

I clutched the bundle gratefully. After an hour of standing over the hot oil, the smell had permeated my shirt. Not exactly the most attractive scent in the world.

A familiar ayah, sung in a child's voice, rang out in the air as I stepped out of Mahnoor's room, changed into an old peach T-shirt and faded jeans, freshly washed and spritzed. Mahdi was practicing his Qur'an.

183

I could hear the smile in Hassan's voice. "Good job. Next one?"

I knocked on the door, already open just a crack.

"Come in!"

Four heads popped up as I pushed the door open wider and stepped into the room. Mahdi was excited to spend time with Hassan again, grinning wide. Ibrahim sat next to him. And Haya, who gave me a little smile, patted the spot next to her on the bed.

As soon as I sat down, she passed the small Qur'an she'd been holding over to me, its cover hardly bigger than my hand. "Mahdi's mastered Al-Fatihah, so he wanted to start learning another—Ad-Dhuha."

She'd already opened the Qur'an to the correct page, saving me the trouble of checking the index in the back and deciphering the Arabic numerals. "Isn't it a little long for him?" I studied the page, the Arabic letters swirling before my eyes as I counted. Eleven ayahs. Eleven lines.

"We'll take it piece by piece," Hassan explained. Mahdi burrowed into the fold of his arm like a kitten. "Even if he only manages to learn half, he'll be golden."

"But why—"

"Dua," Mahdi complained, shutting me up instantly. "Less talking, more reciting. Practice with me! Then, when Adam comes home, he'll be so proud of me!"

I'd been about to ask what made them choose that particular surah, but that wasn't important right now. Besides, I still had one left to memorize before I could cross that item off my Ramadan checklist. I smiled. "Right. Let's do it, for Adam."

Readjusting in my seat, I repeated after Hassan. Ibrahim

listened intently, nodding along. Haya, beside me, effortlessly repeated each line from memory. The humility in her voice brought out the sweetness of each word, my chest growing light as I listened.

I must have heard the surah several times throughout my childhood, as my mother played her Qur'an playlists on repeat, but I couldn't place the words. I hadn't been listening closely enough.

My head wasn't in the game. I couldn't focus, making the same error again and again. My shoulders started to droop. I sighed, squeezing my eyes shut. How was I supposed to keep my mind on anything, with everything that was going on?

"Take a deep breath," Hassan commanded, his voice firm, but ever patient. "Hold it for three seconds, then exhale." He waited till I was done. "Now open your eyes and try again."

"For me, it always helped to know what I was reading," Haya said, pointing to the page opposite the one I'd been reading. The English translation of the Arabic text. "Never hurts to give it a try, especially if you haven't read it in a while."

Silently, I traced the words with a finger as I read. I stopped, and so did my finger. Taking another deep breath, I resumed reading. "By the glorious morning light," I whispered to myself, "and by the night when it is still—your Guardian-Lord has not forsaken you, nor is He displeased. And verily, the Hereafter will be better for you than the present. And soon will your Guardian-Lord give you that with which you will be pleased."

My eyes stung, and I wiped at them with the back of my hand. Now I was beginning to understand why this surah had been chosen. Not for Mahdi. For me. For all of us.

Haya rubbed my back, her hand warming my skin through my shirt. "You okay?"

"Yeah," I replied, sniffing again. "It's just . . . I wasn't expecting that. It feels like Allah is talking to me. To us. Reassuring us."

She and Hassan wore matching smiles. "Yeah. That's exactly how it feels."

My chest was light, my mind suddenly clear and calm. It was as if someone had spoken the words into my heart: *Everything will be all right.*

The last of my tears had dried when the door banged open, making us all jump. Mahnoor practically bounced into the room.

"Whoa, what's going on, Pogo Stick Legs?" Haya asked, breaking out into a grin.

"Adam!" Mahnoor stopped jumping long enough to elaborate. "He woke up! Alhamdulillah, he woke up, and he's going to be fine!"

"Yay!" Mahdi bounced in his seat.

"Alhamdulillah!" Ibrahim's voice broke, the relief in his voice obvious.

"Alhamdulillah, that's amazing!" Haya screamed, grabbing Mahnoor by the shoulders and jumping around with her.

My jaw felt like it was about to crack, but I couldn't stop smiling, couldn't stop watching Haya and Mahnoor hop around like a couple of kids in a bounce house.

Hassan smiled. "Looks like Eid came early this year."

"Sure feels like it." I closed my eyes, just for a moment, and whispered, "Thank You, Allah. Thank You so much." The whole time, the grin never left my face.

Haya stopped bouncing so abruptly Mahnoor almost did a face-plant. "I have to tell Azhar. We have to go!"

"We need to leave within five minutes," Mahnoor called after her.

Haya was already running down the hallway, headed for the basement and calling behind her, "I'll tell Azhar to start the car."

"This is amazing," I said quietly, to no one in particular.

Mahnoor smiled, squeezing my hand. "Yeah, it is. Your prayers have been answered!" Her eyes twinkled, her voice taking on a playful note I wasn't used to hearing from her. "Now, go wash your face. You look terrible."

I laughed as I reached up to wipe away the single tear that had fallen from my right eye and was making its way down my cheek. "Yeah, my crying face shouldn't be inflicted on anyone."

C

"How's he now?" I asked, right before Mrs. Mousawi crushed me in a hug. "Assalamu alaykum," I said, managing to free one arm and pat her on the back.

"Wa alaykum assalam." Mom, looking fresh-faced despite the fact she'd been practically living in the hospital for the past couple of days, seized me the moment Mrs. Mousawi let go. "Awake, alhamdulillah, but he's tired, poor thing."

"And his injuries?" I asked, handing the container of pakoray off to Haya.

She took a deep breath first. "Several of his ribs are broken, but alhamdulillah, there was no damage to his organs, especially his heart and lungs. It's a miracle, really."

I released a breath I hadn't even realized I'd been holding. "Thank God."

"Speaking of injuries, what happened to your hands?" She

grabbed the offending appendages and lifted them to eye level, examining the Band-Aids as if under a microscope.

I really need to do something about those so people stop asking. Like walk around with gloves on all the time. But that would look weird unless I start wearing a niqaab to go with them, and that would only attract more attention. Ugh.

"Nothing." I tugged my hands out of her grip. "Long nails. Can I go inside and see him?"

She nodded, though it was clear that she wasn't going to forget any time soon. "Sadia and Yusuf are already inside, and the children must have gone in too. Go on ahead, but don't disturb them, and be out quickly. Adam's still very tired."

"Okay." All I needed was to see him once with my own eyes, confirm that he really was okay. Just one look.

Mahnoor beckoned me inside, and when I lingered just a little too long by the door, she pulled me into the room by my arm.

My heart sank. As tall as he was, Adam was dwarfed by the sheer amount of equipment in the room. The IV by the bed, the needle taped to his arm. The huge bandage wrapped around his head. Mom hadn't mentioned that.

"Mahnoor, his head." I stared at him, my fingers digging into her arm.

"Concussion, but he's healing."

"How?"

"The force of being shot knocked him back on the ground, and he hit his head," Ibrahim whispered, leaning in beside me.

Oh, Adam. I reached for his arm. His skin burned under my touch, but maybe it was just my hands running cold. I glanced up at Mahnoor worriedly. She only met my eyes for a second before she reached out to wrap her fingers around his hand.

Aunt Sadia brushed her fingers through his dark hair as she bent over him, murmuring, "Beta, look who's here to see you."

His eyelids rippled as his features tensed. Painfully slow, his eyes opened and focused on us. His lips, dry and cracked, stretched in a small half-smile. "Hey." His voice was low, hoarse, but still warm.

My grip on his arm tightened. "Hey, yourself," I replied, my voice soft with affection and awe. "I'm glad you're awake."

He let out a little grunt that sounded like a rough chuckle. "I'm glad I am too." After a beat, he added, "Your visit here got some unexpected excitement."

Tears pricked at my eyes, and in that moment, I couldn't tell if they were from relief or despair. Maybe a bit of both. "I'm sorry," I said quietly.

His eyebrows furrowed slightly, his face somewhere between man and boy. "For what?"

"Not spending enough time with you during my visit. But I still have some time left; I'll do better, I promise."

He didn't say anything for a long moment. Then, slowly, he looked at me again, his eyes light. When he smiled, it was a real, full one. "I'd like that, Dua. Thanks."

A knock on the open door. Azhar poked his head through the doorway. "Time for iftar."

I glanced at him for a moment, then back at Adam. He smiled, squeezed my hand, still around his arm, his touch slight but definitely there. "Go, I need to sleep anyway. I'll see you soon."

I patted his hand. "Rest well." I stepped outside, already at a brisk pace, and stopped short.

Somewhere between my heading out the door and turning around to wish Adam well one last time, Hassan had materialized in front of me, and I had to freeze in my tracks just to avoid running into him. "Sorry, I'll get out of your way." I stepped to the side, but he didn't move.

He picked up a date from the plate in his hands and held it out to me.

I held my hand out, palm up, and smiled when he dropped the date into it. "Thanks."

Quickly, I whispered the prayer to break my fast and took a bite of the fruit.

I glanced up to find his eyes on me. He still hadn't moved. Once my eyes met his, the corners of his mouth lifted up easily, familiarly. "You've been busy today. You might want an extra," he said, gently handing me another date. "And keep practicing that surah." Before I could respond, he slipped past me into the room.

"I saw that." Haya raised her brows knowingly, walking up to me and stuffing a pakora into my mouth before I could say anything. "Too cute, bhabhi. Anyway, there's a break room we can pray in. Did you make your wudu?"

I nodded, chewing the pakora.

"Perfect. Let's go."

Five minutes later, as we all bent to put our heads to the floor and whispered *Glory to Allah, the Exalted*, there was nothing on my mind, nothing weighing my heart down. That night might or might not have been the Night of Power, but I couldn't imagine feeling more peaceful than I felt at that moment.

nineteen

"Dua, do you know what day it is?"

"Tuesday?" I guessed.

Mahnoor looked unimpressed. "Thursday, actually. Remember what happens today?"

"No, I . . ." My eyes widened as my voice trailed off. "The uncles are coming!"

"Yes, in approximately"—she paused to look at her watch—"one hour. Now get your butt off the floor. We need to prepare, and everyone has to pitch in."

I made a face as I ran my hands through my hair, smoothening out the tangles. Thanks to Hassan and Haya, I'd finally crossed off the first item on my Ramadan checklist, but I still had more to go. Item #5—*Be a better relative, friend, and daughter. Learn to be more open, patient, and selfless in my relationships.* It still applied, even for something as trivial as household chores. "Fine, what am I in charge of?"

"Dusting."

"Oh, thank God," I muttered to myself, "the one chore I don't mind doing."

"What'd you say?"

"Nothing," I said quickly, before she could assign me a chore I hated. I grabbed the nearest bedpost and pulled myself up off the bed. "Dusting, got it." I power-walked to the bathroom, feeling her eyes on my back the whole time. "There won't be a speck of dust when they arrive."

True to my word, I did my best to ensure there wasn't any dust in the house. I got to work, cleaning the counters, the TV, the tables . . . and, once I found a step stool that was high enough, the top of the fridge. Well, the edge of the top of the fridge.

I was so happy and relieved about Adam's recovery, it was hard to stay still. Once I got down from my step stool, I had to give in to the random surge of adrenaline rushing through my veins. "Rabia?" I called, giving my old rag a shake.

Rabia put a hand to her ear as she looked up from preparing kheer for our younger cousins. "I'm right here. You don't have to shout!"

"Sorry. But I was just thinking, you know what we need right now?"

"A couple of maids?"

"As helpful as that would be, no. Turn on some music!" I pointed toward the boom box next to the stove. "We should be celebrating Adam's recovery, but we're busy, so let's celebrate while we clean!"

She shrugged and reached over to hit the power button, instantly filling the kitchen with the pulsing beat of a Bollywood song.

My hips swayed to the beat as I wiped the kitchen table legs down. At least it was music from the '90s and 2000s, not the old songs from the '70s with crappy audio quality I'd been half expecting.

Rabia stopped, turned the stove off, and just stood there for a minute, watching me doing my dorky dance steps.

"Come on, dance!" I sashayed over to her, but she took off running before I could grab her arms and swing her around.

"Rabia doesn't dance." Mahdi blinked up at me.

"Okay, how about *you* dance with me?" I scooped him up without waiting for an answer.

"Dua, I can dance with my feet on the floor," he reminded me, patting my head like I was a kitten that didn't know any better.

"I know, but this way makes it easier for me to hug you." I squished him into my side and pressed my lips to his cheek.

"On the floor," he insisted, rubbing my kiss off his face.

"Okay, fine." I set him down and turned up the volume. "Now we dance." I moved my hips to the beat in a lazy thumka. Mahdi stared at me for a moment before joining in, making a point of dancing in a much more sophisticated manner than I was.

Five minutes later, Mahdi suddenly stopped and ran past me screaming, "Hassan bhai!"

I froze, waiting much longer than necessary before I turned around very, very slowly. Haya, standing with her elbow propped up on Hassan's shoulder, immediately moved to put her hand over Hassan's eyes. "It's okay, Dua, go ahead. I'll make sure he doesn't look, to protect your privacy."

"No, I'm done, thanks," I replied, holding in a laugh as Hassan slapped her hand away, looking annoyed.

"Azhar's grabbing a few things," Haya said. "He and Hassan left some of their junk in the basement, so we're here to pick it up." The creak of the steps interrupted her. "Plus, you know, help with whatever we can since this house is about to be invaded by Punjabis."

"Oh. Mahnoor's in the basement already with the vacuum, making sure everything's clean before they get here." I paused as my words hit me. Azhar was headed to the basement. Mahnoor was already *in* the basement. We'd been careful to make sure they weren't left alone together after Mahnoor broke off the engagement. Until now. "Let me go and check." I was halfway down the stairs when I heard running behind me. Haya and Hassan were coming too.

We got there too late. Azhar and Mahnoor faced each other, staring down at a broken vase. They stood there, oblivious to us, staring down at the shards of glass like they could see something in the scattered pieces we couldn't.

Haya moved first. "No biggie, it happens," she said, bending toward the mess. "Mahnoor, where's the—"

Azhar reached his arm out to stop her, glaring at Mahnoor. "No, let her do it. She made this mess; now she has to clean it up."

Mahnoor looked stricken, but she said nothing.

Haya batted his arm away. "Azhar, what's wrong with you? It's glass, someone could get hurt."

He clenched his hands, scoffing, "Right, because Mahnoor always cares whether people get hurt."

"Azhar!" Haya put a hand on his shoulder, but he shook it off. "You're upset, I get it, but you need to calm down."

Mahnoor stared at him, a single tear trailing down her cheek. "I . . . I never meant for you to get hurt. I just . . . I . . ."

"You what? You said you wanted to marry me and then turned

around and said it was a mistake. How was I *not* supposed to get hurt?"

"I tried to tell you, Azhar. I just . . ." She couldn't get the words out; her voice was too shaky.

"You tried?" he repeated incredulously. "When? When I proposed? When I put the ring on your finger?" He took a step forward, ignoring the glass. "When you'd come over to my house and I'd try to talk to you? How about when you got up in the middle of dinner to lock yourself in your room?"

She flinched, taking a step back. Her eyes shone with tears; her whole face was wet with them, and her lips were trembling.

"Hey, let's go home," Hassan said, stepping in front of his brother. "Haya will get our stuff and I'll come back later to pick her up."

Azhar didn't acknowledge that he'd heard him, didn't look at him. He kept his gaze locked on Mahnoor. Slowly, his fingers unclenched, the furrow between his brows vanished, and his shoulders sank. "You didn't even try to tell me," he said quietly, his pain reflected so transparently on his face that I couldn't look at him without feeling it too. "You just hid from me. Why? Did you ever care about me?"

She opened her mouth, eyes brimming over with tears, but didn't say anything.

"That's what I thought." He sighed, and I could see the unshed tears in his eyes. He stepped toward her, and this time she didn't move back, not even when he stopped right in front of her, so close he could have touched her.

"Here." He drew something out of his pocket and lifted it to the light. His engagement ring. "This belongs to you." When she didn't move to take it, he bent to place it at her feet. Straightening, he added, "Insha'Allah I hope you find someone you care for, someone who cares about you even more than you care about him." Turning, he said to Hassan, "Let's go."

Hassan waited till Azhar walked up the stairs before turning to Haya. "Are you gonna be okay here?"

"Of course." She wrapped her arms around an already sobbing Mahnoor. "Go."

He nodded. "Take care." His eyes met mine for a second, but I couldn't hold his gaze. Not now. "All of you."

Haya hugged her tight, but Mahnoor still shook as sobs racked her body. "What have I done? Ya Allah, what have I done?"

Rabia ran down the stairs, narrowly missing Hassan on her way down. "They're here, they're here, they're here!" She skidded to a halt in front of the pile of broken glass. "What the . . ." She took in Mahnoor, crying and looking like the only thing keeping her up was Haya's arm around her. "What did I miss?"

"Not much. Let's go and take care of the uncles." I reached for Rabia's arm.

"Okay." She turned and started up the steps, looking back over her shoulder at me as she spoke. "I could use the company. They keep trying to figure out what my grades are and telling me how quickly I've grown up."

I held in my grimace. "Great. I'm sure I'll get that, too, plus questions about college."

She nodded. "Yup."

"Is it too late to go back to the basement and take care of Mahnoor?"

"Yes."

"Oh, joy."

I sat between my aunts for an hour before I couldn't take it anymore. They changed topics like bees collecting pollen from every flower, starting with how big I'd gotten (the desi auntie standard), my hobbies and interests, where I'd gotten the olive green and black shalwar kameez I wore (Mom's closet), school, what I wanted to do *after* school. I checked out somewhere in the middle, after one let it slip that Mom mentioned me starting an MSA. I nearly forgot the whole reason they were there in the first place, although I wasn't sure how supportive their presence actually was.

Even Ibrahim, sitting across from me, looked like his eyes were drooping in boredom.

As Shehla Chachi began to introduce another topic, I jumped up from the couch. "You seem tired," I said quickly. "I'll make some chai."

"Oh, you know how to make chai?" Yumna Tayi said, looking strangely proud. Her smile faltered ever so slightly. "My kids only know how to make instant noodles."

Well . . . not to disappoint her, but I didn't know how to make chai either. I just needed to get out of there. I opened all the cabinets, checking. I found a box of Tapal tea bags and what looked like instant coffee in a clear glass jar. I popped off the lid and sniffed. Not coffee. Tea leaves. I considered looking around for a tea strainer but didn't have the energy. Instead, I gathered brown sugar, green cardamom, and milk.

Mom always crushed the elaichi with a mortar and pestle, but I didn't know if Aunt Sadia had one. I filled a saucepan halfway with water and put it on the stove, watching the flame flicker to life. I cracked the cardamom pods open by hand, breaking each one by the edge of the counter before dropping it into the water. Next, I poured the milk and added the tea bags, bringing the mixture to a simmer.

My phone dinged, the screen brightening with fresh notifications. I tapped on the newest one, opening the email.

> Good afternoon, Dua,
>
> I know you're still on vacation, but you haven't responded to my last message. Let me know how you want to proceed with the Muslim Student Association, and we can get started. I'm already putting a list of resources together that may help. ☺
>
> > Warm regards,
> > Ms. Fritz

I sighed. I barely had the brain capacity to deal with everything that was already going on, and still, I couldn't seem to escape the prospect of the MSA. I pressed the side button. The screen went black, the email going unanswered as my nails tapped out a pattern on the plastic phone case. Queens was much more diverse than Burkeville, and Ibrahim and Adam had still been targeted. If someone wanted to do something to me, I may as well be walking around with a bull's-eye on my back. No one in Burkeville would try to hurt me . . . would they? I picked at my chapped lower lip absentmindedly. What was I setting myself up for, and would it be worth it?

"Hey. Hey, Dua!" I felt myself being jerked back, my world shifting as I stared up into emerald eyes, the rich green irises nearly engulfed by the black of his pupils.

What. Just. Happened? Hassan's lithe fingers were still wrapped around my forearm. My bare forearm, since the shalwar kameez I currently wore had half sleeves. I could feel his touch on my bare skin . . . and I didn't mind it, although I *should* have had other things on my mind. The aunts would *freak* if they came in and saw this, assume something else entirely, and blab it to the whole family. A mountain would be made out of a molehill, and I couldn't afford to ruin my last few days in New York like that. I pulled my arm back quickly, wrenching out of his grip harder than I'd intended. He stepped back, and I saw the tea nearly boiling over behind him. I stepped toward the stove and his hand wrapped around my forearm again, keeping me an arm's length away as he shifted the saucepan to another burner and turned the first one off.

"What are you doing here? I know how to turn a stove off." My voice sounded rough to my own ears.

He looked back at me, a flash of irritation flickering in his eyes. Then, as quickly as it had appeared, it was gone. A muscle twitched above his jaw. "I came to get Haya. You weren't paying attention and you were standing too close. *This*"—he lifted the edge of my dupatta to my eye level—"could've caught on fire."

He had a point. Still. I crossed my arms over my chest. "I'm not saying I don't appreciate it," I began, sounding *exactly* like I didn't appreciate it, "because I do, but I don't need you to come to my rescue."

"So, you think I should've done nothing and let you potentially become a human bonfire?" His voice had a hard edge to it.

My shoulders slumped. "No," I muttered, "I didn't say that."

"I know you can take care of yourself, Dua." His jaw clenched, he looked away from me, glaring at something unseen.

"But sometimes, someone else will want to look out for you. Let them." Squaring his shoulders, he left before I could even think about how to respond.

Slowly, I began to go through the motions, pouring the tea while avoiding the still-hot burner. I placed the cups with saucers on a tray, just like I'd seen my mom do before, and grabbed some cookies. I headed toward the living room, where the aunties were waiting. I stopped for a second, taking a deep breath. I had a lot to think about. "Please, Allah," I muttered to myself, "let this be the last messed-up thing that happens to our family for as long as possible. This Ramadan is turning into an emotional roller coaster." Or a desi drama. Ugh.

I carried the tray over to Mahnoor's room next, heaving a sigh of relief once I was out of earshot of the aunties. The last thing we needed now was gossip or extra drama. The door was closed but unlocked, so I balanced the tray in one hand while I let myself in.

Mahnoor lay on her side in bed, strands of her shiny brown hair strewn across her pillow, tearstains trailing down her face.

"Hey. We didn't eat much during iftar, so I brought chai and cookies. I hope you like Milanos and chocolate chip. I snuck them past the aunties." I came to sit beside her, setting the tray down on the bedside table. "Don't worry about meeting the relatives just yet. I told them you were tired and would see them in the morning, when you're feeling better."

"Thanks." She sat up slowly, tucking her hair back behind her ears, and smiled half-heartedly as I handed her a cup.

"What happened?" I asked, after she'd taken a few sips and reached for a cookie.

She sighed, setting the cookie down. "Azhar came into the

basement so quietly I didn't realize he was there till I turned around. I'd been holding the vase, and when I saw Azhar, it slipped right through my fingers and hit the floor."

"So Azhar didn't say anything?"

She shook her head. "Not till Haya tried to pick up the glass."

I picked up the plate of cookies and set it between us, placing one in her hands and taking one for myself. "I've never seen Azhar that angry before." I paused. "Scratch that. I've never seen Azhar angry, ever. But then I've been here less than a month. Was today normal for him?"

She shook her head again, nibbling at her cookie. "Not at all. I've known him all my life and I've never seen him that upset. I don't think even Haya and Hassan have. Azhar's just not like that, Dua. I knew breaking off the engagement would hurt him. Thinking otherwise would've been ridiculous, but I never expected *this*. He's always been sweet and generous and level-headed, not . . . Oh, God. Dua, what did I do? I broke Azhar."

"Mahnoor." I took a big bite of my cookie, taking my time chewing and swallowing before I continued. "I love you, but seriously, what did you think would happen? The dude wanted to marry you, and he thought you wanted to marry him too. Your parents were planning your freaking wedding! And then you went and called the whole thing off. He's going to need time to cool off."

"I never realized he cared so much," she murmured, putting her head in her hands.

"If he proposed, I'm pretty sure he cared," I replied, taking another cookie.

"Yeah, true. I just . . . I thought this would be easier. I didn't think I'd feel so out of sorts about it."

I sipped my chai slowly. "What do you mean?"

She didn't say anything, just stared down at her lap, deep in thought. The corner of her mouth twitched, and she took a deep breath, letting it out slowly. "Maybe I made a mistake."

"Getting engaged to Azhar in the first place? Little late for that, but yeah, at least you—"

"No," she cut me off, shaking her head. "Breaking it off. Maybe I was wrong to do that."

I dropped my cookie. "You think you shouldn't have broken it off because you've seen what a week of emotional torture did to the guy? What happened to only liking him as a friend? What happened to thinking it wouldn't work?"

She reached into her pocket and pulled out Azhar's engagement ring, twirling it around her finger. "I miss him, you know? How he'd text me every day just to see how I was doing, and how he actually seemed to *listen*. He'd send me something funny if he thought I'd like it. I miss that too."

"You miss *him* or his attention?"

She paused, staring at the ring. "Both, I guess." She sighed. "He's angry with me, but he still wants me to be happy. He doesn't want me to suffer a broken heart even though I broke his. He wants me to find someone I care about, someone who cares about me more than I care about him." She looked up at me. "But where am I going to find someone who could possibly care about me more than he does?"

I stared at her, at the raw feeling on her face, and shrugged. "I don't know. Are you saying you love Azhar?"

She twirled the ring on her finger a few times. "I don't know. But I'm sad he's not around."

And, we're back on the emotional roller coaster. Then again, when did we ever get off?

"What should I do, Dua?"

I gawked at her. *She* was asking *me?* "Um, well ..." A knock on the door interrupted me. Thank God. "Come in!"

Ibrahim poked his head into the room. "We're going to the masjid, since tonight could be Laylat-al-Qadr. Wanna come? One of the aunts is staying home to watch over the little kids."

Mahnoor appeared conflicted as she twirled the ring around her finger, biting her lip.

"Yeah, we're coming," I answered for both of us.

"Great. We leave in five minutes."

Mahnoor's eyes shimmered with unshed tears. "You should come to the masjid," I said. "You need to pray. Ask Allah to guide you, and believe that whatever happens is for the best. Insha'Allah, He'll guide you, and you'll be able to make a decision you won't regret. But take your time. Azhar's not a toy. You can't break off your engagement one second and want to marry him the next."

She studied the ring for a moment, then sighed, slipped it off her finger, and put it back in her pocket. "Seek God in both good and bad times," she said quietly. "From your Ramadan checklist."

"Exactly." I stood up. "Let's go."

The masjid was already crowded when we got there; the men's section on the second floor was completely full, and the women's section was almost equally packed.

Glancing over my shoulder to check on Mahnoor, I slipped

my feet out of my shoes and walked in. Fortunately, there was enough space that we didn't need to squish ourselves together like sardines in a can to pray, unlike the men.

Rabia settled down in a corner, dragging us with her. I watched Mahnoor close her eyes, lift her hands to her ears, and whisper *Allahu Akbar* to start her prayer. I did the same.

Oh, Allah. You alone I worship. You alone are worthy of worshipping. You've always answered my prayers, and I can never thank You enough for that, I think, even as the words from the first chapter of the Qur'an roll off my tongue. *Please, answer this prayer too. Let Mahnoor and Azhar both find their happiness, whether that's with each other or not. Guide them, especially Mahnoor. Let her figure out what she wants, who she wants.*

I finished my prayer, then sat back, pulled out my tasbeeh, and watched Mahnoor. Normally, she'd have been finished by now, but she wouldn't lift her head from the floor, the position where we're supposed to be closest to Allah. Her lips moved as she prayed, staying in place with her forehead pressed to the carpet.

Allah, please answer my prayer. Guide her to her happiness. And please do the same for me.

twenty

I tapped my foot impatiently, looking around at my cousins. I wasn't the only one fidgeting and watching the clock. Today was the twenty-seventh day of Ramadan, which meant three things. One, tonight was the most likely candidate for Laylat-al-Qadr. Two, there were only three days left till Eid, including today, and only four days left till I went back to Burkeville. Three, Adam was supposed to come home today. Actually, he was already on his way.

I sighed, wondering how much longer we'd have to wait. Even the aunts had run out of gossip. Suddenly, Mahdi's ears perked up, somehow hearing the front door open before the rest of us, and he shot toward the sound. Rabia launched herself after him, and we followed suit.

Rabia looked like a snake trying to squeeze the life out of her prey as she hugged her brother, Adam trying to keep a look of pain off his face as he yelped and kept her at arm's length. "Watch the ribs."

"Sorry," she murmured sheepishly. "I'm so glad you're home!"

He smiled weakly. "Yeah, so am I. Hospital food doesn't taste so good."

"Adam!" I called, running to him. I ended up with my arms suspended in an air hug around his middle, since I couldn't quite reach his shoulders.

"Dua." He grinned down at me. "You *just* saw me last night."

"I know, just shut up and let me enjoy this. How are you feeling now?" I asked, pulling back.

He grimaced slightly. "Everything still hurts, but I'm healing and I got the bandages off."

Ibrahim rested a hand on Adam's shoulder. "Welcome home. We're so glad you're safe."

Mahnoor stepped forward for her hug, her arms loose around his shoulders. "Love you," she said simply, her voice heavy with emotion.

"That makes an interesting fashion statement," Adam observed as she pulled back. He gestured to the chain around her neck. She'd put Azhar's ring on it, so it hung down just above her heart. "What's the story there?"

She offered him a shaky smile. "It's a long one. I'll tell you later."

His forehead wrinkled in concern. "Why—"

"Adam, beta!" The uncles and aunts descended upon us in an ambush, loud and exuberant. To his credit, Adam did a decent job of hiding his grimace quickly. "Good luck," I whispered.

He shot me a wary look. "Thanks, I guess. It looks like I'll need it."

"Dua, darling." My mother's hand gently smoothed the hair away from my face. "Get up; it's time for suhoor."

"What time is it?" I croaked, rubbing my eyes. I snuck a look at the display on Mahnoor's alarm clock. "Mom, there's an hour left till fajr. What am I going to eat, the house?" I lay back down and pulled my pillow over my head. "You can wake me up in half an hour. Good night."

"Come on, Dua." She pulled the pillow off my face. "It's the last day of Ramadan. It's special. Please get up."

"Fine." Reaching for her hand, I let her drag me out of bed. "Only because it's the last day."

"Mmm-hmm," she said, clearly not listening as she led me out of the room, our bare feet padding softly on the carpeted floor.

The lights turned on as we stepped into the kitchen, blinding me as several voices cried out, "Happy birthday!"

Once my eyes adjusted to the light, I took in the scene before me. Dad, Uncle Yusuf, Aunt Sadia, the rest of the aunts and uncles, and all my cousins stood around the kitchen table, surrounding the biggest chocolate cake I'd ever seen, with huge grins on their faces.

I felt my jaw drop, and not just because I'd managed to totally forget my birthday.

"We thought we'd celebrate now since everyone will be busy getting ready for Eid tonight," Aunt Sadia explained, smiling the hardest of all.

I tried to say something in response, but the words wouldn't come. My brain was blank.

Mom laughed. "Well, don't just stand there, go and blow

out the candles so everyone can eat." Her hand on my back, she gently pushed me to the table.

I closed my mouth, still speechless as Aunt Sadia handed me a knife. There, between the candles and on top of the fudgy frosting, someone had written *Happy 18th Birthday, Dua!* in sky-blue icing.

"Make a dua before you blow them out," Adam reminded me.

Right. We're Muslim. We don't wish on candles. We pray to Allah for what we want and blow on candles 'cause it's fun. I beamed at him, reaching out to squeeze his arm warmly. I already had one of my biggest prayers answered when he came home. But . . . I bent toward the candles, my lips forming a little O. *Allah, please keep this family together always. Happy, content, and loving of one another. That's all I want.* Closing my eyes, I blew out the candles.

☾

Later, I paused by Adam's room on my way back from washing up for maghrib. Through the closed door, I could hear Mahdi's giggles, echoed by Adam's deeper laughter. I felt a laugh bubbling up in my own throat, and I smiled widely. I knocked.

The giggles paused. "Come in!" Adam's voice floated to my ears. I closed my eyes for a second, appreciating the sound of it. When he was in the hospital, I didn't know if I'd ever hear it again.

"Alhamdulillah," I whispered to myself as I opened the door.

"Dua!" Mahdi yelled, already rushing to hug me.

Adam beamed, leaning over to stage-whisper to Ibrahim, "I don't think we're his favorites anymore."

"What were you all talking about?" I asked, folding Mahdi's hand in my own as I sat across from the boys.

"We were telling Mahdi about your birthday presents. He agrees mine is the best," Adam teased. When I glanced around the room, he added, "Not here, you'll get them soon."

"What'd you get me?" I asked, my curiosity piqued.

"Patience," Ibrahim said, smiling. "You'll find out soon."

Sooner than expected, apparently. There was no hiding Mahdi's excitement as he shouted, "A *pogo stick*, Dua! Adam got you a pogo stick!"

My eyes widened. "Seriously?" I looked at Adam pointedly. The idea sounded exciting, but . . . "I've never used one before. What if I fall?"

"We'll be right next to you," he said. "Promise."

"You're still healing and I don't trust myself not to knock Ibrahim over," I pointed out.

"Okay, then we'll have Rabia there to catch you if you fall, and I'll direct her." He raised his eyebrows. "Any other safety concerns?"

I couldn't help but smile. "Fine, I'll give it a shot."

"Dua, there you are!" Aunt Sadia appeared in the doorway. "I've been looking all over for you!"

"Sorry. What's going on?"

"I've been waiting all month to give you this." A huge smile lit up her face as she pulled out a gift-wrapped package from behind her back.

I stared at it for a moment before reaching for it, taking in the sparkly blue wrapping paper and shiny bow. "Aunt Sadia, you didn't have to," I said, my fingers already tightening around it. I yanked the paper off in one fluid movement and lifted the lid. I pulled out the most gorgeous shalwar kameez I'd ever seen. It was the perfect shade of red, neither too bright nor too dark, with delicate embroidery and small rhinestones all over, and gold trim. With this in my closet, my mom wouldn't have to practically blackmail me into dressing up. Running my hands over the smooth, soft cloth, I looked up at my aunt, grinning so wide I could feel my jaw ready to crack.

She smiled, laying her hand on mine. "I wanted to, sweetie, and you deserved a great gift, so I called your mom and got your measurements months ago. It'll be a perfect fit, I hope."

"I'm sure it will be. It's lovely." I reached out for a bear hug. "Thank you."

"Happy birthday, Dua," she replied, patting my back.

Mahnoor poked her head into the room. "Aww, Mom, I wanted to be here when you gave it to her."

"She loves it," she said, beaming at me as she pulled back. "Get her other present."

"What? There's more?" I asked as Mahnoor entered the room.

"Yup." She made her way over with another gift-wrapped box, this one smaller and wrapped in sparkly red paper with a shiny blue ribbon. "This is from Rabia and me."

I took even less time with this one, sliding the ribbon off and reducing the paper to shreds in my haste to open it. Shoes. Strappy gold four-inch heels that would complement the shalwar kameez perfectly, an ideal Eid outfit. "Thank you, these are gorgeous!"

Adam's eyes twinkled as he said, "I still think my gift is better."

I laughed as I picked up the boxes and headed for the bathroom. "I'm gonna try these on."

"Hurry back," Mahnoor said. "Haya will be here soon."

"Okay, I'll—" My phone beeped and I paused, feet planted firmly in the hallway, shifting the boxes in my arms to check.

Happy birthday, D! May you have many more ☺ *P.S. You owe me a call. P.P.S. It's okay, I'm imagining you enjoying sightseeing right now.*

I smiled at Kat's text. I'd texted to let her know it wasn't a good time, but I *did* owe her a call. Her response was more gracious than most may have offered in her place. I'd have to tell her all about what happened when I got back home . . . and pack a few extra souvenirs along with the keychain she'd asked for.

Hennaed arms wrapped around my shoulders from behind. "Happy birthday!" Haya squealed, squeezing me. "Bhabhi," she whispered into my ear.

"Thanks." I grinned as she pulled back and led me to Mahnoor's room for privacy. I'd given up on telling her to stop calling me that; it only made her more determined to say it as much as possible. At least she was careful about avoiding it around my parents and the aunts and uncles. And Hassan. Speaking of Hassan, I'd barely seen him since that night in the kitchen, and only from a distance. I felt a little twinge of despair deep in my belly. I hoped he wasn't upset with me. If he thought of me at all.

"Haya, Hassan didn't come with you?" Mahnoor asked, following us into the room.

"No, he just dropped me off. He said he had to go get something, last-minute Eid shopping, I think. He'll be by later to pick me up. Don't worry, bhabhi," Haya teased, nudging my shoulder. "You'll get to see him tonight."

I shook my head, as if that would somehow make the *I'm-way-more-interested-than-I-should-be* look fall off my face. My inability to keep a straight face was totally going to get me into trouble one day. "Astagfirullah, Haya. It's the last night of Ramadan. I have more important things on my mind." I should, anyway.

"Speaking of important things." Mahnoor glanced at Haya as she played with her fishtail braid. "How's Azhar?"

Haya's smile froze on her face and the skin by the corners of her eyes tightened. "He's . . . okay," she said finally, her features slowly softening. "Doesn't say much, but he's okay. I asked him if he was going to come by later, but he didn't respond."

"Okay," Mahnoor echoed, her fingers wrapping around the ring hanging from her neck.

"Is that . . . ?" Haya leaned in so close her nose was only a few inches away from Mahnoor's neck, her eyes wide as she studied the ring. After a few seconds, she looked up at her and straightened, the question clear in her eyes. "Why?"

Mahnoor, who'd been holding her breath when Haya leaned in, finally let it out. "Because I miss him."

Silence fell over the room as Haya stared at her, dumbfounded. Mahnoor returned the look, her head held high. Now if only Azhar had been here to hear Mahnoor's little revelation. Then again, it was probably better he wasn't. She didn't feel brave enough to say it to his face yet.

I pulled my phone from my pocket to check the time. Just as I thought. We didn't have time for this staring contest. Shoving the phone back into my pocket, I cleared my throat. Mahnoor glanced at me out of the corner of her eye, but I was otherwise ignored. "We should go to the dining room now. It's almost time for iftar."

Haya blinked, slowly turning away from Mahnoor. "Right. Let's go."

Rabia passed me a date as I sat down. "Two minutes left."

"Thanks." I set it down and folded my hands, about to close my eyes and pray when the legs on the chair beside mine screeched as Mahdi pulled himself up to sit next to me. His eyes wide, he propped his chin up on his fists and studied me, like he was trying to memorize my face. I raised an eyebrow. "What's on your mind, little man?"

"Adam said if I want you to stay, I have to think of ways to keep you here," he admitted, still studying me. "I'm thinking."

I glanced at Adam, who smiled as he gave a little shrug. "We got used to having you here. It's not so bad."

Quashing the desire to hug both of them, I settled for stroking Mahdi's hair. "Okay, then. I'm going to pray. Don't want to disturb you while you're thinking."

Folding my hands again and closing my eyes, I tried my best to block out all other thoughts. The time had passed quickly, yet it somehow felt like years since I'd left Burkeville. I'd found amazing friends in my cousins, learned a few life lessons, got to see Madame Tussauds and Central Park . . . and got to see the effects of Islamophobia firsthand. How had all of that happened in a month? After this, Burkeville would feel empty when I got back, even with Kat there. I'd go back to being an only child, back to being the only desi teen in town, the only Muslim my age around. Maybe an MSA at Nottoway High wouldn't be so bad, if I could talk to Ms. Fritz about any possible safety concerns first. With Kat's help, we should be able to rally up a few active members.

Honestly, this Ramadan had been so eventful, I didn't want to go back, didn't want to have to leave everyone, not now that I'd just become a part of their lives. I'd fought on the way here, and now I'd be fighting on the way back. I sighed to myself. No, I wouldn't fight this time. It wasn't fair to my parents. They'd promised I'd enjoy myself, and I did. Too much. That wasn't their fault or mine. It was the truth, and there was no fighting it.

Maybe Mahdi was on to something. Maybe I didn't have to leave after all—not permanently. *If you end up at NYU or Fordham, we can work something out,* Haya had said. Not a bad idea—I could slip a few NY schools into my college applications; it wouldn't hurt anybody. And I'd be close to Hassan. My soaring excitement faltered, recalling that the last time we spoke, it hadn't gone so well. Still, one could hope, and a little prayer never hurt.

I bent my head over my cupped palms. *Oh, Allah, this is the last night of Ramadan. I won't experience this for a whole nother year, so please accept my fast, forgive my sins, answer my prayers, and bless me in the coming year. And, if it's good for me, please help me come back someday. Ameen. Allahu Akbar, Allahu Akbar!*

I opened my eyes, whispering the dua for breaking the fast as I reached for my date. I drew it to my mouth, took a bite, and chewed it at the same slow pace, letting every second of it sink in, hoping it would fill the sudden void that had appeared somewhere in the vicinity of my heart.

twenty-one

"Almost done." With a flick of her wrist, Haya put the finishing touches of a flower on the back of my hand, the fragrant henna cool against my skin. "There."

I pulled my hand back to show Rabia, who nodded her approval. "Looks great—I owe you one."

"Do you mean that?"

I glanced up at her. "What's on your mind?"

She toyed with the henna cone for a moment, then set it down. "Okay, this is really last minute, but Sheikh, Rattle, and Roll has a gig tomorrow. We agreed to it way before Ramadan, but Ibrahim's in no shape to perform right now. He's still a little . . . jumpy after what happened." Mahnoor paused in her admiration of her own henna, her expression darkening.

"Yeah," I murmured, my voice barely audible. Maybe he should talk to someone. Adam, too. It might be good for both of them.

"I googled a few therapists who specialize in trauma," Haya

said, as if she could read my mind . . . or my face. "Short-listed a couple and handed the list to Hassan, who's promised to talk to Ibrahim and Adam about it. Hopefully that will help."

"You think so?"

"Oh, definitely. Hassan is the most convincing out of all of us, and he's been a big advocate for mental health awareness within our community. We all got bullied over the years, but since Hassan was the youngest, he seemed to feel it the most. It was really hard for him."

"I didn't know that." Granted, there was a lot about Hassan I was still discovering. My heart ached when I imagined him as a child, hurting and helpless.

"Yeah, but he's doing well now, and he says it's because of everything his therapist taught him. For a while there, he was considering majoring in psychology, but he enjoys graphic design just a bit more."

I studied the henna pattern emerging on my hand. No wonder he'd said what he did about sharing the burden with others. I felt a tiny twinge deep in my belly. Maybe he was right; I had to learn to let other people take care of me sometimes. Especially genuinely good people I could trust. I had little doubt he fell into that category.

"Anyway," Haya continued, unaware of my thoughts as she worked on my henna, "Azhar knows bass, so he's going to cover for Ibrahim, but we're short a keyboard player."

"I'll do it," I said quickly, before I could overthink it.

"Really? Great. Here's the sheet music." Pulling a couple of sheets of paper out of her bag, she slid them over to me. "I know you're a musical genius or whatever, but you can learn it by tomorrow, right?"

Keeping my hands up in the air, I leaned over to study the paper. "Insha'Allah, I think I'll be okay. You can always play a little for me if I'm confused."

Haya grinned wide, the lower half of her face nothing but teeth. "Bhabhi, you're amazing!"

I blushed, ducking my head in my attempt—and failure—to hide it. "*Stop* calling me that!"

Mahnoor bit her lip and shifted uncomfortably, her eyes glassy.

Technically, Mahnoor was the one Haya should have been calling *bhabhi*. "Hey, Mahnoor," I said quickly, "let's grab some stuff from the kitchen. Mom told me that putting a mixture of lemon juice and sugar on henna helps the color last. Maybe it'll work."

Recognizing the reprieve, Mahnoor nodded. "Yeah, let's try it."

Haya didn't glance up as we left the room. Rabia, bless her, didn't give her a chance to—she sat there, pointing out the minute details of a design she liked on Instagram, chattering away.

Once we'd closed the door behind us, I looked at Mahnoor. "Want to go outside? Take a break for a few minutes?"

She nodded. "Definitely." She led the way, hennaed hands raised in the air as we walked through the kitchen. She was only a few steps away from the living room when she stopped in her tracks. I did, too, to keep from walking into her.

"What?"

She lifted a finger to her lips. "Shh!"

I swallowed my questions and leaned forward, trying to hear better. The tune was soft, but familiar. My eyes widened as I placed it. It was the same song I'd found Mahnoor singing, hummed in a deeper voice.

Not a note was out of tune. It was perfect, well-practiced. The lyrics came to mind easily, and I had to bite my lip to keep from humming or singing along.

Mahnoor closed her eyes for a moment, savoring the sound.

It was a man's voice. Not one I could place. I stepped forward gingerly, Mahnoor on my heels, and peeked around the corner.

He stood with a guitar slung over his shoulder, humming the song as he tuned the strings.

The smile on his face was easy, calm, reflecting the same peace Mahnoor had on her face as she'd sung that song.

Mahnoor stifled a gasp. He wasn't tall, but he was handsome. And he wasn't Pakistani, but he knew a Pakistani song well enough to hum it from memory.

Azhar.

Mahnoor dragged me away. In the safety of the bathroom, she turned to me. "Did you?"

I shook my head. "No, I didn't tell him about it."

"Haya?"

"No," I replied firmly. "I didn't say anything to anyone."

I watched her face change as she processed this. "Azhar isn't Pakistani," I said, my voice soft. "Yet he knows the same song you do, a song I didn't even know till I'd heard you sing it. Do you know what this means?"

Mahnoor squeezed her eyes shut, her brows furrowing.

I kept going. "He appreciates Pakistani music, Pakistani culture. Not only that, but your tastes are so similar. He enjoys the same music you do." That said a lot, considering I—and many other Pakistani people, I'm sure—had hardly heard that song before.

I reached out and touched her shoulder. "Mahnoor?"

She looked at me, a question brimming in her eyes.

"What if this is a sign? He may not look like what you'd been expecting in your future husband, but his *interests*, his *character*, and his *heart* all match up with your ideal. Maybe Allah chose Azhar for you."

"And I rejected him," she gasped, tears shining in her eyes. "No wonder I haven't gotten a moment's peace since." She rubbed her arm across her face. "He must be here to pick Haya up. I can't see him now, and I can't let Haya see me like this."

"Hey, it's okay. You do what you need to. Figure yourself out. I'll tell Haya."

She sniffled. "Thanks, Dua. I'll hang out in Adam's room until they leave."

"You're welcome."

I entered Mahnoor's room alone. As I opened my mouth to deliver my news, Haya's phone beeped. She bent over her lap, her lips silently forming the words. Her shoulders drooped the slightest bit; then she straightened. "Well, looks like my ride's here." She looked up at me, her eyes dark. "Say goodbye to Mahnoor for me?"

"Sure," I said. "Come on, I'll see you out."

"I'll see you tomorrow for Eid," Haya said quietly, loosely wrapping an arm around me. It wasn't quite the Mousawi bear hug I'd come to expect.

"Insha'Allah." I stayed outside where I was and stared after Haya and Azhar till I could no longer see their taillights, and only then did I slump into the lone old chair by the front door, turning my face to the sky.

Staring at the skyline was peaceful here; I hadn't thought so at first, missing the sight of the stars dazzling from our backyard.

But maybe they shouldn't be compared at all. They were too different, each beautiful in its own way.

"Assalamu alaykum."

I jerked out of my reverie, almost falling out of my chair. Hassan stood on the steps directly in front of me, his eyes shimmering in the dark. "Wa alaykum assalam," I replied, steadying myself without using my hands. "You just missed Haya and Azhar."

"That's okay, I'll see them at home. I stopped by to see Ibrahim and Adam."

He didn't say anything for a long moment. My stomach bubbled in discomfort, but the moment wasn't as awkward as I'd expected. I glanced at him shyly, thankful my hair shielded my face. If I concentrated, I could still feel his hand wrapped around my arm. "I want to apologize for being rude that day in the kitchen. You were just trying to help, and clearly I needed it."

A beat passed; then he said softly, "That's okay. Sometimes help is tough to accept, even when we need it the most."

I nodded. "You're definitely right about that. I just . . . I was worried someone would see and get the wrong idea."

His shoulders stiffened, getting my drift. "Then I owe you an apology too. I don't want to put you in an awkward situation with your family."

"Thank you," I said simply, not knowing what else to say.

He rubbed the back of his neck as he cleared his throat. His mouth tilted up on one side in a lopsided smile. "So . . . do you spend a lot of time sitting outside staring up at the sky?" His eyes sparkled in the dim light. My heart beat harder and I looked back at the sky as I willed it to relax.

"Yeah, actually," I replied, feeling my mouth curl into a little smile. "At home, whenever life feels too overwhelming, I go outside, watch the night sky, and count the stars. The beauty of the universe never fades, and by the time I lose count of the stars, whatever's bothering me doesn't seem like such a big deal anymore."

He turned his head to follow my gaze for a moment before looking back at me. His silence was expectant, like he was waiting for me to go on.

After a beat, I continued. "Ever since I got here, there's always been someone around to listen or talk or just *be there* with me, so I haven't done any major counting all month."

"So, you're sitting by yourself right now because . . . ?"

I bit my lip, gathering my thoughts. "You know," I said slowly, studying the wood beneath my feet like it held all the answers, "when I first got here, I didn't know how I was going to adjust. There was almost no privacy, too much noise, too much pollution. Even too many food options to choose from!"

He quirked a brow at that, and I added, "I'm indecisive sometimes."

He chuckled. "Aren't we all?"

I continued, reassured. "Anyway, I thought I would hate each day more than the last and would just be waiting to go home. But the opposite happened. I adjusted before I even had time to realize it. The differences didn't bother me as much as I thought they would. New York doesn't feel so alien now."

" 'Cause you stopped fighting it," he said quietly, folding his arms over his chest. "You accepted it, so it accepted you."

Images of subway cars and gigantic pizza slices surrounding me in a circle and hugging me came to mind. Smiling, I shrugged and replied, "Maybe. I don't really know how or why, but I'm going to miss it." I looked up at him. "That's why I'm out here, to savor my last days here. Who knows if I'll ever get a chance to do so again?"

"You don't have to totally leave New York behind if you don't want to. New York has lots of great schools to choose from. You can come back, make a life here, pursue your music. Insha'Allah," he said softly, his eyes darkening.

"Insha'Allah," I repeated, my voice as low as his. "I'll have to think about it." Taking one last look at the sky, I sighed as I got up. "Time for me to go in; it's getting chilly." I walked past him and reached for the doorknob, stopping just in time. "Oh." My henna was still wet.

"Ahem." He cleared his throat, standing directly behind me.

Wordlessly, I took a little step to the side.

His eyes on mine, his mouth curled into a little smirk as he twisted the doorknob and pushed the door open. We stayed like that for a couple of seconds, staring at each other, till he cleared his throat again and said, "You can go in now."

I blinked, suddenly as brain dead as a rock. "Oh. No, it's okay, you go first."

He flashed that crooked smile again. "Then who's going to close the door after you?"

Good point. I stepped past him into the house. "Thanks."

"You're welcome." He stepped in behind me, leaving plenty of room between us. "Oh, and happy birthday."

I smiled. "Thanks."

The peace in his face flickered, and he glanced at the floor as he rubbed the back of his neck again. "Um . . ."

I slowed, my heart leaping into my throat. "What?"

His eyes crinkled at the corners as they met mine. "Azhar sent an Eid gift for Mahnoor. He picked it out before, you know, and he wanted her to have it." He pulled a tiny lavender gift bag from his pocket, sparkly white tissue paper poking out of the top. "He meant to bring it over, but I had to hang on to it a little longer. Can you make sure she gets it?"

"Yeah, of course. Uh . . ." I glanced at my fingers. Maybe I could hook a strap through a crooked pinky, so I didn't get henna on it or drop it.

"Oh." He lifted the gauzy ribbon straps away from the bag, forming a loop. Gently, he passed the loop over my open hand, till the straps nestled safely on my forearm. As quickly as I'd felt the heat of his skin against mine, it was gone.

"Thanks," I murmured, ducking my head so my hair covered my burning ears.

"Thank you." His dimple peeked out at me for a moment; then he quickly looked away and started to head up the stairs. "I'll just see Ibrahim and Adam. Then I have to get home."

"Right." I waited a beat before taking the first step up. "Home."

"Oh," he called back, "there's something in there for you too." I heard the smile in his voice. "Sorry for the delay; it took me a while to find the right one. I hope you like it."

"What?"

But he was already gone.

Mahnoor sat on her prayer mat. She opened her eyes as I entered the room, her fingers pausing on the beads of her tasbeeh. She'd already rubbed off her henna, the designs swirling over her hands. "What's that?" she asked as I set the gift bag down in front of her reverentially.

"I don't know," I admitted. "An Eid gift from Azhar. And something else."

Her eyes widening, she reached for the bag, pulling out two little packets wrapped in purple wrapping paper. She turned one over to show me the white label on the front, my name printed in black swirling letters, the curve mimicking the twists and swirls of the Arabic alphabet. Hassan's work, clearly.

I lifted my chin. "Check yours first."

She set mine down as she opened the other packet. She lifted a slim rose-gold bangle to eye level, two charms along its length. I squinted, studying them. They looked like random shapes to me, kind of like the pakoray I'd made.

She opened the little card with her name on it. *"Mahnoor, I know how much your upbringing means to you. The charms represent the maps of Pakistan and Lebanon. This was my way of showing you that we could build something beautiful with both."* Her voice cracked, and she sniffled as she finished. *"Anyway, it was always meant for you, so I wanted you to have it."* She chuckled half-heartedly. *"Plus, I lost the receipt."* She wiped at her eyes.

I spread my arms out to hug her, awkwardly keeping my hennaed hands away from her. "Are you okay?" I asked after several long moments of her sniffling into my shirt.

She nodded, pulling back. "Yeah, yeah, I'll be okay. Just . . . that was very sweet of him." Her voice cracked and she grabbed a tissue from the box that was always by her bed now, blowing her nose loudly. "Your turn. Open yours."

I studied my hands. The henna was dry enough. "Okay, one minute."

I emerged from the bathroom minutes later, the henna

scraped off. I checked the card first. *Now you have one of your own, so keep it close. Happy birthday, from Hussan and Haya.*

"One what?" Mahnoor asked, her voice booming in my ear.

I jumped, my surprise subsiding long enough for me to glare at her. "Do you *have* to give me a heart attack right now?" I demanded. "And I don't know," I added, ripping the paper open. "I'm not a psychic."

It was a box no bigger than my palm, with a snap closure on the front like the ones on my mom's old jewelry boxes that I used to love playing with when I was little. My heart ached to just sit and marvel at the box for a minute, but I opened it before Mahnoor decided she was tired of waiting and snatched it from my hands.

My jaw dropped as I reached for the necklace nestled inside. The pendant shimmered in the faint light of the room as it dangled from the chain in my fingers, making it easier to admire the beautiful dips and curves of the golden Arabic letters that connected to spell *Allah*.

Now you have one of your own. The memory came rushing back at me. Standing at the keyboard at the Mousawis' house, admiring Hassan's silver Allah pendant, telling him about how I was always forgetting to ask for one for myself.

I looked at Mahnoor, my mouth still open.

Her eyes were as wide as tennis balls. "Mashallah, it's beautiful! You have to wear it on Eid tomorrow. It'll go so well with your outfit and shoes."

"Mahnoor, I can't accept this. Look at this." I thrust it into her face. "It's real gold!"

She didn't even blink. "So? It's probably just gold-plated. Let me see—"

"What do you mean *so*? I can't accept a gift like this from just anyone." Even as I said it, my grip on the chain tightened. I already loved it too much to let it go.

"You're not accepting gifts from *just anyone*, Dua. It's Haya and Hassan. They're not strangers. They haven't known you long, but it's not about how long you've known someone; it's about how well you know them. And they all love you. They wouldn't have gotten you this if they didn't. Don't insult their love by not accepting it."

I narrowed my eyes at her. "Are you saying that because *you* regret insulting their love?"

She sighed and smacked me on the head with my own pillow. "Well, I'm starting to. Now put it away and go to sleep. We have to wake up early for Eid prayer."

"You're not supposed to hit people on their birthdays."

"It's past midnight, Dua. It's not your birthday anymore. Go to sleep before I throw this pillow at your face again." I watched her climb into her bed, gingerly placing her new bracelet on the table beside her, where she could see it.

twenty-two

This Eid was going to be special, something to remember, and I couldn't miss out on any of it. I slipped the red kameez over my head and turned to look at my reflection in the mirror. It was a perfect fit, and the red made my skin look like it was glowing. I pulled the hairband from my ponytail and finger-combed my hair till it fell just right. Not exactly Bollywood celebrity material, but I still looked pretty good.

I stepped out of the bathroom and immediately bumped into Mahnoor. "Hurry up and get ready. The Mousawis are here, and we leave in twenty minutes."

I looked down at myself, then back up at her. Did she not see? "I *am* ready."

She leaned back on one heel, her thumb and index finger cradling her chin as she looked me up and down slowly. "Not quite. You need makeup and jewelry."

"I don't think—"

Arguing, as it turned out, was fruitless. After what felt like eons of Haya, Rabia, and Mahnoor rushing around me, Mahnoor tapped my shoulder to signal me to open my eyes.

I grinned at my reflection. Mahnoor had dusted shimmery gold eyeshadow on my lids, lined my eyes with kohl and added mascara, and put a sheer rusty-red gloss on my lips. My hair shone like black diamonds, loose curls trailing down to the middle of my back. To top it off, my teeka glittered like a crown, resting gently against my forehead. Definitely Bollywood-worthy.

"Girls"—Mom knocked on the open door—"come on, we're getting late." She paused. "Dua, what have you done?"

"*She* did nothing, Aunt Sanam," Mahnoor replied, tucking her hijab into place. "It was all our handiwork."

Mom lifted the hem of her dupatta to dab at her eyes. "You look so grown up. So beautiful, Mashallah!"

I turned away from my reflection. "Mom, are you *crying?*"

"Just a little, dear," she replied, sniffling as she lowered the dupatta from her eyes. "Let's go." And down the hallway she went, sniffling the whole way. I shook my head at the melodrama. I blame desi dramas.

From the hallway, I could see that the living room was jam-packed with people. All the uncles and aunts, the cousins, Ibrahim, Adam, and Mahdi, my parents, and the Mousawis.

Hassan stood next to Ibrahim. He wore a dark green shalwar kameez—probably a gift from Ibrahim or Uncle Yusuf—that highlighted his broad shoulders and made him look taller. The light stubble on his jawline made it seem even more defined, which sent my heart ramming so hard into my ribs I thought it'd burst right out of my chest.

I knew the second he noticed me. He'd been laughing at

something Ibrahim had said, but the moment he saw me, his smile faded and the twinkle in his eyes dimmed as they widened.

I forgot all about watching where I was going, forgot about the uncles and aunts and cousins. Trapped by his gaze, I could do nothing but peer into the depths of his eyes. He seemed just as mesmerized as I was, not breaking eye contact for a second, his eyes unblinking. What was he thinking?

My klutziness chose that unfortunate moment to rear its ugly head. I'd been so busy having a staring contest with Hassan, I hadn't been watching my feet. My ankle twisted on a misstep, knocking me into Mahnoor's side.

Hassan's mouth opened and he reached an arm out, but Mahnoor got to me before he did.

"Whoa!" She caught my arm, stopping me from falling to the floor. "You okay? Maybe the heels were a bad idea."

Still bent at the waist, gripping her arm tightly, I shook my head, grateful my hair had fallen over my face, obscuring it from view. It had to be as red as my clothes by now. "No," I said quietly, straightening. "No, I'm fine. The heels are fine."

He was still watching me. I could see him in my peripheral vision, but when I finally brushed my hair out of my face and turned, he looked away. His eyes shifted as he glanced at something off to the side and then looked back at Ibrahim, his mouth moving as he said something I couldn't hear over the chatter of the aunts.

My heart dropped into my stomach, and I suppressed a sigh as Mahnoor, still holding my arm, led me outside to the van. "So clumsy. Of course, I can't walk and be remotely romantic at the same time," I muttered to myself as I sat down, rearranging my clothes so they wouldn't wrinkle. "Where are we going, anyway?"

"The American Muslim Community Center," Haya replied, sticking her head through the door. "It's also where we're going to perform after breakfast."

My jaw went slack as I stared at her.

"See you there," she added, waving even as she jogged to her car.

"Allah help me," I muttered under my breath.

⸺ ☾ ⸺

"Allahu Akbar!" the booming voice of the imam announced.

"Allahu Akbar," I repeated, raising my hands, then letting them fall back down to my sides. Unlike our normal prayers, on Eid day, we repeated Allahu Akbar four more times before the imam began to recite a passage from the Qur'an.

I listened attentively, willing my mind to focus on the melodious Arabic words the imam recited, instead of letting my thoughts run away. All I could think about was that I was going to leave New York soon, and I was going to leave my family and the friends I'd made behind.

"We all believe in God," the imam was saying. "One God, the Lord of the universe. We believe in Him, we worship Him, but for many of us the hardest part is to trust Him. And yet, that is the ultimate faith, to rely on Him alone, to put all your trust in Him. He is the only One who will never let us down, yet some of us find it easier to trust our mortal friends before we trust the One who created us. What does that say about our faith?

"In the holy Qur'an, God has promised us that He will test us throughout our lives, either with poverty or riches, our parents or our children, anything at all. But what is the point of all these tests? He is testing our faith! The only way we can pass these tests is by having complete faith in Him, and our faith in Him cannot be complete until we trust Him wholeheartedly."

Closing my eyes, I wrapped my fingers around my new pendant.

"There is no faith without trust," he continued, "and there is no trust without faith; they go hand in hand."

I opened my eyes and stood, realizing the khutbah was over.

"Eid mubarak." Mom reached out to hug me the moment I had my shoes on, before I was even steady on my feet.

"Eid mubarak," I replied, smiling as I hugged her.

Releasing me, she turned to the gaggle of aunts behind her to greet them one by one.

I went toward my uncles, who were standing all in a row together, looking like they were just waiting for their hugs.

"Eid mubarak, Uncle Yusuf." I squeezed him tightly. "Thank you so much for inviting us," I whispered. "I'm never going to forget this trip."

"Eid mubarak, Dua. Thank you for making this Ramadan memorable for all of us." He smiled as he kissed the top of my head.

Smiling, I moved on to Dad, then the rest of the uncles, wishing them all a joyous Eid.

"Dua, come on." Mahnoor appeared beside me, grabbing my arm. "Everyone is waiting for us. I got you a plate."

"Thanks."

"No problem," Mahnoor replied, though she froze, stiffening beside me.

"Something wrong?" I asked her.

When I didn't get a response, I followed her gaze. Azhar. He looked very handsome, cutting a striking figure in dark rinse jeans, a cream-colored shirt, and a dark blazer. But the frown on his face stood out most of all.

"Dua." Mahnoor looked at me. "There's someone I have to talk to, and I could use some emotional backup. Do you mind just standing behind me a little bit?"

"Sure," I agreed instantly, though I wasn't quite sure of what was about to happen.

"Great. Let's go." Slowly, Mahnoor headed to the other side of the room, not stopping till she was directly in front of Azhar. She looked up at him with wide eyes, but I could see the determination in her shoulders.

He glanced at her for a second, then looked away, using the plate of food in his hand as a distraction. His jaw was clenched so tightly, it had to hurt. "What do you want?" His voice was low, raspy.

"Thank you for my Eid gift," she said quietly. "It's beautiful." She extended her hand out to him, offering a water bottle. He continued to look away from her, but she didn't move. Had he looked at her arm, he would've seen the bangle shining on her wrist.

I felt a pang in my heart for them. They were both suffering, and they were the cause of each other's pain.

He was quiet for a minute. Then, softly, "You're welcome."

"I want you to know the truth." She sighed. "I thought if I married you, I'd lose a part of myself."

"What?" The shock and pain on his face were so clear, it almost hurt to look at him. "How?"

She looked shamefacedly at her shoes. "I'd always thought I'd marry someone of Pakistani descent, you know? Someone who would just get it, who would get me. I made a senseless assumption—that only a Pakistani guy could share and appreciate all the beautiful things I love, the poetry, the music. I thought I'd have to forget those things, leave them behind, to start a life with you. I didn't realize you recognized how important my heritage is to me, but I knew yours mattered to you too."

"You just didn't think they could coexist? That *we* could coexist?" His voice cracked. "I never wanted to change you, Mahnoor. I just wanted to be with you."

"I'm sorry," she said quietly, looking up at him, her gaze begging him to look her in the eye. "I was wrong."

"To break off the engagement or get engaged to me in the first place?" he replied, still keeping his gaze trained on his food.

"You know I wouldn't be standing here right now if it was the latter."

He shook his head, his body twisted away from her. "I can't do this again. I have to practice before our set." Setting the plate aside, he turned to walk away. He'd already managed a couple of steps when Mahnoor reached out.

"Wait." She tightened her grip on his arm and he froze, almost as if in shock. Initiating physical contact wasn't like Mahnoor, and certainly not where other people could see her touching him. He had to know how difficult this was for her. "Azhar, please, just listen to me for a second. Don't just walk away."

He sighed, running his free hand through his hair. "What do you want?" He sounded tired.

She ran her fingers down his arm, clasping his hand firmly in her own. "You mean so much to me."

He stared at her hand, soft and small against his own, at their entwined fingers. "You really mean that?" His voice was soft with hope, yet it still held a note of fear.

"More than I've ever meant anything," Mahnoor admitted.

Turning back toward her, he met her gaze. "But are you sure? Mahnoor, I love you, but if there's a chance you might change your mind, I can't go through that again. I just can't. And I can't put my family through that either. Or yours."

"I know. I hurt you, and everyone else, and I'm sorry for that." Her eyes were wet, as if she was near tears. "But wallahi, I promise, by God, I will not change my mind again. I want to marry you, Azhar Mousawi. I want to build a life with you, insha'Allah."

He lowered his gaze, but not before I'd caught a glimpse of how red his eyes were. He hunched his shoulders, vulnerable, ready to give in, but still afraid to say yes. "Mahnoor, even when we were kids, I couldn't imagine spending the rest of my life with anyone else. But I guess you always saw me just as your best friend's brother. The day you said yes to my proposal was the happiest day of my life, and the day you broke off our engagement was the worst."

"You're right, and you have no idea how truly sorry I am for putting you through that." Her eyes closed, and she lowered her head, her cheeks flushing. "I didn't know what I wanted. I thought I did, but . . . what I wanted was just a fantasy, a faceless figment of my imagination.

"I thought we were too different, but then I realized—or, Allah showed me the truth—that we're more alike than not. Azhar, you know my favorite song by heart. The rest of my family's barely heard it. Yet, somehow, you knew. You connected with it, just like I did."

"What?" He furrowed his brows and took the smallest step away from her, though she still held on to his hand. "Wait. You're saying this is all about a song?"

"No," she said quickly. She paused, studying the floor as she gathered her thoughts. "The song, the bracelet are what finally opened my eyes, but there's so much more than that. You stopped coming around, and everything just felt off, like something was missing." Her grip loosened, his arm slipping through her fingers. "Then, when Adam was in the hospital and you came over, I could see the pain in your eyes, and it *hurt*. All of a sudden, I could clearly see my future without you in it, and I didn't want it." She swallowed.

"And then I couldn't face you. How could I? I'd put you through so much. How could I ask you to let me back into your life again?" She took a deep breath, her gaze on his. "Azhar, I promise, if you give me one more chance, I will spend every day of the rest of my life making it up to you." She held her hand out, her palm facing up. "Please, just one more chance."

He stared at her outstretched hand for a moment. Then, slowly, he lifted his gaze to her face. "You can have all the chances in the world," he said, his voice low but strong, "but answer one thing."

Her eyes shone with unshed tears. "Anything."

"Do you love me?"

"Yes," Mahnoor said, nodding. "I love you more than I can fully express. When you're with me, I feel like there's nothing I can't face. A day hasn't gone by that I haven't missed you, and I don't want to go another day like this."

He heaved a little sigh, of relief, of joy after a long period of darkness. "I've missed you too," he said, finally reaching for her hand. "God, I've missed you."

"And?" she prompted, raising an eyebrow.

His smile glowed. "And Eid Mubarak. But your timing is awful. I'm hungry, and I still have to practice before the show." A beat passed. "But we'll work on that, insha'Allah. Better late than never."

"So, I'll see you after?" she said as she returned his smile.

"Definitely. I've got a ring for you to go along with that bracelet."

twenty-three

Mahnoor was still blushing as she turned away from a now-beaming Azhar. I followed as she half led, half dragged me to the table where Haya and Rabia sat with food ready for us.

Rabia swallowed her last bite of chicken puff and wiped her mouth, the skin between her eyebrows crinkling as she looked at me. "What's with that look on your face? What happened?"

I glanced at Mahnoor. As happy as I was for her, it wasn't my right to tell.

She just smiled and offered her sister a pastry from her own plate. "Dua is just really, really happy to finally be eating during the day again," she explained, winking at me. She would tell. I knew she would, but in her own time. Unless Azhar spilled the beans first.

"Well, eat up, because we perform in about forty-five minutes," Haya said, first looking at me, then at Rabia. "We'll have a super-quick rehearsal before we go on."

I swallowed the last of my jalebi and pushed my plate toward Mahnoor. "Here, you can eat the rest."

"Yes, because tons of sugar in the early morning is exactly what I want," she muttered, already reaching for it as the rest of us got up.

It was only then, as we headed toward it, that I saw it: the stage at the front of the room. My stomach turned cartwheels. It was just one song. One. Nothing to get nervous about, right?

Hassan and Azhar had already set up the instruments and equipment. Thankfully, the room we were performing in was empty, and would be until we were ready to officially start. We'd have all the time we needed to practice in peace. My fingers itched the moment I laid eyes on the keyboard, and as I sat down in front of it, I could feel the longing to touch the keys through my whole body. Still, I reached for my sheet music folder, refusing to let myself play till I was ready.

Haya tapped me on the shoulder a few minutes later. "Are you okay?"

"Yeah, why?"

She pointed downward. "You're shaking."

My gaze followed the direction of her pointed finger. The stool I sat on looked like it was going through an earthquake. I forced my legs to still and set the folder down. "How are all of you okay?"

She blinked down at me. "What does that mean?"

"This is a major gig for you, and you're totally calm with having a complete noob like me performing with you. How are you not freaking out right now? This band is your baby. What if I ruin it?"

Sighing, she bent and wrapped her arms around me. "Don't worry." She smiled. "I know you can do this. And even if something does go wrong—and insha'Allah it won't—so what? We're among friends here. They know what happened to Adam; they'll understand. You're not going to ruin anything. You're talented. Just relax, practice, and let the music flow."

Let the music flow. I'd never really had permission to do that before. "But—"

"Put everything else out of your mind. You can do this."

I still felt myself shaking a little, but I nodded. "Okay, I'll try. Thanks for the pep talk."

She grinned. "Anytime. I'm going to regroup with Azhar and Rabia. We're all a bit out of practice." She turned and dashed off to the other end of the stage.

Setting up my sheet music, I reached out to touch the keys. My fingers faltered, hovering above them. Part of me yearned to relax and let the music flow, like Haya said. But the other part of me was crippled by fear, the anxiety forming a tight knot in the back of my neck.

"What's wrong?"

I looked up to find Hassan had abandoned his drum set and stood over me, his unreadable gaze steady on the keyboard. When I didn't respond, he shifted his gaze to me.

I looked back at the keyboard quickly. I'd stopped shaking, for the most part, thank God. "I've never actually played in front of anyone else before. No one other than my parents and my piano teacher," I admitted quietly, clasping my hands in my lap.

"You played in front of me."

The reminder was enough for me to reach for my pendant, giving my restless fingers something else to hold on to. "Only because I didn't know you were there."

He studied me for a moment, rubbing his chin. "We can try playing together."

I blinked up at him, my heart jumping into my throat. "What?"

He smiled. "Relax, it'll just be the two of us. You'll get a feel for the song, and I'll point out mistakes—if there are any." His smile widened. "I have a feeling there won't be."

"Okay." I barely managed to get the word out, my nerves choking my chest.

He sat in front of the snare and adjusted. Once he was satisfied, he picked up his drumsticks and straightened his back. He looked over to me, warmth twinkling in his eyes as they met mine. "Ready?"

I stared at the sheet music. He would begin, and then everyone else in the band followed his lead. I gulped and forced a nod.

"Bismillah. In the name of Allah, the Beneficent, the Merciful," he said softly. Each beat was deliberate, powerful. I watched him quietly, mesmerized at how he was simultaneously attentive yet strikingly relaxed, his body engaged in its own transcendent journey as he played. As I watched him, I felt peace settle in my belly, my own being following in recognition of his euphoria. I let myself be transported, to where there was only us and the music.

My fingers stroked the keys reverently, longing to join in so ardently, I almost missed my cue. Hassan lifted his chin, looking pointedly at me. His smile, the open acceptance on his face, felt like home. Closing my eyes, I whispered all the prayers I knew under my breath as I began to play. I felt myself becoming weightless as the bass pulsated in my ears, the rhythm echoing in the beat of my heart. The melodic chime of each chord rose to match him beat for beat, blending with the deeper sound of the percussion while, somehow, maintaining its unique integrity. My fingers wandered the keyboard in their own flawless dance, my body falling in sync with the melody as it flowed from my fingertips. Each note was smooth, sweet and pleasing to the ear. The more I played, the better I felt. Every chord touched my soul, lifting it above all worry, filling it with joy and peace.

It was just the two of us, his drum and my keyboard. Yet, amazingly, even without Haya's singing, without Rabia and Azhar's guitars, the tune still felt somehow whole. Complete. And as I let myself get lost in it, I felt completed.

I stilled as we ended, in awe of the experience. My eyes remained closed for a long moment, honoring it. When I finally opened my eyes, Haya, Rabia, and Azhar broke out into beaming smiles and applause, Haya whistling to show her approval. Yet, the only thing that mattered right then was the pride in Hassan's eyes, the unrestrained joy in his smile.

I felt myself beaming back, radiant. Everyone was right. I could do this.

"I think we're ready," Haya said softly.

Our audience trickled into the room, our families pooling together at the front. Mom looked excited, but Dad's eyebrows were furrowed, and I couldn't tell what he was thinking. I bit my lip, some of my nervousness flooding back. Then I spotted Adam. It was impossible not to—he towered over everyone else. Meeting my eyes, he smiled wide and lifted his hand in a thumbs-up. As I returned the smile, my body relaxed.

Haya's face lit up as she bounded to the center of the stage. I could almost see her stepping into her performer persona like a second skin. "Assalamu Alaykum and Eid Mubarak, everyone!" she announced into the microphone.

"Wa alaykum assalam!" the crowd replied, cheering.

"Are you guys ready to celebrate Eid?" she asked. She was a natural at stirring up excitement.

"Yes!" came the overwhelming response.

"Awesome. We are Sheikh, Rattle, and Roll. Now, we might be a little rusty because we didn't practice much during Ramadan, but we'll do our best to put on an amazing show for you guys, so just sit back and enjoy the music!"

Rabia counted us down, Haya smiling at Hassan as he began, every movement measured, precise. Rabia followed, her fingers gracefully skimming her fretboard, adding brightness to the song. I joined in next, each crisp note melting any last vestige of nervousness or fear. Haya had a look of utter joy on her face as she began to sing, rising and falling in perfect tune as she brought the lyrics to life. Azhar came in next, adding depth that beautifully complemented her sweet voice. Her body swayed lightly as she sang; at first, the lyrics were subtle, suggesting this was just any old love song. But as she continued, the true nature of the song came through, reverence and adoration spread like honey through her dulcet tones. I looked out into the crowd, noting how our audience leaned forward, reeled in. I felt light as I watched the other bandmembers, how each one mirrored the same devotion in their own ways. As if he knew I was looking for him, Hassan lifted his head and met my eye. He smiled with his whole being as he mouthed the lyrics. With a matching smile, I let my eyes close and just listened as Haya sang of Allah as the ultimate source of love, neverendingly compassionate and merciful. My body seemed to melt and merge with the keyboard as I felt the same transcendent feeling come over me, forgetting about the crowd as the drumbeats swept me along in their bold tempo. It took me back to the innocence of my childhood, while somehow holding the promise of something entirely new and miraculous.

The second item on my Ramadan checklist flashed through

my mind. *Discover myself. What does Islam mean to me, and how can I use it to figure out who I am and the future I want for myself?* I sighed, my whole body relaxing on my exhale as I realized that I finally knew the answer. I never wanted to let go of this feeling.

☾

"Red Mango?" Haya said hopefully as soon as our instruments were packed.

I waited a moment before answering. Somehow, I felt both tired and energized, my heart simultaneously full and light. We'd done it. *I'd* done it—and our performance had been a success, alhamdulillah. After a minute of reveling in that sense of joy and accomplishment, I grinned at Haya. "Let's go."

Looping her arms through mine and Mahnoor's, Haya led the way, eyes sparkling as she talked about brownie bits and cheese-cake bites.

Azhar stared at Mahnoor on the subway, and whenever she'd meet his eyes, he'd smile, making her blush.

"Allah bless them," Haya whispered to me, leaning in close. "Mashallah, they're so cute."

"Yeah. I wish someone would look at me like that." I sighed happily.

"Someone already does," she whispered.

I looked over at Hassan, standing just a few feet away. He hadn't been close enough to hear Haya, but he must have already been looking at me—our eyes met, and he smiled.

I couldn't help but smile back and he held my gaze for a long moment, before finally turning back to face straight ahead as we reached our destination and the train doors opened.

"What do you think you're going to get, Dua?" Haya asked, her mind already elsewhere.

"Anything but chocolate or vanilla," I said as we walked through the door of the frozen yogurt shop. "I want something different." I perused the offerings, making my choice quickly.

"I think we should let them have a table all to themselves," Hassan said, pointedly looking at Mahnoor and Azhar as he stood beside me while I got myself some Caribbean Coconut.

I glanced back to see Mahnoor smile widely at Azhar. I turned back, giving them some privacy. "That's a great idea."

I reached for my wallet as the cashier noted my treat's weight, but the second I glanced down to grab some cash, Hassan sidled up next to me and swiped his debit card. My mouth opened in protest, my inner desi coming out. "Hey, that wasn't necessary." He'd already done enough for me.

He merely smiled, his eyes twinkling as he stuffed the receipt into his pocket. "Too late, already paid."

I lowered my head to hide my blush. "Well, thank you. I'll pay you back next time."

His smile flashed at me as he sat down beside Haya. I sat across from Adam, who eyed the chocolate syrup and chopped peanuts on my froyo. Brow quirked, he glanced down at his own. "Did I forget something?" He dug around with his spoon.

I stared at the mountain of toppings. "How would you know?" Did he even *have* actual froyo underneath?

"Taste, of course." He scooped a little into his mouth. His forehead smoothed, and he smiled. "Perfect."

Smiling back, I cupped my chin in my palm. "Well, you don't hold back."

"I used to," he admitted, a serious tilt to his mouth. "My usual order is chocolate with chocolate sprinkles and chocolate syrup. Today, I wanted to try *everything*."

"What led you to that decision?"

Adam quirked his eyebrow. "What's the first thing you think when you hear someone got shot?"

My stomach sank for a split second. I didn't hesitate. "It's the worst thing I can imagine."

He poked the air triumphantly with his spoon. "Exactly. The worst thing I could ever imagine happened to me. So now what?"

Confusion laced my voice. "What?"

"This life-changing thing happened to me, Dua. I couldn't be the same afterward if I wanted to—and I *don't* want to. I was sure I was going to die that day, but I didn't. So why stop myself from trying all the flavors? This is the only life I have, and no one's going to care about going after the things I really want more than I do."

"That's pretty brave of you," I said wistfully.

He furrowed his brows. "I'm hearing a big *but* coming," he said, right before stuffing a huge bite in his mouth.

I handed him a napkin for the resulting smear of sauces on his lower lip. "I don't know if I can be as brave as my dreams need me to be."

He blinked. "Are you talking about music? I saw you up there on the stage. You were *in the zone*."

I nodded.

He was silent for a beat. "How badly do you want this?"

"Very," I said quickly, before I could overthink it.

"Then go for it."

I sighed. "Come on, Adam. You know how desi parents are—they think anything artsy is a waste of time and tuition. They won't agree."

He blinked. "Sounds like you're making excuses to deny what you really want, trying to avoid disappointment before it actually happens."

I shook my head vehemently. "You're oversimplifying the situation."

"And you're overcomplicating it," he countered, so matter-of-fact that I stilled. "It's not your job to change your parents' heart, it's Allah's. And sometimes we focus so much on asking Him for help in tough situations, we miss out on how we can actually help things along. Allah gave you this talent for a reason, Dua. Maybe He's waiting on you to take the first step."

I couldn't help smiling. "Well, *damn*, Adam. You could be a motivational speaker."

He shrugged, lifting a spoonful of brownie- and cheesecake-studded froyo. "Maybe I'll put that next on my list."

I swirled the froyo and chocolate syrup around my cup, thinking back to the rush of euphoria, the freeing contentment as I'd played earlier. I watched Adam, recognizing the same weight-less exuberance in his movements as he relished every bite. With a pang, I realized I already missed that feeling. I made a vow to myself in that moment that I would do everything I could to hold on to it.

twenty-four

I woke long before my alarm went off for fajr. Today was the day we were leaving for Burkeville, leaving New York and everyone here behind. I squeezed my eyes shut, one hand searching my chest for my heartbeat. It was hard and fast against my palm in my excitement at returning home and seeing Kat, but at the same time, I was sad at the thought of leaving when I'd found so much love here.

Slowly, I got out of bed.

"Mahnoor?" I stopped in front of her bed, where she slept on her side, her hands tucked under her pillow. She'd spent half the night talking to her future in-laws and setting things right. I'd try waking her in a few minutes if she didn't get up soon.

I headed to the bathroom to make my wudu. I made my ablution with extra care that morning, the water cold to wake me up quickly. The first tears came when I pressed my forehead to the prayer rug. I blinked them away as I sat up, trying to focus on the words that came out of my mouth instead of on the wetness of my eyes. Still, I couldn't shake the feel of the tears that dripped off the edge of my chin or my damp lashes as they brushed against my skin.

Another Ramadan was gone forever. I finished my prayer and leaned back, lifting my hands to supplicate. "Oh, Allah," I whispered, "this time passed so quickly. I hope You have shown mercy and forgiven me my sins. Please forgive me, Allah. I know I don't thank You enough and I take things for granted a lot, but I know I can't even take another breath if not for Your mercy. And thank You for turning this trip that I was dreading so much into an experience I'm never going to regret. This Ramadan was . . . transformative." My voice faltered for a moment. "I just wish I could come back again soon. So, Allah, please, if it's right for me, please make it happen. Ameen." I swept my hands over my face and opened my eyes.

I need comfort food, I thought as I rolled up my prayer rug.

Minutes later, I sat at the kitchen table with a mountain of steaming biryani on my plate, shoveling it into my mouth. Aunt Sadia had really outdone herself this time. Each mouthful of rice and chicken, mixed with a blend of fragrant spices, was perfect.

"Assalamu Alaykum." Ibrahim slipped into the chair opposite mine.

"Wa alaykum assalam," I replied, scooping up another mouthful of biryani. "What's up?"

"I smelled biryani."

I stopped chewing. "I hope you're not expecting me to get some for you. I'm a little too busy stuffing my face."

He shook his head, smiling. "No worries, I'll get some myself. Isn't it a little early for biryani, though? The sun hasn't even risen yet."

My mouth full, I lifted both of my feet up onto my chair and shifted so the plate was propped on my knees. Swallowing, I replied, readying my spoon for the next bite, "Today's the day I'm going to leave. Who knows the next time I'll get to have Aunt Sadia's biryani?" I stuffed the last bite into my mouth.

"Oh, I'm going to miss this," I said, sighing as I leaned back in my chair. "Just chilling with everyone. With *you*. You're so calming."

He half smiled, looking thoughtful. "I'll miss these times too."

I sighed again and grabbed my empty plate as I got up. "I have to pack, and I've been putting it off."

"Not ready to leave? I would've thought you were looking forward to having a room to yourself again," he teased.

I paused in the middle of rinsing off my plate. "You'd think so, wouldn't you?" I stashed the plate in the dishwasher quickly, and since I was in an especially affectionate mood that morning, I squeezed him in a tight hug around his shoulders before heading to the bedroom.

I almost hit Mahnoor getting into the room, she was standing so close to the door. "Were you waiting for me?"

"Isn't it obvious?" she asked, following me as I walked to my assigned section of the closet to get my clothes.

"You look happy today. I hope it's not 'cause I'm leaving." I couldn't resist teasing her.

"Oh, shut up, you know it's not that." She began to sort my clothes into neat little stacks, her lips turning up at the ends. Azhar's engagement ring was gone from her neck, now sparkling on her left ring finger.

"When's the wedding?"

"We haven't decided yet. Azhar and I agreed to sit down and just talk before we decide on anything." She beamed at me. "But we're thinking it's going to be kind of soon, like less than a year, insha'Allah."

I grinned back at her. "You're going to make a gorgeous bride. You better have the wedding during one of my breaks, so I can come."

"We will. I don't want to worry about classes when I'm getting married either." She made a face.

"Dua, why are you going?" Mahdi ran through the door and into my arms.

I hugged him tightly. "I have to go home, Mahdi," I said softly, running my hands through his hair, cradling his head in my lap.

"Make this your home," he said quietly, tears pooling in the corners of his eyes.

I wiped at his eyes gently. "My life is in Virginia, sweetie. I have to go home with my parents and go to school."

"I'm going to miss you," he murmured, sniffling.

"I'm going to miss you too." I brushed his hair back from his forehead and planted a kiss on the soft, smooth skin there. "Why don't you sleep now? It's still early. I'll be here when you wake up."

"Promise?"

"Promise. I won't leave without saying goodbye to you."

He rubbed his nose on his sleeve. "Can I stay here?"

"Sure." I gave him another kiss and shifted, moving his head from my lap to the pillow. "Go to sleep," I sang softly, running my fingers through his hair. My own eyelids were starting to droop. Still singing under my breath, I snuggled down next to Mahdi and closed my eyes, holding his tiny hand in my own.

"Goodbye, Uncle Jibran, Uncle Hamza, Uncle Dawood." Mahdi clung to my sleeve as I went around hugging and saying good-bye to all the aunts, uncles, and cousins gathered in the living room. I spent the most time saying goodbye to Uncle Yusuf and Aunt Sadia, squeezing them as tightly as I hugged my own parents.

"Dua," Uncle Yusuf said softly when I pulled back. "It's been a pleasure to watch you grow this Ramadan."

It has? "Uncle Yusuf, you had a look on your face when you saw my Ramadan checklist. What was that?"

He smiled wide. "You had quite an ambitious list for your first time, but you've exceeded any and all expectations. You're tenacious, Dua, and that is an amazing quality to have. From now on, remember your list, and try your best to live by it."

My body hummed with pride at his warmth. "I will, Uncle Yusuf. Thank you." In that little bit of advice, there was love, a sense of belonging. Of family.

Between the rest of the aunts, it took almost ten minutes to say my goodbyes as they crushed me in bear hugs and pinched my cheeks, loudly wondering to themselves when they would see me again. I pulled Mahdi into my arms for a hug, resting my head on his.

"The Mousawis are here," Mahnoor announced as she walked into the room, everyone two steps behind her.

Haya didn't even wait for me to put Mahdi down before she engulfed me in a hug. "I'm going to miss you so much, Dua," she whispered into my ear, sniffling. "You're amazing." After a solid minute or so, she pulled back. "We'll text each other every day and FaceTime at least once a week. No arguments."

No arguments here. "Okay, sounds good."

"Come back soon, habibti." Mrs. Mousawi tearfully seized me in her crushing hug.

"Insha'Allah." I held in my own tears as I patted her on the back.

"My turn." Mahnoor held on to me with surprising intensity as she hugged me. "Same thing as Haya goes for me; we need to text each other every day and FaceTime regularly. You're more than a friend, Dua," she whispered. "You were there to listen when I couldn't tell anyone else what was bothering me. Thank you so, so much. I'm really going to miss you, my confidante."

"Okay, let's go," Dad interrupted, lugging his and Mom's suitcases into the room. Uncle Yusuf was right behind him with my bags, minus the one duffel bag I held on to.

"But we haven't finished saying goodbye yet," Rabia said, wiping at her eyes with the back of her hand. "Mahnoor's hogging Dua."

Dad's eyes softened as he looked at her. "Let's just go outside, or none of us will ever leave. You can finish saying your goodbyes there."

Gripping Mahdi's hand tightly, I followed Mom as she walked out the front door. The whole house came with us, relatives pouring out and spilling into the driveway as my uncles helped Dad put everything in the car.

"You're a great baking buddy," Rabia began, launching herself into my arms, the force of her tackle knocking my duffel bag to the ground. "And I can't wait to see you again. I hope I didn't talk your ear off, but I had a great time. We need to do this again sometime, and soon!"

"Oh, Rabia." Still clutching Mahdi's hand in one of my own, I reached up with my free arm and wrapped it around his sister.

"I'm going to miss your constant chattering when I get home. And your cupcakes."

"Rabs, stop choking her." Adam smiled wanly. "Have a safe trip, Dua. Don't forget our conversation."

Like that was a possibility. I smiled back. "Thanks, Adam. Take care of yourself."

He opened his arms, and I went in for my hug. He wrapped his arms around me, giving me a warm squeeze. "You still owe me a soccer match," he whispered.

I grinned. "I've been waiting for you to heal. I guess I'll need to come back for that, then."

He nodded. "Don't wait too long."

"I'll try my best."

Ibrahim rested an arm along my shoulder. "The next time you give me music as a gift, it'd better be yours."

"Sure, but you may have to remind me," I said, certain my eyes held the same twinkle of mirth as his.

He grinned. "You know I'm always here, whenever you need me. I always have been."

"Thank you." I looked down at Mahdi. "Your turn, little man." I knelt down and half smiled as I placed my hands on his shoulders. "I'm sure you know this, but you're very special, Mahdi, and I think I'm going to miss you most of all." I reached up to stroke his cheek. "I'm going to keep in contact with everyone, so whenever I'm on FaceTime, I want to see you, too, okay?"

"Okay." He sniffled, wiping his nose on his sleeve. "Please come back soon. I'll miss you, and seeing you on the screen isn't the same."

Awww. I clutched him to my chest, my tears finally escaping as I hugged him. "I'll try, Mahdi," I whispered. "I'll try." I held on to him longer than I had everyone else, trying to memorize the feel of his warm little body in my arms.

"Dua!" Mom called me.

I took a deep breath and let it out slowly before pulling back, ignoring my tears as I smiled at him. "Remember what I said about FaceTime, okay?" I kissed him once more and nudged him toward Mahnoor, who immediately bent to scoop him into her arms.

I turned and reached for my duffel bag, but another hand got to it before mine. Hassan smiled down at me, his dark brown hair falling over his forehead, eyes twinkling. "It's okay, I can do it."

"I got it," he replied, slinging it over his shoulder. "Besides, this gives me an excuse to talk to you."

"A very thinly veiled one, but sure." I smiled as I stood.

"So where do you want this?" he asked as he walked me to the car, unnecessarily loud.

Regardless of the lack of subtlety, it worked. Dad stopped eyeing him and went back to stuffing Mom's bags into the trunk.

"Back seat's fine." Tears dripped down my chin, and I reached up to wipe them away.

"What are your plans for the rest of the summer?" he asked, ducking his head into the car as he carefully placed my bag on the floor.

"Spending time with Kat, mostly. Planning for the MSA. Then, college applications."

"You'd have a lot of great options here: Juilliard, Barnard College, Columbia, Sarah Lawrence, NYU." He arched his eyebrows at the last one.

"Mmm-hmm. And I'm sure you're not emphasizing NYU just

because you go there." I tried to keep a straight face as I folded my arms over my chest, but I couldn't stop my smile.

He chuckled. "Of course not. But you should consider it. They could definitely use your talent in the music program."

I pretended to think about it as if it had never occurred to me before. "Maybe."

"Think about it. Seriously."

I smiled. "I will. Promise."

"Good." He grinned back, stepping aside to give me room to get into the car. His arm slipped past mine as he did; I felt my palm suddenly weighed down, squared edges of something pressing into my skin.

"Thanks for all your help," I said loudly as I slid into my seat, gesturing to my bag. "I never really thought about how heavy makeup and jewelry could get."

He almost laughed; I could see him holding back. "Sure. Have a safe trip. Assalamu alaykum."

"Wa alaykum assalam," I replied, letting him close my door for me as Mom slipped into the front passenger seat.

"Buckle up, ladies," Dad said as he turned the engine on. "It's time to go home."

I waved frantically to everyone even as I whispered the prayer for starting a journey under my breath, even as Dad reversed the car out of the driveway and started for the main road. They all waved back, different people, different faces, but the same wet look in all of their eyes as they watched us leave. I faced forward only when I couldn't see them anymore.

With a sigh, I leaned back and glanced down at my lap, opening my palm. My breath hitched in my throat. It was . . . me. I stared at the small digital print, at the rich caramel of my skin against the vivid emerald of my shalwar kameez, noting the softness of my hair, the silky smoothness of my dupatta. The fingers of my left hand caressed the keyboard while the right brushed up against my neck, at the golden glint of my new pendant. I saw myself as Hassan had seen me when he first caught me playing, dark lashes fanning my cheeks as I closed my eyes.

"Did you enjoy yourself, Dua?" Mom asked.

"Hmm? Yeah, I did." The print usurped every bit of my attention. The look on my face was of pure contentment, enraptured by the music in my heart and at my fingertips. *This* was the unbridled joy I felt when I touched the keys, and he'd captured it perfectly. It was a feeling I never wanted to let go of, one I longed to live every day.

"Good. So, have you given any thought to the MSA?"

I looked up, slipping the frame into my duffel for safekeeping. Suddenly, I knew exactly what to say. "Yeah, I have." My voice was firm, but calm. Here goes nothing. Bismillah. "Nottoway High really does need an MSA, and I'm going to head it."

They beamed. "How wonderful! That's great, beta!"

"On one condition," I finished.

Their eyebrows furrowed, their faces bearing matching puzzled expressions. "What?"

"I'll start an MSA, but in return, I want you to consider a request of mine. I want to study music at college. As a major. Or, at the bare minimum, as a minor."

Concern flashed across their faces.

Mom glanced back at me. "Really, Dua? Music?"

I nodded, surer than ever. "Yes. It's all I've ever wanted to do."

She sighed, a rushed breath of bewilderment. "Dua, you were

wonderful with the band yesterday, but you don't have to study music to be in a band, surely?" She glanced at Dad, who shrugged. "You can do that on the side," she added. "Start a band of your own while you study something more practical, like business administration or science."

"If I decide to go down that route, I'll have plenty of time to figure it out in the future, insha'Allah," I said firmly. "But I enjoy music, and I have a talent for it. I don't want to regret not exploring all my options. Let me try for music, see what I can really do when I'm not holding myself back."

Dad peered at me in the rearview mirror, brows furrowing at the edge of determination in my voice. "Were you holding yourself back yesterday?"

I shook my head. "No, not yesterday. But I have before," I admitted.

He glanced away from me, voice lowering. "I don't remember hearing you play like that before, subhanallah." He quieted, studying the road like it contained a particularly challenging puzzle. After a long minute of silence, he looked at Mom. "Okay."

"Okay?!" I squealed.

Mom gaped. "Really, Khalid?" She glanced at Dad. He nodded, just once, and she sighed. "Well, I guess we're considering it, then." She looked back at me. "Have you looked into any programs? What would you do with a music degree? You'll have to discuss it with your guidance counselor, too, see if she has any ideas. Did you set up an appointment with Ms. Fritz yet?"

A smile played about my lips. So many questions. Fortunately, we had a long drive ahead. Plenty of time for me to answer, and plenty of time to figure out the road ahead.

twenty-five

Nine Weeks Later

Something fell out of my duffel as I pulled it out of the overhead compartment. I tucked it into my back pocket for later, intent on getting off the plane as quickly as possible while not dropping the precious box of homemade jalebi Mom had made as an Eid Al-Adha treat, with a few extra tucked in a smaller tin just for Adam.

Rabia nearly knocked me over with the force of her hug when she spotted me. I recovered my balance, laughing as Mahdi latched on. One by one, the rest of the family joined in. In their arms, my heart swelled with joy and love, a void filled before I even realized it existed.

It wasn't until hours later that I emptied my pockets. I unfolded the paper, smoothing it out in my lap as I read. My Ramadan checklist, with every item complete with a little check next to it. I smiled as I read the first item, recalling my Qur'an lessons with Hassan. He texted me at least a couple times a week to remind me to practice the surahs I'd memorized and see how I was coming along, or just to see how I was. Kat and I had a running joke that Hassan was the MSA's invisible co-president, because whenever I got stuck or had questions, he had plenty of suggestions, or just listened as I used him as a sounding board.

Sometimes, he'd send a nasheed he thought I might like, a piece of digital art he'd just finished, or video clips of Mahdi trying to play keyboard. Once, he even sent a photo of the outside of NYU Steinhardt and a link to their piano studies page. Sadly, he wasn't in the photo, though Haya posed beside the building rather enthusiastically.

His brilliant eyes and crooked smile appeared in my mind's eye. I closed my eyes and lay down, letting the image stay as I fell asleep.

☾

Mahnoor looked up from her latte as I approached her table. She studied my face for a long moment; satisfied, she smiled. "I'm guessing the tour went well?"

I grinned. "Really well! I have a good feeling about this place." Dua Sheikh, Bachelor of Music in Piano Studies from NYU. It had a nice ring to it. "Let's hope I get in."

"You will, insha'Allah," Rabia replied between bites of chocolate chip cookie.

"May Allah will whatever is best for you," Mahnoor added, smiling at the glint of her bracelet. "Ready to go? This brownie isn't satisfying my sweet tooth; let's get some kulfi from Jackson Heights on the way home."

My smile brightened at the thought of dense, creamy kulfi. It'd been so long since I had a decent one. "Yes, please."

"Chalein, let's go. The weather's beautiful, and I thought of something you'd like to see."

C

I relished my first mouthful of kulfi as I looked up at a large silver globe, three rings surrounding it. Cardamom, cream, and pistachio in perfect harmony. Yum. I leaned back, enjoying the sun on my face, eyeing the trees with leaves just barely tinged yellow and orange.

"Here it is." Rabia thrust her phone in front of my nose as she read aloud. "'The Unisphere is the largest globe in the world, created to reflect the theme of Peace Through Understanding.'"

Hmm. I mulled that over for a moment. The globe had been made in the 1960s, and we still had a long way to go to achieve peace.

"That's so weird, we've been coming here for years and I totally forgot about that." She shook the remnants of her kulfi off her fingers and looked pointedly at Mahnoor, who had her head bent over her phone, ignoring the drip of her treat. She was likely pinning wedding ideas, as she had been doing every free moment she got. "We'll just toss these and be right back." Rabia stood, dragging Mahnoor away, still engrossed in her phone.

I sighed, my shoulders rounding as I marveled at the design of the Unisphere—and the sweetness of my kulfi. *Peace through understanding.* We could all use more of that in the world. It was the whole point behind starting the MSA back home. Now that I'd jumped headfirst into preparations for the club launch, it felt less like something that originated because of my parents' wishes, and more like something I'd needed for myself. At least within the confines of the MSA, I got to choose the image of Islam I presented to others— an image that was more authentic, different from what they saw on the news or angry blogs. I smiled to myself a little. It was one step closer to peace, one step closer to owning my voice.

My phone trilled with a new text. My smile widened automatically when I saw Hassan's name. He'd sent a digital sketch, black and white. A girl sat on a bench with her head tipped up toward the Unisphere. Long hair flowed down her back, shoulders relaxed, a stick of kulfi clasped between the fingers of her right hand.

I glanced at my own hand for a second, my eyes roaming the Unisphere before I turned and perused my surroundings.

Haya waved to me, flashing a smile before saying something to Rabia, whose mouth was already going a mile a minute. Mahnoor was finally looking up from her phone, beaming up at Azhar, whose whole face glowed. But where was Hassan?

I cast my gaze farther, my hope blurring at the edges and heartbeat quickening as I searched strangers' faces for the one I longed to see most . . . There!

Hassan's eyes twinkled, his grin bright as his gaze met mine. I sat on my free hand, quashing my fingers before they played out the romantic Bollywood song that was suddenly in my head. I didn't need any distractions in that moment, my heart light as I watched him walk toward me. He looked as handsome as ever in a plum-toned T-shirt—my favorite color!—that accentuated his broad shoulders, a black backpack slung across them. His facial hair was slightly thicker than the last time I'd seen him, outlining his jaw sharply, and the light breeze adorably tousled his dark brown hair.

I forgot to respond to his salaam in all my gawking.

"Assalamu alaykum," he repeated, still smiling down at me in the most disarming way.

I didn't know what to do with my hands, my kulfi, or my words. Only the cold drip of my ice cream brought me back to my senses. I blinked. "Wa alaykum assalam." I skooched over, making room for him on the bench.

I held out the bag with extra treats as he sat down, slipping the backpack off before reaching in for a mango kulfi, an evidently permanent smile on his face. His warm, sweet cologne wafted over me with every movement, my heartbeat quickening again as I just stared at him, in awe that he was really in front of me after all this time. Could I poke him to be sure? I narrowly stopped myself, reminding myself that it fell under the category of unnecessary touch.

"How are you?" I asked instead.

"Better now that you're here." His eyes twinkled at me.

I blushed at his straightforwardness. "I'm glad to be back, even if it's just a few days. I've missed this place."

"We've missed you too. It's not the same without you. Sheikh, Rattle, and Roll is *definitely* not the same without you." Softening his voice, he added, "*I've* missed you."

Was that my heart I felt melting, or just my ice cream? I couldn't stop my shy smile. "I've missed you too," I admitted softly, eyes on the ground.

He was quiet. Did he hear me? I lifted my gaze slowly. His smile was like the sun, bathing me in its radiance. "Alhamdulillah," he whispered, as if to himself.

I giggled at the unexpected response. It was too adorable, warming—like a perfect cup of chai. "Alhamdulillah," I echoed, wrapping my fingers around my now-favorite pendant.

He turned in his seat to face me. "Haya said your NYU tour went well. What's next on the list?"

"Juilliard, of course, then Mannes School of Music, Manhattan School of Music, and Purchase College."

"So, you definitely want to move to New York?"

I nodded. "Yeah, I feel at home here."

"Perfect." He grinned, cupping his chin in his palm. "So, when should I send my parents over to talk to yours?"

"Well, I think next week they're— Wait. What?" My brain scrambled, processing the question a few seconds late. "You mean like . . . talk to my parents as in . . . You're saying you want to propose?"

"Very much so."

The butterflies in my stomach fluttered, but . . . "Did Mahdi put you up to this?" I asked, raising an eyebrow.

He mimicked the action. "Maybe. But I can't say that was the only factor. We'll take it as slow as you want; I just want your family to know my intentions are halal." He lowered his eyes for a moment. For once, it was his turn to blush. "Of course, only if you're interested."

The corner of my mouth turned up in a shy smile. "Yes. Definitely interested."

He looked up, mirroring my smile, his eyes sparkling. "Alhamdulillah," he said again.

My phone trilled once more, but I didn't dare look. I didn't want to interrupt this moment.

After a beat, Hassan cleared his throat. "Why don't you take a look?"

Something about the earnestness on his face made me check my phone. Another sketch. My breath caught in my throat. This one had a play button on it. When I hit play, a familiar mandolin tune began. The girl on the bench wasn't alone anymore, now joined by a boy with short, dark hair, their heads inclined toward each other, a cartoon heart suspended in the air between them. In the sky above their heads the clouds parted, words slowly materializing one by one in fancy cursive: DUA . . . WILL . . . YOU . . . MARRY . . . ME?

I looked up from my phone to find him studying my face, his head tilted adoringly. A smile broke out on my face. "Yes." I said it softly at first, then louder. "Yes!"

His dimple peeked out, his smile growing to match mine. We sat in the sunshine like that for a minute, silently reveling in a mix of joy and awe. I couldn't stop smiling, visions of a future life, full of happiness, love, and music, swirling before my eyes. My heart felt light as I whispered a prayer. I touched my pendant lightly, my personal reminder of Allah being closer to us than our jugular veins. In that, I felt immense hope and trust. *Oh, Allah, make these dreams our reality. Or something better.* "Ameen," I whispered, sharing a smile with Hassan.

Acknowledgments

I can't remember a time when I didn't know I was a writer. Unwaveringly, I dreamt of having my work published. That childhood dream has come to fruition, and I couldn't have done it without the wonderful individuals who saw the potential in me and in this book. First, I thank my family and my loving husband, Raheel, for always believing in me and pushing me to pursue my dreams—the loftier, the better.

Friends who have become family also deserve a big thank-you. I am eternally grateful to Masuma Virji and her family for being my first readers (shout-out to Naushad bhai for coming up with the perfect band name!), to Hadwa Abboud for being the first "Dassan" shipper, to Faria Ali for her endless enthusiasm, and to Sarah Aslam, my chai and book buddy.

To the teachers who recognized the writer in me and helped me hone my skills—Mr. Ed Sandt, Ms. Shawn McDonald, and Mr. David Bucco—thank you. I will always remember and appreciate your encouragement and good humor.

Last but definitely not least, my extraordinary team. To my agent, Jamie Vankirk, thank you for your persistent dedication.

You are a rock star! To Wendy Loggia and Alison Romig, thank you for your passion, your recognition of Dua's story, and your absolutely brilliant suggestions. The three of you helped me polish this story into a novel I am truly proud of and ecstatic to share with the world.